CAPTURING
FOREVER

Acclaim for Erin Dutton's Work

"*Designed for Love* is…rich in love, romance, and sex. Dutton gives her readers a roller coaster ride filled with sexual thrills and chills. *Designed for Love* is the perfect book to curl up with on a cold winter's day."—*Just About Write*

"*Sequestered Hearts* is packed with raw emotion, but filled with tender moments too. The author writes with sophistication that one would expect from a veteran author. …A romance is about more than just plot and character development. It's about passion, physical intimacy, and connection between the characters. The reader should have a visceral reaction to what is going on within the pages for the novel to succeed. Dutton's words match perfectly with the emotion she has created. *Sequestered Hearts* is one book that cannot be overlooked. It is romance at its finest."—*L-word Literature.com*

"*Sequestered Hearts* by first time novelist, Erin Dutton, is everything a romance should be. It is teeming with longing, heartbreak, and of course, love. …As pure romances go, it is one of the best in print today."—*Just About Write*

In *Fully Involved* "…Dutton's studied evocation of the macho world of firefighting gives the story extra oomph—and happily ever after is what a good romance is all about, right?"—*Q Syndicate*

With *Point of Ignition*… "Erin Dutton has given her fans another fast paced story of fire, with both buildings and emotions burning hotly. …Dutton has done an excellent job of portraying two women who are each fighting for their own dignity and learning to trust again. The delicate tug of war between the characters is well done as is the dichotomy of boredom and drama faced daily by the firefighters. *Point of Ignition* is a story told well that will touch its readers." —*Just About Write*

Visit us at www.boldstrokesbooks.com

By the Author

CAPTURING FOREVER

by

Erin Dutton

2016

ISBN 13: 978-1-62639-631-9

This Trade Paperback Original Is Published By
Bold Strokes Books, Inc.
P.O. Box 249
Valley Falls, NY 12185

First Edition: August 2016

CREDITS
EDITOR: SHELLEY THRASHER
PRODUCTION DESIGN: SUSAN RAMUNDO
COVER DESIGN BY SHERI (GRAPHICARTIST2020@HOTMAIL.COM)

Acknowledgments

As always, thanks to the dedicated people at Bold Strokes Books for helping me put forward a polished, beautifully packaged version of the stories that start as images in my head. Dr. Shelley Thrasher continues to be my editor, my teacher, and my guide on this amazing journey.

Sarah Bridget Kerry, thanks for an insightful beta read just when I needed it. You helped bring another layer to my story and I'm so, so grateful.

Thanks to Kelly for your information about fostering and adopting. I hope I captured the experience accurately. It's such a generous thing—offering a home, stability, and love to children who desperately need it. Much respect for what you and Becky have done for your family.

To the readers—your support, messages, and feedback are crucial to my process. I will always be a writer, but you help me continue to be an author.

On a personal note, a part of me believed I would never be legally allowed to marry in my state of residence. Now all of that has changed. By the time this book is published I will have promised to honor and obey the love of my life in front of our family and friends. Christina, this is where I would go on and on about how I waited all of my life to meet you and just how much I adore you…but I'm going to save all of that for my vows (not really). I hope you know how much I love you and how I've always looked forward to the rest of our lives together. Walking this road with you by my side was already the plan, and being able to call you my wife while we do it just makes it that much sweeter.

Dedication

For the first time, but not the last…to my wife,
you are my forever.

PROLOGUE

Twenty-one Years Earlier

"What are we waiting for? Let's get started." Jacqueline Knight split the deck of cards into two stacks. Then, bracing them against the table, she shuffled them back together. After a full week of exams, she'd jumped on board when her roommate, Kendra, suggested this gathering. She needed a night of stress relief before she headed home for the holidays.

"I have one more coming." Kendra took a bowl of onion dip from the fridge and set it out next to the bag of chips on the counter. None of their guests cared about the sparse snack offerings, since they had plenty of beer, and everyone had already put a big chunk of their allowance for the week into the pot for tonight's poker game.

"I can see that." Jacqueline glanced pointedly at the empty chair directly across from her. "How long are we planning to wait?"

"Chill, Knight. You're stressing me out." Kendra dismissed Jacqueline's irritation in her typical laid-back manner. Kendra had become the one exception to Jacqueline's desire to keep her life organized and orderly. Jacqueline liked schedules and clear expectations, but Kendra, a music major, abhorred those restrictions.

"She's one of your free-spirit friends, isn't she?" Jacqueline ignored several offended looks from around the table. The rest of their guests, mostly Kendra's friends, fit in the same category.

"She's great. I only met her a couple of weeks ago, but I think you'll like her."

"That's not an answer to my question."

"She's an art major."

"I knew it."

"She's a photographer and actually quite brilliant with a camera."

"But not with a watch, huh?"

Before Kendra had a chance to answer, another voice answered from the doorway behind Jacqueline. "I can handle the digital ones easily enough. It's the ones with the little symbols where the numbers should be that really confuse me."

Jacqueline closed her eyes, embarrassed at having been caught dogging a girl she hadn't even met yet. Suddenly, she wished they hadn't left the door open to the hallway. But crowding eight people into the living area of their dorm suite tended to make the place feel stuffy.

"Hey, Casey." Kendra laughed and tossed Jacqueline a smug look.

"Sorry I'm late." Casey rounded the table. When she smiled, something clutched in Jacqueline's chest. The expression transformed Casey's face, bringing light and warmth into features that just a moment ago had appeared almost haughty.

"No worries." Kendra pulled her into a one-armed hug. "You look amazing. Girl, you didn't have to dress up for us."

Casey swept her hand down the front of her light-gray blouse and black slacks. A maroon paisley scarf added a pop of color around her neck. Her golden hair had been pulled back from her face, but several wavy tendrils fell free and brushed the sides of her neck. "I promised a friend I'd hit up her student exhibit tonight and didn't have time to go back to my room and change."

As Kendra reeled off the introductions, Casey made eye contact around the table until she reached Jacqueline. Good God, this girl had the bluest eyes Jacqueline had ever seen, and now that smile was focused on her. Jacqueline would have to be made of stone not to melt a little. "Casey Meadows. It's nice to meet you."

"You, too. Now sit. We're ready to start." Caught off guard by the way her heartbeat accelerated under Casey's gaze, Jacqueline's words came out gruffer than she intended. Casey's smile faded as she dropped into the chair, but, to her credit, she didn't take her eyes off Jacqueline.

"You could have started without me."

"Yeah, I wanted to. But Kendra's too nice." Jacqueline dealt cards to each of the eight players at the table.

"If you're really as good at poker as you're trying to make me think, then you should thank her for inviting me." Casey slapped several bills down on the table in front of her. "Here's more money for you to win. And since you're so warm and welcoming, I'm more likely to come back and play next time, too."

Two hours later, Jacqueline was certain she'd been hustled. Everyone but her, Kendra, and Casey had busted out, leaving all of the chips stacked neatly in front of them. She'd expected competition from Kendra but now suspected Casey could outplay both of them. Yet Casey had stayed conservative, betting small even when she clearly had the upper hand. Was she strategizing? Or did she think it might be rude to clear out the hostesses quite so handily? Jacqueline's curiosity regarding Casey's style of play nearly outweighed her frustration at getting beat.

Jacqueline picked up the cards she'd just been dealt, careful not to give anything away in her expression. She glanced down at a pair of queens, then flicked her eyes across the table. She hadn't had much success reading Casey during previous hands but found that she enjoyed just looking at her.

Casey rested her elbows on the table in front of her and leaned forward as she organized her cards. The motion caused her shirt to gap against her chest, but that damn scarf blocked Jacqueline's chance to glimpse a sliver of cleavage. When Jacqueline forced her attention back to Casey's face, Casey narrowed her eyes. Caught, and seeing no reason to deny her interest, Jacqueline put on her most flirtatious smile. Casey lifted her chin and gave a sexy little wink, and judging by the jolt of arousal that had Jacqueline squeezing her knees together in response, she'd been outplayed again.

"Do you want to make this interesting?" Casey's grin hinted that she understood exactly what she'd just done to Jacqueline.

"What did you have in mind?"

Casey gestured to her chips, then to Jacqueline's smaller pile. "I've got you covered. I'll put my entire stack against yours, even up, but if I win, you also have to give me your phone number."

Several dramatic gasps sounded around the table, and Jacqueline rolled her eyes. *Damn art majors.*

Kendra shrugged and threw her cards into the center of the table. "Well, I don't have shit, and I already have your phone number. So, I'm out."

Jacqueline didn't hesitate. "I call."

Casey laid two kings on the table in front of her and threw three cards facedown on the table in front of Kendra. "I'll take three."

Since they'd both committed their entire stacks, they had no reason to hide the cards pre-draw. Jacqueline followed suit, showing the two queens she'd felt confident in until just a moment ago. "Help me out, Kendra."

"Are you that afraid to give me your number?" Casey spoke as if they were the only two women in the room, and for a moment Jacqueline was jealous of her confidence. She'd never been very good at flirting, typically either awkward or chickening out altogether.

She smothered her insecurity. "You won't be getting anything but the losing hand."

Kendra flipped over three cards in front of Casey, none of which improved her hand. But her kings were still ahead. Jacqueline didn't realize how hard she was biting her lower lip until she saw Casey's eyes flick down to her mouth, then back up. She relaxed her jaw and ran her tongue across her lip to ease the indentations from her teeth. Casey's composure seemed to slip as she followed the motion, but then she turned her attention back to Kendra.

Kendra showed Jacqueline's first card—a five of diamonds, no help, and then came the seven of hearts.

"Don't celebrate yet," Jacqueline said as Casey's smile widened. "Kendra loves to be dramatic. She'll save the best card for last. Now, give me the queen."

Kendra lifted the card so only she could see it and shook her head. "Not a queen."

Casey turned her triumphant gaze to Jacqueline, and for a moment, Jacqueline didn't care if she won. Casey's eyes glittered like the afternoon sun dancing on the surface of a lake, and Jacqueline would tank every hand she'd ever played to see that expression again. But something in Kendra's eyes had given the hand away. Jacqueline would win it—the card had to be a five or a seven, giving her two pairs and besting Casey's kings. Kendra laid down the seven of diamonds with a flourish.

"Damn," Casey muttered.

"Told you. She can't resist the chance to perform." Jacqueline swept Casey's chips back next to hers.

Later, as the group started shuffling toward the door, Jacqueline began to gather up red plastic cups from around the table and let Kendra deal with the good-byes. They were Kendra's friends, after all. She certainly wasn't avoiding Casey, which was a good thing, because she'd have failed miserably. She spun around with her collection of cups and beer bottles and almost crashed into her.

"Whoa. Sorry about that." Casey grabbed Jacqueline's upper arms to steady her.

"S'okay." Jacqueline's still-full hands twitched. She should try to extricate herself from this accidental embrace. As she moved, the backs of her fingers brushed the front of Casey's blouse. The fabric was incredibly soft, and suddenly she couldn't stop wondering if her skin was softer. She stared at Casey's scarf and wished she had her hands free. She'd grab the ends of that scarf and pull Casey closer. She wanted her fingers spanning Casey's slim waist, squeezing her—

"Jacqueline." Casey's voice carried a trace of laughter, and a sly smile stretched across her beautiful mouth.

"I'm—uh, let me just put these—" She backed up and cringed when her butt hit the table behind her. Her face flushed with embarrassment and she sidestepped toward the trash can. After she emptied her hands, she turned around. Casey rested against the counter, one hip cocked higher than the other and her arms folded across her chest, blatantly surveying Jacqueline.

Jacqueline glanced down at her flannel shirt and blue jeans and wished she hadn't opted for comfort over fashion just this once. She'd had a long week and didn't feel like dressing up, so she'd freshened her makeup and decided the swirling winds she'd faced while walking between classes that day had left her hair unsalvageable for anything but a messy ponytail. Now she couldn't stop thinking about what Casey saw when she looked at her. Maybe she was wondering just how a woman could care so little about her appearance.

"So, I'd say thanks but—you took all my money." Casey gave her a wink that made her face feel even hotter.

"Then *I* should thank *you.*" She injected a teasing note into her voice, surprised and pleased that she could compose herself enough to flirt back.

"Well, you certainly seemed to enjoy it."

"Oh, I did."

"It was nice meeting you—mostly." Casey stuck out her hand.

Jacqueline laughed and took it, intending a quick handshake. But when Casey's palm slid against hers, Jacqueline held on, reluctant to relinquish the fire that traveled up her arm and through her body, like a flame following a trail of gunpowder.

"Are you really going to let me leave without getting my number?" Casey stepped closer and lowered her voice, the intimate tone flowing smoothly over obvious confidence. She didn't even seem to be trying, and she had Jacqueline ready to melt again.

"I believe the bet was for *my* number, and you lost." Jacqueline jerked her hand free. Disappointment flashed across Casey's face, then was quickly covered by bravado.

"The way I see it, we both lost that hand."

"How do you figure?"

"Because when you wake up tomorrow still thinking about me, you'll have to track me down through Kendra. And she'll know you're into me—"

"I'm into you?"

"Yes. And you know how gloaty she can be."

"First, I don't think gloaty is a word. And second—I'm into you?" Kendra did like to be overly involved in Jacqueline's life. And finding out Jacqueline might be interested in one of her artsy friends would just make her day.

"Yeah, you are." Casey moved forward until their breasts nearly touched. Only an inch or two shorter than she was, Casey was the perfect height, and Jacqueline couldn't help thinking how well they'd fit together. Casey's eyes appeared almost navy in the shadows of the room. "So, ask for my number."

"You're kind of bossy."

Casey crossed to the door to Jacqueline's bedroom and grabbed the dry-erase marker from the whiteboard hanging on the outside of the door. She wrote her name and phone number across it in a flowy-girly script. "Despite your stellar first impression, if you call me," she shrugged, "maybe I'll give you a shot."

CHAPTER ONE

Present Day

Jacqueline looped the handles of five plastic grocery bags over her hand. She lifted her load, pressed the button to lower the trunk of her Lexus, and snatched the two remaining bags out before it finished closing. Though the plastic bags already limited the circulation in her fingers, she didn't bother redistributing their weight as she hurried up the short walkway in front of her father's home.

When she reached the front door, she tapped the toe of her shoe against it in lieu of knocking. "Dad." Her fingers were numb, and her palms tingled under the constricting strips of plastic. She kicked again, harder this time. The door swung open, and she turned sideways and slipped past her father. "I told you I was bringing your groceries today."

"Sorry, Jacq. I must have fallen asleep in my chair." He followed her into the kitchen.

"At noon?" She hefted the bags onto the counter and turned to study him. "Are you feeling okay?" His hair had been thinning for years, and the comb-over she'd been trying to talk him into abandoning looked even more sparse than usual. He'd given up golf last year—or was it two years ago—complaining of back pain, so maybe he'd lost some muscle mass since then, due to his increased inactivity. But other than that, he looked fine to her. Was he napping out of boredom? Six years ago, after her mother died, she'd encouraged him to meet up with his buddies at the VFW. He'd always been proud of his air-force service during Vietnam and enjoyed visiting with fellow veterans. But she couldn't recall him mentioning them recently.

"I'm fine. Can't an old man fall asleep in front of the television in peace? Doesn't matter what time it is. I don't have anything better to do."

"I brought you that list of activities from the senior center." She opened the refrigerator and began pulling out the expired food before she put in the new supplies.

"Now, why would I want to go hang out with a bunch of cackling hags?"

"You could make some friends. I'm sure you'd find some surly old veterans like yourself there."

"Very funny."

"I got one of those rotisserie chickens you like. You should eat that in the next couple of days. After that, there are plenty of your favorite frozen dinners—"

"I'm not an invalid. If I want something different, I'll go out and get it." His tone was gruff but not angry as he left the kitchen.

She nodded, clenching her jaw against her protest, and continued stowing the food. She'd started getting his groceries last winter when he'd had pneumonia and had carried on even after he was well again. Though he readily allowed her to continue shopping for him, he never liked for her to suggest he depended on her to do it.

"I'll be in Atlanta for the rest of the week. Do you need anything else before I go?" Travel had been an integral part of her career for well over a decade now. As regional manager of human resources for a major national shipping company, she traversed Tennessee, Kentucky, Virginia, and North Carolina regularly. Company-wide meetings forced her even farther away several times a year. Next week she'd be at the divisional office in Atlanta for a quarterly meeting with her boss.

"If I think of anything, I'll call Casey."

"Dad, I'm here. You don't need to call Casey."

"You just said you're going out of town." He'd already settled back into his favorite chair by the time she returned to the living room. His hand covered the television remote that rested on the arm of his chair, but the flat-screen hadn't been turned on. She'd replaced his old tube television with a brand-name 55-inch LED model several years ago.

"I am, but—" She couldn't argue. She wouldn't be around this week. Before they'd split up, she'd always loved that her father and Casey were close, especially since Casey had lost both her parents only two years after she and Jacqueline met. But Jacqueline hated that sometimes it seemed Casey was closer to her father than she was. She couldn't really fault either of them since she spent more than half the month out of town. So instead, she nodded stiffly and squeezed his shoulder as she headed for the door. "I'll call you tonight."

"Be safe."

She waved a hand as she exited. He'd been calling out the same good-bye since she first started driving away by herself at sixteen. With the exception of one minor car accident in her twenties, she'd managed to comply.

In the driveway, she slid behind the wheel of her car. She'd loaded her suitcase and her leather laptop bag in the trunk that morning. By the time she merged onto the interstate, just minutes later, her brain had already switched completely into work mode. She would arrive in Atlanta in time to check in at the hotel and make her first meeting. But, for the sake of efficiency, she would also be monitoring a conference call via her car's integrated Bluetooth feature while driving.

❖

"Come on. Give me that smile that makes everyone melt." Casey looked through the viewfinder of her favorite Nikon and shook a rattle over her head. The baby propped up in the fall-themed tableau giggled, and Casey fired off a series of shots. She'd hoped to get some photos outside, but the day had turned too cold for the baby, so she'd be doing the whole shoot in the studio. "There we go. Just a bit longer, little man. Okay, Mama, put him in his last outfit." She adjusted a couple of settings on her camera as the child's mother swept him up and carried him to a small loveseat against the wall behind Casey. "Sean, let's get the next setup ready."

"Sure thing, Mom." Sean loped into the frame and began loading the decorations into a large plastic tote. He'd always loved hanging out in her home studio. In fact, even from the time Casey and Jacqueline had taken him in at five years old, he'd been so fascinated with her cameras that she'd been convinced he would follow in her footsteps.

When, at ten years old, he'd declared that he wanted to be a veterinarian, she'd been certain that was just a childhood phase. Now, entering his second year as an animal-science major in preparation for veterinary school, he'd proved her wrong. Though their road hadn't always been smooth, she couldn't be more proud of the caring young man he'd become.

Those first few months, fresh out of a nightmare of a foster home, he'd been timid and extremely distrustful. Slowly, Casey and Jacqueline had won him over and soon found out he was warm and anxious to please. In the early years, when Casey gave him busywork in the studio to keep him occupied, she offered a small allowance as a reward for good behavior. Not long after his twelfth birthday, she and Jacqueline had split up. That first year, he'd begged to stay on and work with her for the summer. The petty part of her had celebrated the fact that he seemed to be choosing her over Jacqueline. But in the eight years since, she'd learned to share his affections.

In preparation for the next series of shots, Sean rolled out a piece of artificial turf marked with white yard markers. As the baby's mother dressed him in the onesie decorated like a football, Sean assembled the smaller version of a football goal post that he'd built for her out of PVC pipe and spray-painted yellow. She found the layout a bit boring, but this particular shot had been set up exactly to the mother's specifications. Casey hadn't been able to convince her that there were other, more creative ways to shoot a football theme.

She planned to take a few like this, then switch it up a little to better fit her style and let the client decide which she liked best in the end.

"Do you need anything else before I head out?" Sean asked.

She pulled him into a hug, which he merely tolerated at first, but then he wrapped his arms around her shoulders as well. "Would it be too much to ask that you not go?" She pressed her cheek to his chest and swallowed against the tightness in her throat. Her baby boy had topped six feet by the time he graduated high school.

"Mom, classes start next week. You know I like to get moved into the dorm and settled early." Last year, she and Jacqueline had both helped him move into the dorm at Middle Tennessee State University for his freshman year, neither willing to forego such a milestone. This year he would be handling the move-in himself, taking all that he could fit in the Camry that Jacqueline had given him for his birthday.

"I got spoiled having you around all summer." She reluctantly released him and resisted the urge to ruffle the dark mop of hair he'd let grow shaggy over his forehead and ears.

He smiled, and for a moment Casey glimpsed the boy who had somehow managed to keep his beaming smile despite being taken from his birth mother and placed in foster care at five years old. The first time she'd seen him, she'd been taking photos for the Department of Children's Service website as part of a charitable donation. She'd met several caseworkers and the children in state's custody at a park to get some candid shots for the DCS website to showcase the kids that needed loving homes.

That night, at home, she hadn't been able to shut up about the little curly-haired boy who'd stolen her heart. Within days, and after several serious discussions with Jacqueline, she'd scheduled the necessary parenting classes to gain approval as a foster parent. She figured Sean would've already found a home in the time it took for her to become fully qualified. But as soon as she finished, she inquired about him and found he'd been placed only temporarily. She and Jacqueline had brought him home days later. For over two years, they endured frustrating supervised visitations with his birth mother, which often left Sean disappointed and cranky for days afterward. Finally, his mother's parental rights were terminated. He had officially become theirs three days before his eighth birthday.

Sean slung his backpack over his shoulder, but before he could ease away, she cupped her hands on either side of his face and pulled him down for a kiss on his cheek.

"Did you already say good-bye to Mama?"

He nodded. "She had to get Poppa's groceries today. Then she's headed out of town this afternoon. I went by her place last night." He was used to living his life around Jacqueline's schedule. They both had been. Not long after making Sean legally their son, Jacqueline had accepted the promotion that pulled her away from home at least two weeks a month.

Casey had assumed most of the daily responsibilities for Sean. After trying unsuccessfully to juggle her own schedule with his, she'd quit her position at a growing art gallery. She'd converted their garage into a home studio and invested in enough new equipment to launch her own photography business.

As Jacqueline advanced through the ranks, the amount of travel required increased. If Casey dared complain, Jacqueline promised someday it would pay off and they'd spend more time together. But they'd split up before that day had come. And now, eight years later, Casey didn't get the sense that Jacqueline had slowed down at all.

"Text me when you get there." She wanted a phone call, but that would be too much to ask. Sean had been trying to assert his independence lately. During his freshman year, he'd seemed to experience some of the same separation anxiety she had. But this year, he'd seemed braver, more ready to conquer the world.

"Sure thing." He headed for the door, pausing long enough to call over his shoulder, "Tell Nina I said bye."

She smiled as the door closed behind him, suspecting he only mentioned Nina for her benefit. She'd been seeing Nina for a year and a half, and though he'd been away at school for most of it, when they did spend time together, neither of them showed interest in getting to know the other. Somewhat solitary by nature, Nina had told her when they first started dating that she didn't want kids. But they'd agreed to see where things went. After all, Sean was grown; it wasn't as if she'd need to parent him.

The next round of photographs went smoothly. In fact, the baby slept through most of them. She even managed to snap a few with her own, more-minimalist take on the football theme. Though she wished she'd captured a bit more variety in his expressions, she knew better than to suggest they wake him in order to catch a couple with his eyes open. Most likely, the parents would choose only one photograph in this outfit to include in their purchased package. Certainly, this young mother wouldn't think one more option would be worth the effort of getting the boy back to sleep afterward. Especially since she'd likely end up picking a proof in which he was sleeping. Casey had theorized that parents liked pictures of their babies sleeping to remind them of how cute they were during those times when they just wouldn't stop crying. Of course, she'd made the mistake of mentioning that joke in front of only one mother before she learned that, in fact, it really wasn't funny.

She'd just clicked her shutter release one final time when the baby started to stir. The mother, already engrossed in packing up their belongings, mumbled and began cooing at him from across the room. Casey set her camera aside and carefully picked him up. She cradled him close, swaying from side to side as he settled back down. She brushed a finger against his downy cap of brown hair and breathed in the heavenly scent of baby lotion. She wandered around the open area in front of her backdrop, humming a quiet nonsensical lullaby to the boy.

"Thanks so much," the mother whispered as she lifted him from Casey's arms moments later.

"Sure." Her voice sounded rough, and she cleared the emotion from her throat quietly. "I'll email you the proofs soon."

"I can't wait to show my husband. His parents will be in town in two weeks. I'd love to have some to send home with them." She slung the diaper bag over her shoulder and headed for the door. "I wish I could email pictures to them, but they're still in the Stone Age and his mother insists on prints."

"Certainly. If you get back to me with your selections rather quickly, I should have no problem getting some done for you. Do you need help out?"

"Thanks, but I'm getting pretty good at juggling all this."

Casey held the door open while the woman left, then closed it behind her and retrieved her camera. She ejected the memory card, then slid it into her desktop and set it to upload the hundreds of shots she'd just taken. Since she had back-to-back appointments tomorrow, she'd be editing these photos well into this evening so she could get the proofs out.

She passed through the door that separated her studio from the rest of the house. Since she'd already established her business here and Jacqueline spent so much time out of town, they agreed that she would keep the house in the split. They'd listed the house with the school as Sean's residence so he wouldn't have to change districts, and he'd usually stayed with her during the week.

Jacqueline had moved into a high-rise condo downtown. At the time, she'd seemed thrilled, citing her shortened commute to the office and the lack of lawn care and outside maintenance. At first, Casey wondered if she'd faked any of that enthusiasm to cover up her real feelings or to make the transition easier for Sean, but since she still lived there, maybe she really did like it. She'd let Sean decorate the second bedroom for himself. He'd loved spending weekends and his school breaks with Jacqueline, thrilled by the pace of downtown and the view from the twentieth floor.

"Honey, I'm home," Casey called to the empty house as she stepped into the living room. She'd started doing that when Sean left for school last year, because it somehow made her feel less lonely.

A few months ago, she'd said it out of habit once when Nina was with her. Nina had used the opportunity to suggest they move in together. Casey asked for a couple of months to think about it, citing Sean's return home for the summer as an excuse to not rush things. She supposed she'd now be facing that conversation again.

She liked Nina and enjoyed the time they'd spent together, but once she got past missing having Sean in the house, she actually looked forward to having the place to herself again. Until last year, when Sean left, she'd never lived alone. She'd gone from her parents' house to sharing a college dorm room, then to an off-campus apartment with Jacqueline.

Without Sean, at first, she'd been lonely and the house seemed too quiet. But after a while, she'd learned to appreciate the time for herself. She'd begun to explore photography for her own enjoyment for the first time in longer than she could remember. She'd started hiking and shooting nature—lakes, trees, flowers, birds—any frame with no people in it, really. She feared that letting Nina further into her life meant relinquishing those new pieces of her freedom.

She popped open a bottle of wine and poured a large glass, deciding now was not the time to examine her relationship with Nina. She'd had four sessions today, all children, two of which clearly didn't want to sit for portraits, and was exhausted. She needed a quick break to recharge before getting back to work.

She headed down the short hallway to the left of the kitchen. Pausing in the doorway to Sean's room, she automatically cataloged the things missing from the room—his laptop, the iPhone docking station that seemed to constantly be playing music, and most of the clothes from his closet, judging by the empty hangers visible through the open closet door.

He'd left the framed photograph on his dresser of him standing between Casey and Jacqueline last year when they'd dropped him off at college. Casey mentally compared it to the one in her own bedroom that was taken the day they'd officially adopted him. He'd changed immensely, as expected, growing up and filling out into a young man. And Casey critically picked out the signs of aging in her own features. New lines bracketed her mouth. Her face was a bit fuller—much the same as the rest of her body—and the dimples brought out by her smile appeared deeper.

Jacqueline, too, had softened over the years. Her waist was a little thicker, and her breasts and hips were rounder. Her dark hair was as lustrous as ever, but she wore it shorter now, an inch or so shy of brushing her shoulders. Just before the picture had been snapped, Jacqueline had thrown her arm around Sean's shoulders. Their wide smiles touched their nearly identical brown eyes in such a way that if she didn't know better, she might have sworn they were related by blood.

The room still smelled like Sean's favorite cologne, and she blinked back a mist of tears as she closed the door and continued down the hall to her own room.

CHAPTER TWO

Jacqueline rolled her golf cart to a stop behind the one in front of her just next to the tee box on the first hole. She stepped out of the cart and twisted her upper body slowly, pulling one arm across her chest. She'd had some back issues in her thirties, and now, in her forties, if she didn't stretch she'd be more susceptible to injury or, at the very least, some next-day soreness.

She drew a deep breath, enjoying the scent of fresh-cut grass. A light breeze cooled the heat from the full midday sun. If she closed her eyes she could almost convince herself she was out here for pleasure and not business. She chuckled to herself. A round of golf purely for her own enjoyment—that would be a rare treat.

Owen Tanager, her boss and playing partner for the day, slid out of the passenger seat and pulled out his driver. "Are we doing yoga or playing golf, Jacqueline?" He strode to the tee box.

Before she could reply, another one of their foursome spoke up. "Show her how it's done."

Owen laughed at the jab from one of their competitors for the day. He'd roped two of the local managers into spending the afternoon on the course with them. The losers would pay for dinner and drinks later. Owen teed up his ball and took a blistering practice swing. His fitted polo showed off his strong shoulders and back and highlighted the V-shaped torso he worked hard to maintain. Jacqueline admired his commitment to fitness, especially since he had fifteen years on her, though, in fairness, he spent more time with his personal trainer than she ever would. She'd given up wasting money on a gym membership she wouldn't use, and rarely even made time to use the hotel fitness centers when she traveled.

With a big swing, Owen sent his ball soaring down the fairway. But the trajectory painted a sweeping fade to the right, and his ball bounced into the tree line. None of the other players said a word as Owen stalked back to the cart and shoved his driver back into his bag.

"Pick me up, partner." Owen patted Jacqueline's shoulder.

Filled with confidence, she grinned as she teed up the ball. During their first outing together, she'd let him win, on the advice of a colleague, and he'd barely noticed her for the entire round. The next time she'd played with him, she hadn't held anything back, besting him by several strokes in the end. She ignored the it-was-nice-knowing-you looks her coworkers gave her and held her head high. He seemed pissed. But the next time she was in town for a charity tournament, he'd promptly claimed her for his team.

She glanced down the fairway once more, then swung her driver. The sound and feel of the ball coming off the face of the driver indicated she'd hit the ball as well as she could. It landed in the center of the fairway. Since she played from the men's tees, one of the other two would likely out-drive her in distance, but often, the rest of her game was tight enough to compensate.

Two hours and ten holes later, Owen and Jacqueline dominated their opponents. As they'd pulled so far ahead that their score was unreachable, Owen had started teasing the other two. He began talking about where they'd go for dinner and what expensive dish he might make them pay for. His attitude was a bit arrogant for Jacqueline's taste. She preferred to enjoy her victory more privately. Though there wasn't really much on the line in this match, she liked to win. She loved the adrenaline rush that grew with each passing hole—a feeling rivaled only by really good sex. *It's about time for that, too,* she thought as she stowed her club in her bag and climbed into the cart.

Maybe she could catch Marti in town. Over the years, Jacqueline had been involved with a number of women, always casual and usually short-term. She remained upfront about what she wanted, careful not to lead them on. She wouldn't date a woman in Nashville, convinced, with all of her travel, they'd have some of the same issues that drove her and Casey apart. So she made mostly superficial connections in the cities she frequented. She wasn't interested in relocating a woman to Tennessee, and she didn't do long-distance. Eventually, her terms had brought them to a point of separation either when the other woman wanted more from her or met someone else who could provide a real relationship.

Marti was different. As a flight attendant, she also spent nearly as much time away as she did at home. She wasn't looking for a wife, just good sex and companionship when she was at home in Atlanta. Jacqueline had been involved with her for three years, and they'd actually developed an uncomplicated friendship.

She grabbed her phone from the cup holder of the golf cart and sent a text inviting Marti to a late dinner one night this week. As she stepped out of the cart, she shoved her phone in her pocket, then grabbed her nine iron and approached her ball in the center of the fairway. She was settling in for her next shot when her phone vibrated against her thigh, indicating what she was certain was an affirmative response from Marti. She swung her club and sent the ball arcing toward the green. The ball landed, took a short hop, and rolled to within ten feet of the hole.

Owen tapped his palm against her shoulder. "That's my girl." He winced, as if he'd just realized that he'd made such a condescending remark to his human-resources manager. "Okay. You know I didn't mean it like that."

Jacqueline nodded and shoved her club back into her bag. Though his comment was definitely inappropriate, the calculated apology would leave her looking like a hysterical female in front of the other guys if she challenged him. Besides, Jacqueline believed in picking her battles, and this wasn't one she wanted to wage. She'd been playing this game for too long to screw it up now. Owen's boss had been hinting around about retiring, and Owen was favored to move into his spot. If Jacqueline wanted to stay in play for Owen's job, she wouldn't be raising hell about a sexist comment.

Despite the veneer of polish at the executive levels, the shipping business was built on eighteen-wheelers and forklifts. When she wasn't meeting with the suits, Jacqueline spent most of her time with the hourly employees, truck drivers and dock workers. Thanks to mandatory annual sexual-harassment training, she heard fewer crass remarks and offensive language than when she first joined the company. But in the end, she worked in a blue-collar industry dominated by male employees. She still caught the occasional lewd or sexist comment when someone thought she wasn't in earshot.

❖

Casey balanced a large plastic storage bowl filled with chili in her hands while locking the deadbolt on her front door. She'd slung a tote bag containing a bottle of wine, a loaf of Texas toast, and a Ziploc baggie of homemade brownies over her shoulder. Despite her cargo, she opted to walk the three blocks to her standing Wednesday dinner engagement. Though the temperature still held at just over eighty degrees, the evening air lacked the humidity typical of Tennessee in late August.

As she passed the park, she nodded at several parents watching over their young children from a bench near the playground. She'd walked Sean to the same park to play more times than she could count. The green space so close to the house had been one of its major selling points. She'd been happy she was able to stay in the neighborhood after she and Jacqueline broke up. She'd been prepared to fight for the house, but surprisingly Jacqueline had acquiesced without protest and, in fact, had insisted on paying part of the mortgage so that Casey and Sean wouldn't have to worry about money. Casey had argued, not comfortable with Jacqueline supporting her, but Jacqueline had insisted that her contribution was for Sean. She'd also admitted that with all of her traveling, having Sean and Casey close to her father eased her mind.

Casey had worked hard to build her business and decrease her dependency on Jacqueline's money. She'd reached a point of self-sufficiency several years ago and had started putting any money that didn't support Sean into a savings account. She'd presented him with a chunk of it each year as he started college. She planned to sign the account over to him upon his college graduation. She felt good about separating herself financially from Jacqueline. But she'd never let go of her connection to Teddy.

As she reached Teddy's house, she knocked once, then, using her key, opened the door in order to save him the walk to the foyer. "Teddy?"

She found him in the living room, in his chair with the sports section. She didn't know anyone else who read an actual newspaper. Her attention span was so short, she typically heard the latest sound-bites from the local television network while editing photos and drinking her morning coffee.

She touched his shoulder and returned his greeting on her way to his modest kitchen. The outdated countertops and cabinets inspired a wave of nostalgia for her mother's kitchen. Teddy even had the same ivory-colored appliances she'd grown up with. She dumped the chili in a big pot, set it on the stovetop to warm, and turned on the oven to heat the bread. After pouring two glasses of wine, she headed back through the doorway to the living room. While most of their neighbors, herself included, were opening up the floor plans in these old houses, Teddy had retained the walls that defined each separate room and made the footprint feel smaller.

"Anything good in there?" She nodded toward the now-folded paper on the lamp table beside him as she handed him a glass.

"Never is." He sipped, then nodded his head in approval. "Something smells good."

"Chicken chili. It's been wafting through the house all day. I can hardly wait for the bread to toast." The small plate of cheese and crackers she'd called lunch in between clients today hadn't kept her stomach from growling throughout the afternoon. But her day had already been jammed before she'd agreed to squeeze in a senior portrait session that required her to drive twenty minutes outside of town to an abandoned barn.

"Did Sean get away before you started crying all over him?"

"Yes. Smart-ass." She gave an exaggerated sniff. "I'm getting better at this."

"Oh, honey, you never get better at letting them go. You just learn how to hide it."

"Now there's something I've never been good at." The sarcastic comment slipped out before she could censor it. She usually avoided talking about Jacqueline with Teddy. He'd never stopped treating Casey like a daughter, and that couldn't have always been easy for him.

"You weren't alone in that."

"Sorry." She stood and headed for the kitchen to check the bread. "Today has me feeling nostalgic."

He nodded absently, his eyes taking on a distant look. The ball of emotion in her throat grew larger as she continued into the kitchen. She hated these moments of vulnerability that reminded her of his advancing age.

"Get a grip, Casey." She rolled her eyes as she bent to take the bread from the oven. Mostly, she was simply emotional and being melodramatic. But a small part of her couldn't help focusing on all of the little ways he'd been acting differently. Where she'd once seen only a strong family provider, this past year, she'd caught glimpses of frailty—both physically and mentally.

As she spun toward the counter, she nearly ran into Teddy, now standing in the middle of the kitchen. She jerked the tray close to her to keep from burning him, and the bread slid toward her, several of the pieces ending up trapped between her shirt and the edge of the cookie sheet. She maneuvered the hot pan onto the counter while trying to salvage the bread.

"Geez, Teddy. Don't sneak up on a girl like that."

His eyes darted from the bread to the front of her shirt, and a slight tremor shook his hand as he swiped his forehead. He appeared more shook up by the near miss than she did. He stared at the three slices of bread now on the floor.

"I hope you weren't craving bread." She gathered them up and threw them in the trash, then bent to clean the crumbs from the floor. Despite her attempt at levity, he still appeared bothered. She straightened and touched his shoulder. "Hey, it's fine. Did you come in here for something?"

"No—I—" He looked around, obviously now at a loss as to why he'd entered the kitchen.

She steered him toward the dining room. "Sit down. I'll bring your dinner."

When she set a bowl of chili in front of him a minute later, he said, "I can't seem to remember anything these days. Getting old sucks."

She laughed.

"Just you wait."

She groaned as she settled slowly back in her chair, further proving his point. "Are you not feeling well?" She laid her paper napkin across her lap while covertly studying him for signs of illness.

"Aches and pains. Let's stop talking about how old I am." He waved his fork dismissively.

"I'm not too far behind you. If I didn't write everything down, I'd never know where I was supposed to be or what I'm doing."

"That's because you work too hard."

"Says the man who had two jobs for most of his adult life."

"Raising Jacq wasn't cheap."

Casey laughed with him. "She does have expensive taste. But I don't have it easy either. You've seen Sean eat."

"You have a point there. I've stayed out of the business between you. But I'm sure if you needed money for Sean, Jacq—"

"No. She's always done more than her share for him financially." She set her fork down and wiped her mouth, her appetite waning with the change in topic. "Sometimes, the extra work is more about filling the hours than the bank account." She didn't want him worrying about her finances. And her statement was partly true. She readily admitted she'd been experiencing a bit of empty-nest syndrome. But more than that, she found a degree of satisfaction in capturing the perfect memories for couples and families.

CHAPTER THREE

By the time Casey left Teddy's house, the sun had long set, but she refused the offer to take his car. Still, she kept a vigilant watch and maintained her pace through the dark patches between the circles of streetlamp glow. She carried her keys fisted in her hand, with one sticking out between her middle and index fingers. They lived in a relatively safe area outside of the metropolitan area of Nashville, but as the city continued to grow and change, so did the neighborhoods around it. One of the homes down the block from Teddy had been broken into just last week. The residents weren't home, and their security alarm had apparently scared off the suspects before they could get much from the house.

Casey worried more about Teddy than about herself. But he and his late wife had bought the house just before Jacqueline was born, and he'd likely die in it, just as she had. Casey had lost her parents in a car accident while she was in college. Teddy and his wife had been nearly as instrumental as Jacqueline in getting her through their funerals and the months following while settling their estate.

She and Jacqueline had been separated for two years when Jacqueline's mother had passed away. She marveled at how differently her family had dealt with their grief. Teddy had withdrawn from everyone except Sean, who, at only fourteen, had probably processed his loss most easily of any of them. She hated that he'd said good-bye to so many people in his life already. As much as she knew he loved his adopted family, he also seemed to hold a piece of himself back, as if expecting he might lose them at any time.

Casey spent the days and weeks following the funeral trying to take care of everyone, while privately dealing with losing her second mother. She forced home-cooked meals on Teddy, smothered Sean with love, and sent largely unanswered texts to Jacqueline just checking in. Jacqueline, like her father, had isolated herself. Casey suspected she'd thrown herself even more into work, but she hadn't known how Jacqueline was handling her downtime, when she couldn't escape her grief.

She'd found out one night when Jacqueline had responded to her text by calling her cell phone. Jacqueline had sounded exhausted and slurred her words. She probably should have demurred when Jacqueline asked her to come over, but she'd never been able to refuse Jacqueline when she needed something badly enough to ask for it. Jacqueline was almost a full bottle of wine ahead of her when she arrived at the apartment. She made a cursory attempt to catch up but still had most of her faculties about her when Jacqueline, sappy and sentimental, moved into her arms. Casey struggled to keep the embrace friendly and comforting. But then Jacqueline had kissed Casey's neck, and she'd been lost. When Jacqueline started taking Casey's clothes off, she'd tried to be honorable, given that Jacqueline seemed to be walking that line between just drunk enough and just sober enough. Apparently, Jacqueline remembered how to touch her in order to short-circuit her brain, and she'd given herself over to that sensation, perhaps too easily.

As she unlocked her front door, she closed off those dangerous memories and forced her thoughts back to Teddy. She'd been getting more concerned about him but hadn't decided how to proceed. She settled on the couch and picked up her cell phone, then set it aside, delaying her next move.

If she took them separately, she could discount his moments of confusion in the same way he did, the rigors of aging. And maybe that's all they were. She wasn't a doctor. But when they were coupled with his newfound clumsiness, she couldn't disregard them altogether. Just this evening, he'd stumbled as he made his way into the living room. She'd been close enough to grab his elbow and halt his fall. He'd immediately blamed Jacqueline for moving the lamp table next to the couch. But the table had been in the same place for as long as Casey could recall, and she couldn't see any indentations in the carpet to indicate it had been moved.

Any time she tried to have a serious discussion with him, he dismissed her. The one time she'd pushed even further, he'd retreated to his workshop in the garage. She'd backed off and tried never to chase him out there again, mostly because she didn't like the idea of him messing around with power tools just to spite her. Her next step was to call in backup.

She didn't want to distract Sean from his studies, so she'd have to contact Jacqueline. They'd gotten pretty good at co-parenting. But for some reason, Teddy was a sore spot between them. Jacqueline seemed to resent her continued involvement in Teddy's life, appearing to think that when Sean got old enough to maintain his own relationship with his grandfather, Casey should have simply cut off contact with Teddy. But Casey had stopped letting Jacqueline's opinions steer her life long ago.

Decision made, she picked up her phone and scrolled through her contacts until she found Jacqueline's name, then pressed send before she could change her mind. Jacqueline answered after three rings.

"Hey, it's Casey."

Jacqueline's quiet laugh vibrated through the phone. "Yeah, I know. I still have your number in my phone."

"Right. Am I calling too late?"

"No. It's fine."

Judging by her curtness, Casey didn't fully believe her. But calling her on it would only lead them off the track of her intended conversation. Jacqueline wouldn't want to admit that Casey could still read her tone of voice.

"I saw your dad this evening and he seemed a little off. Has he been feeling okay?"

"As far as I know. He hasn't complained about anything. He seemed all right when I was there Monday."

"He said he was fine and I didn't push. I just—he seemed a little fuzzy—confused, maybe. He's more unsteady on his feet lately. And I noticed his hands seem stiffer than usual."

"He's got arthritis." Jacqueline sounded irritated. "He'll tell you himself that he's no spring chicken. But I will say, he doesn't like being questioned about how he's feeling."

"Yeah, I know." Now she wished she hadn't called. Jacqueline clearly thought she was being silly. "I'm sorry I bothered you."

"Casey." Jacqueline's tone indicated she thought Casey was trying to pick a fight. She should have known she wouldn't get anywhere with this call. But before she could act on her urge to hang up the phone, Jacqueline sighed. "I'm sorry. Thank you for calling. Really. I'll try to talk to him this weekend."

"Thank you. Let me know if I can do anything to help." Casey grasped for a civil topic to leave the conversation with. "Sean said you're in Atlanta."

"Yep. Until Friday."

"You sound tired." They'd spent a lot of time on the phone together over the years. Casey used to be able to tell what kind of day Jacqueline had had within seconds.

"Then I can imagine how it sounds when I say I'll be in Memphis most of next week."

"It's good to know some things never change." Casey chuckled.

"I like to think the company would fall apart without me."

"I'm sure it would. I won't keep you. Good night."

"Good night." Jacqueline ended the call and stared at her cell. She'd hoped she'd been imagining the decline in her father's health, but clearly she wasn't the only one noticing.

"Is there a problem?" At the sound of the soft voice behind her, she turned away from the window. Marti sat up in bed. Though there was no need for modesty between them, Marti held the sheet against her chest with one hand. Her otherwise ivory skin still held a flush from her orgasm. Jacqueline had stirred from her own postcoital nap when she heard the ringtone she'd assigned to Casey's number.

"Sorry if I woke you." She held up the phone. "That was about my dad."

"You got out of bed with me to talk to your father?"

"Worse." Jacqueline smiled. She strode naked back toward the bed, enjoying the way Marti's eyes followed her. "I got out of bed to talk to my ex about my dad."

"Wow. I'll try not to be offended."

"You shouldn't be." Jacqueline picked up a robe from a nearby chair and wrapped it around herself. She glanced at the clock on the nightstand and resisted the urge to slide back between the sheets. She usually returned to her hotel room, citing her need for a good night's sleep before another busy day. But she didn't really feel like dressing just to head across town and fall into a different bed.

Marti carefully picked her fingers through her knotted hair, wincing as they stuck and tugged. "I don't know why you insist on tangling your hands in my hair."

Jacqueline laughed. The first time she'd seen Marti striding down the aisle of a plane, every long auburn tress had been perfectly under control—smooth, coiled, and pinned against her head. The first time they'd been together, Marti had released her hair and let it fall to her shoulders. Jacqueline harbored a secret thrill every time she watched Marti writhing beneath her, so consumed by pleasure she didn't care that her hair wrapped itself into a tousled mess.

"Let me help you with that." She sank her fingers into the hair at the base of Marti's skull and pulled her close.

"You're not really going to help, are you?" Marti asked between kisses.

"That depends on your definition of help," Jacqueline murmured as she let her robe fall to the floor and climbed back into bed.

❖

"What a week, huh?" Casey opened a pizza box and slid a slice each onto two plates. Her schedule had been nonstop all week, and she'd lacked the energy to dress for the restaurant where they'd had reservations. "Thanks for settling for pizza."

"Please, you got pepperoni and black olives. I can't be mad when you ordered my favorite." Nina settled on one end of the couch and accepted a plate from Casey. She hadn't argued when Casey had texted to say she didn't feel like going out. Instead, she'd arrived after work and asked Casey for some more-comfortable clothes. Casey had ordered the pizza while Nina changed from her business attire. She liked Nina in her suits, but she'd always found her approachably sexy in the sweats and oversized T-shirt she wore now. Her dark, pixie-cut hair, stuck up in places where Casey imagined she'd run her hand through it during her frustration with the rush-hour drive from downtown.

Casey sat next to her. She picked the olives off her slice and pushed them to the side of her plate, staring at the almost donut-shaped indentations in the remaining cheese. If only she could convince herself they'd been mini-donuts and not bitter rings of what looked like fungus that tainted the taste of everything they touched.

Nina noticed her grimace as she bit into the slice. "You could have gotten them just on half."

Casey shrugged. The kid who'd taken her delivery order over the phone had struggled to get her address correct. By the time she'd ordered the food, she'd lost all confidence that he'd get their order right anyway.

"So, tell me about your week. I feel like we've barely spoken since last Sunday."

"Same as usual. More shoots than I can handle and a ton of editing in order to get proofs out in time."

"I guess I shouldn't complain that business is good for you." Nina's tone indicated she wanted to do just that. "I'd hoped we could have a serious talk this weekend, but it doesn't seem like you're up for it."

Casey set her plate aside and rubbed a hand over her face. She really wasn't. She'd known for a while that Nina wanted to move their relationship forward. And why wouldn't she? As lesbians who'd dated for well over a year and hadn't U-Hauled yet, they must have set some kind of record.

"We've been dating for almost two years." Nina's petulant-child voice wasn't one of Casey's favorites.

"Clearly we're rounding up," she murmured.

"What?"

"Nothing. Go ahead."

"I just—I need to know, where's this going? Are we going to live together? I want that. Do you?"

"I—" She glanced around the living room. She'd put away most of the photos of her and Jacqueline when they split up. But a few remained, those treasured photos with Sean in them. She'd never wanted him to think she aspired to wipe his other mother from their lives. Even without the photos, Jacqueline's imprint remained on their home. She'd brought home many of the pieces in the house while traveling.

Nina set her plate aside. "Not here. I understand why that would be weird for you. Well, I'm trying to. But it's been, what, eight years? When does it stop being her house?"

"I'm sorry." Nina didn't deserve to pay for Casey's past. *God, I'm such an ass.* Nina had every right to expect more of their relationship. And if Casey didn't want to lose her, she needed to make some concessions. "You're right. Not here." She took Nina's hands in hers. "Maybe we could look for a place together, one that's ours."

"Yeah?" Hope warmed Nina's eyes to honey brown, and the beginning of a smile pulled at the corners of her wide mouth.

Casey nodded.

Nina surged forward and wrapped her in a warm hug. Casey cupped the back of Nina's neck where the fringe of her hair touched her skin. Nina pulled back, took Casey's face between her hands, and stared into her eyes as if searching for something. Casey tried to block everything except her affection for Nina from her mind. Apparently pleased with what she found, Nina guided her close for a kiss.

CHAPTER FOUR

By the time Jacqueline fought her way out of Atlanta's evening rush hour Friday afternoon and made her way over Monteagle Mountain, she'd arrived home late that night. She'd spent Saturday ensconced in her apartment, catching up on laundry and household chores. Her precious weekend passed far too quickly.

From time to time, she'd considered hiring a maid service. But giving the key to her apartment to a total stranger made her nervous. She already tried not to think about the security desk downstairs where a copy hung in a locked case alongside all of the others for the building. Besides, she enjoyed cleaning. She liked the combination of accomplishment and fresh lemon scent that permeated her rooms after she finished.

Sunday afternoon, she hit the grocery store, armed with her father's list and feeling almost grateful that she'd be out of town in the coming week and didn't have to also get her own groceries as well. She dreaded those trips to the store when she had to lump her items together on the belt in two separate stacks. On those occasions, she supervised the bagging so she didn't have to then sort the items again before dropping off her father's food.

By the time she pulled up in front of his house, she'd exhausted her patience with the busy store patrons, the apathetic clerk, and the Sunday drivers impeding her progress on the street. She just wanted to drop in for a few minutes, then go home and enjoy a quiet night before heading out to Memphis the next morning.

"He doesn't even need half this stuff anyway," she grumbled as she hauled the bags out of the trunk.

For the past couple of months, she'd noticed while putting away his groceries that he hadn't eaten much of the food she'd bought the week before. Yet, when he gave her his list the next week, it contained all the same items. His freezer was beginning to look like he might be preparing for the apocalypse. And there was no chance the stray cat he insisted on feeding on his back porch would run out of food anytime soon. By all appearances, the little mongrel ate more than Teddy did.

She maneuvered her right hand, loaded with plastic bags, as close to the doorframe as she could and extended her thumb just far enough to hit the doorbell.

"Dad," she called, more out of frustration than the hope he'd hear her, but the door didn't open. After a few more seconds of silence, she huffed and set down some of the bags. She flexed her fingers to restore blood flow, then dug in her purse for her keys. "Dad." She tried again as she pushed the door open.

He'd picked a great time for a nap. She'd told him in advance she'd be bringing his groceries and didn't plan to stay long. She hadn't even repacked her suitcase yet. As she rounded the corner into the kitchen, her irritation turned to panic when she saw him lying on the floor.

She dropped everything and knelt at his side. When she touched his shoulder, his eyes fluttered open, and though they were unfocused and glassy, relief made her limbs weak. "Dad? Can you hear me?"

He tried to roll over, then winced and moaned.

"Okay. Try not to move." She crawled across the floor to where her purse had landed and searched for her cell phone, then managed to dial 9-1-1 despite her shaking fingers. She gave the address and answered what felt like a hundred questions about her father's condition. When she couldn't verify his level of alertness, the operator offered to stay on the phone until paramedics arrived, but Jacqueline had lost patience with the well-meaning woman and hung up. She shoved her cell into her back pocket and settled back on the floor next to her father.

She sat there talking quietly to him, nonsense that she wasn't sure he followed, as he still seemed extremely disoriented and managed barely an incoherent mumble in response to any questions she asked. She stared at his chest, willing him to keep breathing, and didn't move until the paramedics arrived and she had to let them in.

She'd always thought of herself as a person who handled crisis well. Typically, adrenaline made her more focused and sure, instead of paralyzing her like it did some people. But while watching paramedics lift her father onto a stretcher, she used every ounce of her concentration to remain standing upright, though she did manage to lock the front door as she followed them outside. She nodded numbly when one of them asked if she'd be following them to the hospital and hurried to her car.

A few minutes later, she pulled onto the street behind the ambulance. Through the back windows she could see one of the paramedics moving around her father, who still looked pretty unresponsive, but she couldn't tell what he was doing. Several times, she had to jerk her eyes away from the rear of the ambulance and force them to the traffic and road conditions around her again. She wouldn't be any help if she got T-boned on the way to the hospital.

"Mom."

Casey glanced up from her laptop screen, surprised when Sean came through the front door. She'd settled against the arm of the couch an hour ago, laid her legs along the length of the cushions, and promised herself she wouldn't do any work tonight. She'd lasted nearly an hour before she'd pulled her computer onto her lap to answer *just one email.* "What are you doing here?"

"Mama called. Poppa went to the hospital in an ambulance."

"What?" She shoved her laptop onto the coffee table, turned, and put her feet on the floor.

"He fell, but she said he's okay. I'm on my way up there. She asked me to stop by his house and get his slippers. They're admitting him, and you know how particular he is about his slippers." He stood in the middle of the living room, looking a little lost. His eyebrows were pinched with worry and his shoulders stooped in a way she hadn't seen since she and Jacqueline first split up. He'd never been able to hide his anxiety from her.

"Okay. Have you been over to Poppa's yet?"

"No." He didn't move.

"Do you want me to go with you?"

He nodded. "And to the hospital?"

"Of course, sweetie." She headed for the kitchen to grab her purse and her car keys. She wasn't about to let him drive. In fact, she wasn't very happy with Jacqueline for calling him at school and encouraging him to come home upset.

Minutes later, she pulled her car into Teddy's driveway and Sean jumped out. She stared at the front of the house and hoped, as Sean had relayed, he truly was going to be okay. Someday she'd have to face losing him, but neither she nor Sean was anywhere near ready.

From the first day they'd brought him home, Teddy had been a surrogate father and a grandfather all rolled into one. Sean had taken to him, probably more quickly than he did even to Casey or Jacqueline. And, after raising just one daughter, Teddy had clearly loved having someone around who wanted to learn guy stuff.

Sean climbed back in the car, holding a small duffle bag on his lap. "I got him some fresh clothes, too. For when they let him come home."

Casey smiled, pleased with what a thoughtful young man Sean had become. He didn't say anything more during the drive to the hospital, and Casey didn't press him to. But she hoped whatever he was thinking so hard about as he stared out the passenger window didn't weigh too heavily on him.

When they reached the hospital, Casey continued to take charge while Sean trailed along behind her. She followed the signs until they found the room number Jacqueline had texted to Sean. But when they reached the correct hallway, she let Sean enter first.

A lamp in the corner combined with a subdued glow coming from somewhere behind the bed provided enough light to see the room's two occupants. Teddy lay in the bed, covered to his chest, his eyes closed and his face peaceful. His right arm lay outside the sheet, encased in a splint to his elbow. But she didn't see any other obvious injuries. Jacqueline slumped in the chair beside him, pulled close enough that her hand rested on the bed next to his. Jacqueline's eyes were also closed, but her body radiated tension. Her fingers twitched like they often did when she wasn't fully asleep, but she seemed to be hovering just under wakefulness.

Casey stepped inside the room and pulled the door closed behind her, hoping to keep the bustle from the hallway outside from disturbing them. But as the latch clicked, Jacqueline jolted awake. The motion caused Teddy to stir as well. Sean moved immediately to his bedside, but Casey hung back and offered them both a small smile in greeting.

"How are you feeling?" Sean touched his shoulder.

"Not bad enough to warrant all this fuss."

"Would you rather I'd left you on the kitchen floor to fend for yourself?" Jacqueline asked as she rose and pulled Sean into a quick hug. He held her for longer than Casey expected, as if he needed the embrace as much as she did. "He's okay, buddy." She cupped the back of his neck quickly before releasing him.

Sean nodded, his jaw muscles working against the emotion in his sweet eyes.

"Since you came all this way, sit and tell me about school." Teddy waved his good arm at Sean and then toward the chair at his bedside. After Jacqueline stepped out of the way, Sean sat down, bent close, and began talking to him.

As Jacqueline moved farther from the bed, Casey spoke quietly to her. "Hey, I hope it's okay that I tagged along."

"Of course."

"What happened?"

Jacqueline shrugged. "I went to take him his groceries and found him on the floor."

She lowered her voice. "Was he unconscious?"

"For a bit, but we don't know exactly how long he was there before I found him. His scans came back clean, but since he hit his head when he fell, they want to monitor him overnight."

"You could have called me when you found him. I would've come over and helped. You know I'm only a couple minutes away." She hadn't meant to sound as accusatory as she did.

Jacqueline shrugged. "Once I'd called the ambulance, I didn't have much to do but keep him still and wait."

"I'm right around the corner."

"I know where you live, Casey."

Jacqueline's expression remained stoic, so Casey tried another avenue. "How's he really doing?"

"Not as well as he's projecting. They're giving him something for the pain, but I think his wrist is hurting. He's too tough to show it, especially now that Sean's here."

"We won't stay long. He'll need his rest."

"Sean's his grandson. He's welcome to stay however long he wants to." Jacqueline gave her a sheepish look. "Sorry. I realize how that sounded. You're welcome as well." She rubbed her fingers across her forehead. "It's been a long evening. And judging by the looks of that chair I'll be sleeping in, it's going to be a rough night, too."

"Maybe they can get you a roll-away or something in here."

Jacqueline shook her head. "I won't be sleeping much anyway." She closed her eyes briefly, and when she opened them, a piece of her armor vanished and Casey glimpsed her pain. "I was so scared."

Casey glanced across the room and caught Sean's concerned gaze. She gave him a reassuring nod and he visibly sighed.

"Sean, can you keep Poppa company for a few minutes while I take Mama to get some coffee?"

"Yeah."

Casey turned to Jacqueline, who she could already tell was gearing up for a fight. "Come with me."

"I don't think—"

"There's a family lounge just down the hall, and I'm sure I saw a Keurig when we passed." Casey took Jacqueline's hand and led her out the door. Despite her resistance, Jacqueline continued to hold her hand as they walked to the other end of the hall, releasing her only when they'd entered the otherwise empty room.

Casey crossed to the beverage station along the opposite wall. She positioned a foam cup under the dispenser and loaded a K-cup into the machine. "We've established that Teddy is a stubborn old goat. But how are *you* holding up?"

"I'm fine." She shook her head as she spoke. "Or I will be. Now that I know he's going to be okay."

"Was he able to tell you what caused the fall?" Casey dumped two single-serving pods of creamer into Jacqueline's coffee and motioned her to an empty table nearby.

"Thanks." Jacqueline took a careful sip from the cup. "He doesn't remember anything right before the fall, or even what he was doing in the kitchen. The last thing he can recall is that he was on the couch doing the crossword out of yesterday's paper. I don't even know for sure how long he was there before I arrived, but the doctor doesn't think it was very long."

"Well, thank goodness you were there."

"Yeah. I was leaving for Memphis tomorrow. When I think about being out of town and him lying there all alone—"

"Don't do that to yourself." Casey covered her hand. "I can check on him more often. And maybe we can get him one of those life-alert pendants."

Jacqueline shook her head. "No. If he's unconscious and can't push the button—he can't be left alone. I'm going to hire a nurse or something."

Casey couldn't help but chuckle. "I'm not sure he'll be receptive—"

"He'll have to suck it up and deal." Jacqueline surged to her feet. "For now, I'll be here. I called Owen, and he got someone to cover the meetings in Memphis for me. I'll stay with Dad this week until I can figure out what to do."

CHAPTER FIVE

"Are you ready to go home?" Jacqueline followed an aide pushing a wheelchair into her father's room. His doctor had been in with discharge instructions over an hour ago. They'd waited another thirty minutes after that for the paperwork, and now even she was itching to get out of there.

"As if I have any say in my life anymore."

"Dad, we talked about this. You shouldn't be alone right now. I'm going to try to adjust my schedule, but when I can't be there, I'll hire someone to stay with you." She managed not to sigh in frustration. They'd argued half the morning about her plan. The doctors hadn't found anything to indicate that he'd passed out prior to falling, but he didn't remember slipping or losing his balance either. He'd recommended her father follow up with his primary-care doctor. And until Jacqueline got some further reassurance about his competence to stay alone, upright, *and* conscious, she didn't want him left alone.

"I don't need a babysitter."

"Clearly." She waved a hand at the splint on his wrist.

"I was walking through my kitchen. Since when did that become a high-risk activity?"

"You don't even remember what happened. And you could have been seriously hurt."

"Well, I certainly don't need that thing." He snapped his good hand toward the wheelchair. "There's nothing wrong with my legs."

"Hospital policy." The aide didn't seem amused.

"Get in the chair," Jacqueline demanded.

He pouted but complied. He remained quiet during the elevator ride to the lobby. She knew he hadn't conceded but was biding his time until they were alone again.

When they reached the lobby, Jacqueline gave her ticket to the valet, and they waited only a few minutes while he pulled her car up to the front. Her father refused any help getting in the car, and the aide didn't wait to see him in safely before he whisked the chair away.

As she'd predicted, she had barely exited the circular drive of the hospital when her father started in.

"I'm not an invalid. I can make my own decisions."

"I never said you couldn't."

"But you want to force a nurse on me."

She slipped her sunglasses on and took a breath before answering, reminding herself that he was frustrated and most likely feeling emasculated. "I don't want to. This isn't a power trip for me, Dad."

He didn't respond, instead staring stubbornly out the side window. She glanced at him, then back at the road.

"Can't you just do this, for me?" Her words came out harsher than she intended, and he stiffened in response.

"You'll go back to work, and then we'll see who's in charge."

She shook her head. "Now I know where Sean gets that tone from."

❖

Wednesday night, Casey took her usual walk through the neighborhood to Teddy's house. She'd spoken with Teddy on Monday evening to make sure he'd gotten home and settled. Since then, she'd left him in Jacqueline's capable hands. Though Jacqueline's forced vacation hadn't happened under the best of circumstances, she actually hoped it would be good for them both. She suspected that deep down, when he wasn't being grumpy about being under her watchful eye, Teddy would enjoy having Jacqueline around this week.

She hadn't actually confirmed that she and Teddy would have their usual dinner date this evening. In fact, she'd avoiding calling in case he said he wanted to cancel. She'd worried about him. Several times in the past two days, she'd stopped short of rearranging her day so she could go over there between shoots and check up on them.

As she expected, Jacqueline's car was in the driveway. And when she rang the bell, Jacqueline answered it.

"Hi. I wasn't sure if Teddy and I were still on for dinner. But I wanted to check on him anyway, so I took a chance and walked over."

"Come in." Jacqueline stepped back. "You and Dad had dinner plans?"

"Casey and I always have dinner together on Wednesdays," Teddy said from the living room. "And of course we're still on. Get in here."

"Why didn't I know this?" Jacqueline followed Casey into the living room.

He shrugged. "You're not usually here on Wednesday."

"I thought we could order in Thai this week, since it's Jacqueline's favorite." Casey gave him a wink. She'd effectively shut down any chance Jacqueline would protest.

"That's low," Jacqueline murmured.

She pulled out her phone and unlocked the screen. "So I shouldn't call and order? I still have that place you like on speed dial, you know."

"Well, since you're here."

Casey gave her a smug grin.

"Jacq, open some of that wine Casey likes."

Jacqueline looked to Casey for approval.

"I have an early shoot tomorrow. Unless you plan to join me, don't bother opening a bottle for just one glass."

Jacqueline headed for the kitchen. By the time Casey placed the order and hung up her phone, Jacqueline had returned with two glasses of Moscato. She handed one to Casey.

"Thirty minutes." Casey sipped, savoring the sweet, fruity flavor. She always kept a couple bottles of her favorite label at Teddy's house.

"Great." Jacqueline's cell phone rang and she glanced at the display. "I have to take this." She stepped back into the kitchen as she answered in her most professional tone.

Casey settled on one end of the couch and chatted with Teddy, trying to gauge how he was feeling without asking outright. He was more alert than he'd been in the hospital. In fact, aside from the splint on his wrist, she could almost convince herself he'd returned to normal. But even Teddy's normal hadn't been the same in the past several months. A fact she was reminded of ten minutes later when he started to nod off during a lull in their conversation.

"Should we wake him?" Jacqueline whispered as she returned from the kitchen.

"Let him rest. We have a few minutes until the food arrives."

"Thank you for this." Jacqueline sat at the other end of the couch.

"For what?"

"For having dinner with him."

Casey smiled. "These evenings probably mean as much or more to me than they do to him. You don't have to thank me for that."

"Do you—um, does Nina come over with you?"

Casey shrugged. "Sometimes. A couple times. Teddy invited her."

"Good."

"Good?"

"Yeah, I mean, I'm glad he's made her feel welcome." Jacqueline's expression grew pensive, and when she took a breath, Casey suddenly felt anxious about what she might say. But when she did speak, Casey got the impression she might have changed her mind about what to say at the last second. "How is she, by the way?"

"She's fine." They rarely talked about their respective relationships, though she would admit to some curiosity about Jacqueline's dating habits over the years.

"Sean says you might be moving in together."

She nodded. She'd mentioned the possibility to Sean during their last phone call. He didn't offer an opinion one way or the other, and she didn't necessarily need one, but she didn't want him blindsided if it happened. *When*—when it happened. "We've been talking about it. I suppose once we'd made some decisions, I planned to tell you."

"Tell me?"

"Nina thinks—um, we've talked about getting a new place together."

"What's wrong with your house?"

"Nothing's wrong. We want someplace that's ours."

"Yours?"

"Yes. Hers and mine, together. Don't you remember how much fun you and I had picking out the house together?"

"Yeah. I do." Jacqueline's eyes grew serious.

"Well, Nina and I want to experience that, too."

Jacqueline stared at her, and then her expression darkened. "You want to sell the house."

"Yes."

"You can't."

"I think you lost the right to decide what happens to the house when you sold it to me."

"I hardly had a choice. You kicked me—"

"I didn't—"

"We couldn't keep living together once you broke up with me. And I wasn't going to have you and Sean move out."

"We agreed—"

"Yes, I know. I know, damn it. We agreed. Except you didn't give me much choice. What else could I do but go along with your decisions once you quit on us."

"I felt as if I didn't have a choice either. I'd been losing myself for a while, Jacq. And when I tried to talk to you—and then after Elle—"

"I don't want to talk about that." Jacqueline slammed her wineglass on the coffee table so hard that Casey flinched, surprised the stem didn't snap in half.

Teddy came awake with a start and looked at them both, his gaze bleary with sleep and confusion. "What's going on?"

Jacqueline rose more calmly than Casey would have thought she was capable of, given her previous outburst. She gave Casey a cold look, then headed for the front door.

"Jacq," Teddy called. Then to Casey he said, "What the hell happened?"

Casey shook her head as the front door slammed shut behind Jacqueline. "I think it'll just be the two of us for dinner."

❖

Jacqueline's furious strides ate up nearly two blocks before she slowed enough to realize she had no idea where to go. She couldn't return to the house—not yet, anyway. So she kept walking, covering ground she'd barely traveled in the past eight years but that somehow still felt like a piece of home. She'd grown up in this neighborhood, first in her father's house, and then in the smaller place she and Casey had bought together.

Did she remember the excitement of picking it out together? Yes, she did. Like it was yesterday. Just as she remembered the first night they'd spent there and how they'd christened the place on an air mattress because they hadn't moved their bed yet, and they couldn't wait another moment to be with each other in their new home. How long had it been since she'd truly just had to have someone? And when had she stopped letting Casey know that she wanted her that badly?

When she reached the park, she stopped to sit on a bench within sight of the playground but far enough away to avoid having to interact with either of the two women watching over their children. One of the kids, a fair-haired little girl, ran to the slide, and Jacqueline swallowed hard when a grin lit up her face. Though she knew the resemblance wasn't that close, the girl suddenly reminded Jacqueline of Elle. She'd reacted so badly when Casey had brought her up earlier. But she couldn't have stopped the rage and pain that had boiled up in her if she'd tried.

When Sean was ten, Casey had begun talking about fostering another child. Jacqueline took a bit more convincing, but eventually she'd relented. After all, if Casey really thought she could handle two kids while Jacqueline was out of town, who was she to tell her otherwise?

They'd taken the necessary steps to renew their status as foster parents, and within months, they'd taken in Elle. She'd been a joy from day one—a bright and bubbly five-year-old and so trusting for a girl who'd had a rough start. Her friendly smile and unending optimism had reminded Jacqueline so much of Casey when they'd first met. She'd fallen in love immediately. And so had Casey and Sean.

Elle had been with them for just over a year. Thirteen months—the first six of which were full of tumultuous supervised visits with her birth mother, which only made Jacqueline want to draw Elle closer and hide her away. When, before every meeting, Elle had started to beg them not to make her go, and to cry afterward, Jacqueline had pled with their caseworker to get them a court date. She wanted the woman's parental rights terminated and Elle with them permanently. The caseworker assured them she was doing what she could "within the system" but that Elle's mother hadn't proved herself unredeemable.

In fact, during the next several months, her visits transitioned from supervised to unsupervised. When they were told the mother had been granted a weekend visitation, Jacqueline had tried to refuse. She wouldn't let that woman take her baby for two whole days to a place she'd never seen and was supposed to accept based on the caseworker's word that Elle was safe. In the end, she'd helplessly let her go for the weekend. She hadn't thought she could feel more powerless, but then the system had given Elle back to her birth mother for good.

You are the child's protector. The concept had been drilled into her head years ago, before Sean, during the required parenting classes. Above all else, the safety and welfare of the child should be her priority. And it was. She'd taken those words as an oath and would have ripped herself apart to protect Sean and Elle. In fact, on some levels she had. She'd certainly destroyed her relationship in the aftermath.

She'd known that Sean missed Elle and didn't really understand what had happened. But she'd been so unable to deal with her own grief that she'd basically left comforting Sean to Casey. And though Casey certainly had her own emotions to deal with, Jacqueline blamed Casey for bringing the heartache upon all of them by talking her into fostering again. For a while afterward, she hadn't missed an opportunity to remind Casey that it had been her idea.

Losing Elle hadn't caused their breakup, but it had certainly piled on to the problems they'd already been having. They hadn't lasted even another year after that.

Jacqueline stood, careful not to look at the little girl again. She headed out the other side of the park, away from home. Thinking about Elle had ripped open old wounds, and she couldn't go near either Casey or her father until she'd put those feelings back where they belonged.

Forty-five minutes later, she turned the corner onto Casey's street—her old street. She'd wandered the neighborhood long enough to get herself under control, purposely shutting out any hint of nostalgia.

But when she stopped in front of the house and saw Casey sitting on the top step of the front porch, a fresh wave of emotion swept over her. She still didn't want to talk about Elle or the many other complicated issues that her father's aging and spending time around Casey were bringing up. But she could apologize for how she'd acted. That much she did owe Casey.

"Hey." Casey gave her a small smile. She'd planted her feet two steps below her butt, and she rested her elbows on her slightly raised knees. She held a beer bottle in one hand, her wrist swinging loose.

"I'm sorry. For blowing up and for taking off. Not that it's an excuse, but I've been over there with him nonstop for the past two days, and he's driving me a little nuts."

"And maybe you're a bit stir-crazy. Assuming you didn't work over the weekend, it's been five days, hasn't it? How long has it been since you spent this many days away from work?"

Jacqueline nodded, admitting Casey might be onto something. Since they'd split up, she'd taken only one vacation. Even then, she took her laptop on the weeklong trip to the beach and worked from her resort-hotel room.

"Did I completely miss dinner, then?"

"You did. And Teddy forced me to take most of the leftovers." Casey nodded to a container on a chair behind her. "He said if you were going to act like a child you could eat peanut butter and jelly for all he cared."

Jacqueline rolled her eyes. "Sounds like him. Do you want to share some of that?" Suddenly she was starving, and either she could smell the food or seeing it had made her imagine she could.

"Grab a fork from the kitchen and it's all yours."

Jacqueline hurried inside, intentionally not lingering inside her old house long enough to let her emotions get out of control again, then returned just as quickly. She scooped up the food, then settled on the step next to Casey and opened the lid. She inhaled deeply, practically tasting the spicy flavors as she drew in the scent. "I really do love Pad Thai."

"That's why him sending me away with the food was a great punishment."

Jacqueline shrugged and took a bite of noodles. "Or he knew I'd end up here with my hat in hand."

"That'd mean he raised you right."

"He did." She speared her fork into the food, set the container aside, and turned her body to make sure Casey could see she was sincere. "The house thing caught me off guard, and I reacted badly."

"I wasn't trying to upset you. Especially not when I brought up—"

"No. It's my fault." Jacqueline interrupted before Casey could turn the conversation to Elle. "You don't owe me any explanations. And the house is yours, to do what you want with."

"I know that. But I thought you should hear it from me."

"When Sean said—well, I guess I assumed she'd be moving in with you." The idea of Nina living in her house—Casey's house—wasn't any easier to accept.

"I didn't exactly go into detail with him."

Jacqueline nodded, then covered Casey's hand with hers. "If you're happy, then I'm happy for you. For both of you." She stared at their hands, resting on Casey's thigh. How many nights, when Sean was young, had they sat on this porch together and watched him in the yard with one of the neighborhood kids? Then she remembered how those evenings had dwindled as she'd traveled more, and she wondered if Casey had still sat out here—alone. It hurt to know that she hadn't paid enough attention at the time to know the answer. Since she couldn't ask now, she slid her hand away, stood, and took a few steps down the walk away from the steps.

Casey narrowed her eyes, as if trying to work out the answer to her own question. Jacqueline was so certain their conversation was going to take a different turn that she was almost startled when Casey returned to the topic of moving in with Nina.

"It's time for Nina and me to focus on our future. Sean's going on to the next stage of his life. He won't need me—or you—as much."

"I'm really not ready to talk about him being a grown-up." Jacqueline laughed softly. "It'll just make me feel old."

Casey smiled. "We are old." She tilted her head toward the stair next to her. "Now sit back down and finish eating."

CHAPTER SIX

Jacqueline caught a bead of condensation as it ran down the outside of her water glass and dragged her finger back up to the rim. She glanced at her watch, then at the door. The waiter made eye contact from across the room, but she waved him off again. She wasn't on a super-tight schedule, but she didn't have all day either. Kendra had texted that she was running late. And though it might save time, Kendra would be mad if Jacqueline ordered without her.

Jacqueline had cursed a couple of other drivers in the dense traffic from her office to the popular West End lunch spot. Kendra wouldn't be quite so harried when she arrived, as Jacqueline would bet she'd call an Uber car to pick her up at her Music Row office. She hated driving and avoided it whenever she could.

When she strode through the front door looking relaxed and confident, Jacqueline knew she'd spent the last fifteen minutes checking her email in the backseat of a car rather than silently willing the car in front of her to "just go" so they could make the light before it turned. As Kendra wove her way through the tables, Jacqueline stood.

"You look cute," Jacqueline said as they embraced. Kendra's black jeans, maroon blouse, and black leather jacket accentuated her voluptuous body. A soft, light-gray scarf was wound loosely around her neck.

"You look—tired." Kendra laughed. "How's Teddy?"

"He's hanging in there. Sean came home a day early for the weekend. Which is why I was able to sneak away to meet you for lunch."

"I'm glad you did." They both sat, and Kendra waved the hovering waiter over. "I assume you've had time to look at the menu. I already know what I want."

Jacqueline ordered a turkey-and-avocado sandwich with truffle fries, while Kendra opted for the Swiss chard and oyster-mushroom tacos.

"Did you go vegetarian on me?" Jacqueline asked after the waiter had left.

"It's the most low-cal thing on the menu. Gavin's trying out some new menu items, and I've been his guinea pig every night this week. Pig apparently being the operative word." She patted her belly gently. "If I don't watch it, I'll blimp out."

"You're beautiful. And lucky your boyfriend is an amazing chef. Is he here?" Jacqueline made a show of lifting her chin and looking toward the door to the kitchen.

"He's back there somewhere." Kendra hitched a thumb over her shoulder. "I'm sure he'll make an appearance eventually. You know he's a bit of an attention whore and will want you to have a chance to properly congratulate him."

"For a few new menu items? That's great and all, but I don't know if it's reason for a celebration."

"No. For popping the question." She stuck out her left hand, now adorned with a giant solitaire.

"Oh, my God, that's great." Jacqueline sprang out of her seat, hugged Kendra, and gushed over the ring. "I'll forgive him for keeping you from me for the past couple of weeks. But he better not think he can get away with it again."

Kendra laughed. "It wasn't him. I've been holed up in the studio with Brooke Donahue, putting the finishing touches on her album." Kendra had been Brooke's producer on both of her albums.

"Oh, she's totally forgiven. I love her." Jacqueline returned to her side of the table and they sat down.

"I know. She knows. Remember when you hit on her at that fund-raiser I was kind enough to invite you to."

"I didn't hit on her. I simply told her how much I enjoyed her music."

"Would you break your rule about dating local for her?"

"Maybe. But not my rule about dating married." She had—once—after a very lengthy dry spell. Giving in to loneliness, she'd let a gorgeous woman seduce her into ignoring the wedding-ring set on her elegant finger. But the guilt had eaten her up. As it turned out, she still had some morals after all. She'd never crossed that boundary again.

"That's probably a good thing. Addison is completely in love with Brooke, and she might kick your ass. It's pretty clear how happy they are."

Jacqueline shrugged.

"What was that?"

"What?"

"The shrug and the look." Kendra waved her fork at Jacqueline. "Happy fades."

"Wow. That's a lovely sentiment to hear as I'm about to tie myself to Gavin essentially for the rest of my life."

"Essentially?"

"Yeah. I mean I can still walk away unscathed. Until we have kids."

"That's the truth."

Kendra squeezed Jacqueline's hand. "I'm sorry. I didn't mean—"

"No, please. I'm the one who should be sorry. You have this amazing news, and I don't want to bring it down with my ancient history."

"If it really were history, you wouldn't be upset about it."

"Kendra—"

"I knew something more than Teddy was bothering you when you called last night."

"Let's talk about your wedding. Oh, and babies—are you going to have babies right away?"

"I'm not getting any younger. I told Gavin if he wants one, it needs to be soon."

"I'm going to be an awesome godmother."

"I haven't asked you to be a godmother."

Jacqueline pretended to look offended. "Who else would you ask?"

"Maybe I'll ask you *and* Casey. That way if something happens to us, at least you'll have to finally get over yourself and be honest with her."

She didn't bother with the protest that Kendra would certainly ignore. "I wouldn't even know where to start."

"Hmm—how about, Casey, I've never stopped loving you, and I wish we could give us another shot."

"Kendra."

"I think that sums it up pretty good."

She shook her head. "You know I can't do that. If none of the reasons we split up have changed, then there's no point in trying again. We'll end up the same, only maybe worse."

"Or better. Isn't there a chance you could figure out how to keep it together this time?"

"If it's just a chance, the answer's still no. I could never do that to Sean. He's already been through it once."

"But you love her."

"It's not that simple. I know your squishy heart and wedding-brain want to believe that's enough, but sometimes it isn't." She did love her. But so much trust had been destroyed, and they'd treated each other badly. Jacqueline didn't know if she could give anyone a fair shot at her heart again, let alone Casey, with whom she already had so much baggage.

"Maybe if you talk to her—"

"She asked me to leave, Kendra. Eight years ago. Why do you think that's going to change now?"

"I can hope." Kendra gave her a sympathetic smile. "I introduced you guys, so I feel responsible."

Jacqueline laughed. "You always act like you did it on purpose, too."

"I invited her to poker, didn't I?"

"Not for me."

"Okay. But I did encourage you for three days afterward to call her while you were dragging your feet. You're lucky some other hot lesbian didn't beat you to her."

As soon as Kendra had seen Casey's number on Jacqueline's door, she'd started hounding Jacqueline to call and ask her out. But something about Casey had made Jacqueline nervous, and she'd spent several days with her stomach in knots and fantasies of Casey spinning through her head before she got up her nerve.

"You haven't told Casey that I still—"

"Of course not. I'm a vault."

She knew Kendra still talked to Casey, but she wasn't sure at what level they confided in each other. If Casey had said—no, she wouldn't let her mind or her heart go there. Casey was off the market and definitely off-limits to Jacqueline.

"And, hey, I do not have wedding-brain. That's not even a thing."

"It is. Women who are getting married want everyone else to be, too."

"Please. I don't want you stealing any of my thunder with a shiny new love."

"No new love for me. I promise." Jacqueline signaled the waiter for the check. "When's the big day?"

"We haven't set the exact date yet, but I'm thinking a few months, if we can pull it off. We want a small ceremony. I've already done the big, fancy wedding."

Kendra had met her first husband, a successful music producer, just out of college. Their ceremony had landed on the society page, and she'd been branded the latest trophy wife of a much-older man. While Kendra had been in it for real, the marriage didn't last. She'd left her husband's company and started her career from scratch, determined to make her own name. And she'd stayed out of the dating scene for years, until she met Gavin.

"I expect you and Casey to both stand up with me, so keep it civil until then, okay?"

"She's moving in with Nina." She tilted her head in a fake gesture of indifference. "Actually, she's selling our house—her house—and getting a place with her."

"She told you?" Kendra looked surprised—not that Casey was selling, but that she'd told Jacqueline.

"You knew."

"She mentioned that they were talking about moving in."

"Her idea or Nina's?" She held up her hands as soon as she said it. "Don't answer that. I'm sorry. I shouldn't have asked you. Anyway, she didn't tell me. Sean did, but she confirmed it when I asked."

"I don't think she intended to keep the news from you."

"I don't either. I just wasn't prepared for that kick in the gut. I haven't lived there in years. But it's like as long as she had the house—"

"I know."

She took a deep breath, then expelled it, trying to clear out her emotions as well. "It's okay. It's good."

"Is it?"

She forced herself to nod. "She's happy."

"You deserve to be happy, too." Kendra grabbed her hand.

"I know. But right now I've got my hands full with work and Dad." She'd worry about the rest later. She could try to convince herself that she should be looking for a relationship—someone to grow old with—because that's what people did. But maybe she wasn't meant for that kind of happy ending. She'd just focus on working and making enough money to pay for a fancy nursing home to live out her days in. She smiled to herself, glad she hadn't voiced that thought out loud for Kendra to hear.

❖

Monday morning, Jacqueline loaded her small suitcase and briefcase into her car. Late last week, she'd made arrangements with a senior-care company to send someone a couple of times a day to check on her father. With one worry alleviated, she concentrated on enjoying the weekend before returning to work. She'd made a nice dinner for her father and Sean Saturday night, and then they'd piled onto the couch for a movie night. Sean probably had better things to do on a Saturday night than hang out with his mother and grandfather. But he hadn't let on that he'd rather be anywhere else, and Jacqueline enjoyed the quality time.

This morning, Jacqueline had made her father's breakfast and stayed while he showered and dressed for the day. Now she had him settled on the couch in the living room.

"Okay, so the aide's going to be here in a couple of hours. Do you need anything before I go?"

"I don't want a babysitter."

"Well, I don't want to come home in two days and find that you've been lying on the floor the whole time I was gone. Since you won't agree to around-the-clock care, you're going to let an aide come for a bit each day. She'll help you get lunch and anything else you need. Then someone else will be here in the evening."

Jacqueline had done as much work as she could do from home last week. But she couldn't put off her trip to Kentucky any longer. She'd scheduled her meetings as tightly as possible. She'd spend the rest of today and most of the evening at the Louisville office. Tonight, she'd drive to Lexington, grab some sleep at a hotel, then hit the office there early enough to catch the overnight road drivers before they went home, followed by a full day of meetings. If everything went smoothly, she'd be home by midday Wednesday.

She crossed to him and bent to kiss his cheek. "Dad, please, go along with this for now. I don't want to worry about you while I'm gone."

"Be safe," he grumbled.

"I'll call you tonight." Jacqueline grabbed her purse and left, closing the door decisively behind her. She hated leaving him like this, but she didn't have a choice.

As she backed her car into the street, she slipped on her sunglasses. She hadn't felt this heartsick leaving since the days when she used to have to leave Casey and Sean. Back then she'd told herself that she just had to get used to traveling. So many of the other guys seemed happy to be away from home, commenting on how free they felt being away from their wives. If she complained, she'd be labeled the emotional woman who couldn't hack it on the road.

In recent years, she hadn't minded being away as much. Sean was busy with school, sports, and his friends during the week, and she had no one else to come home to. Today, leaving her dad felt lonely. But she didn't have a choice, so she drove on, forcing her mind to the meetings she'd be stepping right into at the end of her three-hour drive.

❖

Casey poured her third cup of coffee for the day and hoped it gave her the punch she needed to get through yet another new-client consultation. She wouldn't complain about new business, but she usually tried not to schedule more than a couple of newcomers in one day. She had shoots at several different locations later this week, so when three new clients had called last week, she'd put them all down for today. Typically, she liked a little variety in her day—a nice mix of client interaction, editing, and busywork that included answering emails and sending out contracts.

When the doorbell rang, she took another big swig of coffee, then set her mug in the sink. But instead of the expected client, Teddy stood there, flanked by a young woman who looked to be in her early twenties. The butterflies adorning her scrub top clashed with her irritated expression.

"Ms. Meadows?"

"Yes."

"This is rather unorthodox, but I'm Mr. Knight's home aide. He said you were his daughter."

"Really?" She glanced at Teddy and tried not to laugh at the pleading look in his eyes.

"He insisted I leave his house. We can't force ourselves on our clients." She didn't seem eager to question Teddy's assertion of their relationship. "Ms. Knight didn't answer her phone." Teddy mumbled something that sounded like "too busy for me," but the woman went on as if she didn't hear him. "You aren't listed on his emergency contacts, but I didn't feel right leaving him alone. He said you'd be home."

"It's okay." She stepped out of the way. "Come in, Teddy."

"And Ms. Knight?"

"I'll contact her. Thank you." Casey closed the door before the woman could reconsider. She wasn't certain what level of care Jacqueline had requested for Teddy, but this poor girl obviously didn't have a clue what to do in the face of Teddy's resistance.

"What's going on?" she asked him.

"I don't need someone to follow me around the house waiting to wipe my ass." He plopped down on her couch. She sat in a chair adjacent to him, angled forward, and rested her arms on her thighs.

Casey laughed. "I'm guessing those weren't her instructions, so if that's what she was doing, you definitely need to complain to the company."

"Jacq thinks she can just run off and leave me with a complete stranger."

"She didn't exactly run off. She's working—"

"I didn't expect you to defend her after she basically abandoned you for years."

"Teddy!" Casey sat up straighter, shocked both by his words and by the angry scowl on his face. "I'm sure she's doing the best she can."

"I'm a grown man. When I need help, I'll ask for it."

Casey nodded, not necessarily in agreement but to let him know she'd heard him. She understood his reluctance, but she had to give Jacqueline credit for trying to solve a problem that Casey herself had been bringing to her for some time now.

"When's she coming home?"

"Tonight."

"Okay. I'm expecting a client for a consultation any minute now. But you can hang out here for a while. I'll talk to Jacqueline, and we'll come up with a better solution."

"The solution is to leave me the hell alone."

Casey stood. "I'll be in the studio if you need anything."

She grabbed her cell and sent a quick text, letting Jacqueline know Teddy was at her house and asking if they could speak later. Teddy's attitude concerned her. Certainly, he'd had his grumpy days, but given his recent head injury, she wanted to double-check if the doctor had said to watch out for mood changes.

❖

"I'm sorry. He shouldn't have involved you," Jacqueline said, in place of a greeting, as Casey answered the phone. She could tell by the sound quality that Jacqueline had called from her car. She hunched her shoulder to hold the phone while she arranged seasoned, bone-in chicken breasts in a glass baking dish for dinner.

Casey held back an instinctive argument. She didn't mind being involved. She felt like family—Teddy's family, at least. She wouldn't shut him out because things had gotten tense with Jacqueline last week. She'd stayed away over the weekend, even though she knew Sean was over there. Based on past experience, she expected Jacqueline would want some distance from their near confrontation over Elle and that she probably wouldn't be talking to her now if it weren't for Teddy.

"I'll make sure the service knows to call me next time."

"They tried." She flipped on the faucet, washed her hands, then swiped them with a towel. She shifted the phone into one hand and put the dish in the oven with the other.

"I can't always answer right away. It wasn't an emergency. She could have waited for me to call back."

"It's fine. I was close by. He knew I'd likely be here." She leaned against the counter, listening for movement in the living room. Teddy had fallen asleep in front of the television.

"Did he? I can't decide if he's been confused or just downright stubborn, lately." She sighed. "Either way, clearly, I have to have another talk with him about the sitter."

"Maybe start by not calling her a sitter," she said without thinking and braced herself for Jacqueline's response.

But instead of the biting comment she expected, Jacqueline spoke with a softness Casey hadn't heard from her in some time. "I just left Lexington. Traffic permitting, it'll be about four hours. Can he stay with you and I'll deal with him when I get home?"

"Of course. We'll be waiting for you."

"That sounds—um, thank you."

She paused, certain Jacqueline had cut off a thought and replaced it with the sentiment of gratitude instead. "I'm making dinner for him. It's baked chicken. Do you want me to save you a plate?"

"That would be amazing, thanks."

"Amazing? It's just baked chicken. Don't build it up too much."

"I've been eating salads alone in a hotel room for two days. Home cooking *is* amazing." Jacqueline's smile came through in her voice. "I guess I should be happy he made it two days with those poor ladies. I haven't actually talked to the service yet. Has he given any indication of what he put them through?"

"No. I'll let you question him further when you get here. Be safe."

Casey hung up with Jacqueline and dialed Nina's number. They'd had dinner plans, but she'd texted after Teddy showed up to let her know she had to change them. Yet now she wanted to explain the complicated turn her evening had taken in a more personable way.

"Hey, I wasn't sure I was going to hear from you," Nina said when she answered.

"I'm so sorry about dinner. You know I hate texting stuff like that."

"I know. But you can't fight tech progress. And you're a busy, busy girl." Nina's teasing tone warmed Casey.

"Come have dinner with Teddy and me. I know it's not the evening we'd planned, but we can still salvage it."

"I think I'll take a rain check."

"I want to see you."

"It sounds like you're going to have a full house."

"It's just Teddy. Jacqueline won't be here for a couple of hours yet."

"He's her father. It's uncomfortable."

Casey sighed, but she didn't argue. She'd understood Nina's aversion to being around Teddy and Jacqueline when they first started dating. Who wanted to hang out with their new girlfriend's long-time ex? But any lingering insecurity surely should have dissipated by now. Casey had always kind of hoped they would reach a point where they could all spend a holiday or occasion together, for Sean's sake.

Certainly, she eventually wanted to see him get married and start having children of his own. She would be a grandmother someday. And she'd expect that she and Jacqueline might both attend their grandchildren's milestones. What would her life be like years from now if she was committed to someone who refused to be around while Casey was involved in that aspect of her family?

CHAPTER SEVEN

I can't believe you did this, especially after I went to the trouble of arranging everything. I'll probably have to try to find another service now." Jacqueline paced Casey's living room, pausing only long enough to glare at her father occasionally. He'd been sitting on the couch when she arrived, looking completely unbothered, which, given her mood, only fired her up more. Casey had answered the door, then disappeared down the hall, presumably to her bedroom, so Jacqueline could talk to her father. "Are you just trying to make my life harder? The whole time I've been gone, I worried about you. Then, after working all day and driving for four hours, I have to come over here and pick you up because you can't accept a little help."

"You didn't hear the way those *sitters* were talking to me. I'm not a child."

"Then why are you acting like a damn toddler?" She knew as soon as she'd said it that she'd gone too far.

Her mother had often said she only had to look at his face to know what he was feeling. In fact, it was one of the reasons her mother had fallen for him—one thing that set him apart from the other men she'd dated. Now, anger dominated his features. Jacqueline had seen him this mad only a couple of times in her life.

He rose and came to stand directly in front of her. "It seems you've wasted your time coming here. I am your father. And until you decide to treat me with the respect I deserve, I'm not going anywhere with you." He turned and strode down the hallway toward the bedrooms. Seconds later, he slammed the door to Sean's bedroom with such force that the sound echoed through the house.

"Fuck!" She spun around, her fists clenched, and found Casey standing in the doorway leading to the same hall her father had stalked down.

"Jacq—"

"No. No." Jacqueline tilted her head back and raised her eyes to the ceiling, trying like hell to control her emotions. Her anger churned against the fear that she wouldn't be able to figure out how to help him *and* keep her job and her sanity. She couldn't handle all of that and the heartbreaking sympathy in Casey's expression as well.

"He can stay here tonight," Casey said.

She shook her head. "I—I can't—"

"Hey, it's okay." Casey grasped her arm and steered her toward the couch. "Sit down and breathe." Casey sat beside her.

"I'm sorry. This isn't your problem." She inhaled deeply, her body still singing with adrenaline. "If you don't mind, I'll let him stay here tonight. But tomorrow morning, he and I are having a come-to-Jesus. He's going to start cooperating or—"

"Or what?" Casey's quick smile didn't help Jacqueline's mood. "He's not an employee that you can explain an action plan to and expect him to fall in line. He's your father."

"He's got to listen to reason. Don't worry. I'll figure it out."

"I hate when you get like this," Casey said.

The familiarity in her tone irritated Jacqueline. "Like what?" When she started to surge to her feet, Casey touched her forearm, urging her back down.

"Closed off. Like you don't need anything from anyone. Everyone needs help sometimes."

"This is my responsibility."

"I care about him, too. He's Sean's grandfather, and—"

"He worked two jobs." Jacqueline cleared her throat in an attempt to remove the edge of desperation from her voice. "From the time I was a baby until I graduated high school, he worked two jobs so my mother wouldn't have to."

"Jacq—"

"I never went to day care. I had family around. He doesn't want the aides in his house, so I'll have to figure something else out."

"Okay." Casey's quiet acceptance took some of the fight out of her. "Then let me be family again."

She barely held back a whimper as Casey's words ripped her open. She touched her thumb and two fingers against her eyes, willing the burning behind her lids not to turn into tears.

"Let me help you." Casey grasped her wrist and guided her hand down. "Please. He's not just the most important man in our son's life. He's been there for me, too—these past eight years."

She didn't want to need Casey. Not to help with her father. Not to help hold herself together. And when Casey wrapped an arm around her shoulders, she didn't want to collapse against her and give in to the sobs that threatened to push past her lips. But her body betrayed her brain and slumped into the comfort of Casey's arms. She closed her eyes and soaked in Casey's strong embrace and the way she shushed gently while she stroked her hair. She let herself feel protected for just a moment longer before she eased back and composed herself.

She sniffed and swiped her fingers under her eyes. "Wow. I'm sorry. It's been a long week already and I—um—"

"It's okay." Casey released her and shuffled to the side, putting a few more inches of couch cushion between them. She laced her fingers together in her lap. "You had the aides coming to the house a couple of times a day to check on him, right?"

She nodded, appreciating Casey's smooth shift into business mode. "And to help with meals, laundry, and anything else he needed."

"Okay. No problem. I should be able to look in on him at lunchtime so you don't have to leave the office. If you'll send me your schedule for the next couple of weeks, I'll compare it to mine. When you're out of town, or if you're busy in the evening, I can go over for a bit each night, then come home once he's settled in."

Jacqueline shook her head. It sounded like a lot of extra work on Casey. "You don't have to—"

"Let's not go over that again." Casey stood and said, "We're doing this together."

She recognized the tone Casey had used when she was managing their lives and the complex schedules that involved Jacqueline's job, Sean's activities, and Casey's own burgeoning career. She'd made it all work, for years, and Jacqueline wasn't sure she'd ever fully stopped to appreciate that fact.

❖

Thursday, just before noon, Casey knocked on Teddy's door. When she heard him summon her inside, she turned the knob and found it unlocked. After she closed the door, she flipped the dead bolt.

"Do I need to tell Jacqueline to start locking the door behind her when she leaves in the morning?" she called as she walked through the house. She paused at the threshold of the dining room.

He glanced up from the checkerboard he'd been setting up and waved a hand in her direction. "Maybe. Apparently any riff-raff off the street can just walk in here."

She laughed.

"If you two are going to keep ganging up on me, I'll put another chain on the door to keep you both out."

"Seriously, Teddy. This neighborhood isn't like it used to be."

He grunted, and she chose to take that as a positive acknowledgement. "Do you have time for a quick game while we eat lunch?"

"Sure." After Jacqueline left the night before, she'd sent over her schedule, and Casey had spent an hour that morning making sure, for the foreseeable future, she had a little extra time each day around lunchtime to stop by Teddy's between appointments.

Jacqueline planned to stay in town for the remainder of this week. In the next two weeks, she'd managed to limit her travel to a couple of overnight trips.

Casey raided Teddy's fridge and pantry for lunch supplies, putting together a couple of ham sandwiches on bakery rolls with a side of leftover pasta salad. She set his plate in front of him and took her spot across the table.

"Did you and Jacqueline make up?" she asked before taking a bite of her sandwich.

"I suppose."

"She's worried about you."

"She's afraid I'm going to keel over while she's out of town on business."

Just the idea of losing Teddy was like a rope squeezing her heart. When she thought about Jacqueline being away when that happened, a sick feeling spread to her stomach, and she set her sandwich back on her plate. "I don't know how she would live with that."

"She would do what she always does. She'd bury herself deeper in her work, like she did when her mother died. Only this time, I won't be here for Sean, so that will fall on you." He smiled at her despite the sadness shining in his eyes. "You hold this family together."

"I used to. I'm not—I can't be that person for Jacqueline anymore."

"She'll need you."

Casey remembered how Jacqueline had broken down the night before—how good it had felt to be able to offer her a moment of comfort. She would do whatever she could to help out with Teddy—with logistics and schedules, but she couldn't allow either of them to depend too much on that kind of emotional support.

❖

Jacqueline had never been a runner, and she wasn't about to take up jogging at forty years old. But spending almost every evening for a week and a half at her father's house, then driving to her condo and falling into bed, only to get up early, go get him breakfast, rush to work and do it all over again, was taking its toll—physically and mentally. She'd been short-tempered at work and at home, walking the line between frustration and exhaustion with no end in sight.

She needed some stress relief and decided a brisk walk would have to do. After she'd made her father's dinner, he'd insisted on doing the dishes so she stuck around to supervise. Then when he was settled back in his chair and she was certain he wouldn't slip on any water on the kitchen floor, she grabbed the old iPod she'd recently dug out of a drawer.

"I have my phone with me," she called as she headed out the front door. She put in her earbuds and headed down the block.

Three songs in, she'd decided she needed to change the music on her iPod if she was going to keep walking. She'd apparently loaded these songs in one of her melancholy moods, and they weren't exactly inspiring her to get her cardio on.

As she turned the corner at the end of the block, she scrolled through her playlist. She'd gone through some dark times when she and Casey first split up. She'd felt like a failure. She'd let Casey down in so many ways. She'd worried about the impact of another broken family on Sean. She'd told herself that at least he wouldn't hear them arguing anymore.

That last year and a half had been pretty rough. They'd argued about the frequency of Jacqueline's travel, which led to blowups over money. Jacqueline wanted to provide for her family, and if that meant lonely nights on the road, then that's what she'd do. Casey wanted her at home and accused her of putting her job before their family and caring more about the thrill of moving up in her company. The more Casey pushed, the more Jacqueline shut down.

Elle had been the final straw. When, a few months after letting Elle go, Casey had started talking about fostering another child, Jacqueline had refused. They'd had their biggest fight to date over the issue. Casey desperately wanted to help more kids, and Jacqueline couldn't bear to have her heart broken like that again. The long version was much more painful and drawn out, leading, months later—after more harsh words, accusations, and hurt feelings—to their separation.

Despite the tears she'd shed alone in her condo, Jacqueline had let herself need Casey only one more time—when her mother passed away. She'd let Casey blame the alcohol, but truthfully,

Jacqueline had been sober enough when she invited Casey over. She'd known exactly what she was doing when she crossed the line between seeking comfort to needing something more physical. And that night, after Casey fell asleep, when Jacqueline cried, it wasn't over the loss of her mother, but rather because of the void in her heart and life that only Casey could fill. She'd never regretted that night, but she'd paid for it many times in the days afterward when she hugged the pillow that still smelled like Casey's shampoo.

The sound of a child yelling ripped Jacqueline from her pity party. She'd arrived at the park and had no recollection of having walked the last several blocks. She ripped out her earbuds, blaming that damn playlist. Three boys were on the swings, seemingly in a competition to see who could swing the highest. The boy on the end, clearly the front-runner, called out taunts to the other two.

She turned back toward her father's house. She needed to collect her things and head back to her apartment. Next week, Casey would be managing on her own, since Jacqueline would be in Atlanta, attending train-the-trainer sessions on the new consumer-driven insurance plan the company would be switching to in a few months. She'd be responsible for carrying that education to the center managers in her region, so they could pass it on to their hourly employees.

She didn't want to depend on Casey so much. But otherwise, she'd be useless in Atlanta, worrying about her father. He claimed to be feeling better, but he didn't seem to get around as well as he usually did. He denied any pain, even when she badgered him. Since he still refused outside aid, and she didn't have enough flexibility in her work schedule, she had to accept Casey's help. She knew Casey had been at his house for lunch every day this week, but she and Jacqueline hadn't been there at the same time. To show her appreciation for Casey's time, she'd relayed an invitation to dinner with them on Friday night through her father, but he'd said Casey had plans with Nina. So she and her father had ordered pizza, and she spent most of the night trying not to think about whether Casey and Nina were looking at houses together.

Chapter Eight

Casey stepped to the side of the trail to let some runners pass. She still considered herself a novice hiker, but she couldn't imagine a time when she'd want to run the trails. She'd never been super-athletic and pictured herself tripping over a tree root and having to be carried out. She slipped off her backpack and took a bottle of water and a small bag of almonds from one of the outside pockets. Inside, she'd packed her lightest camera and a spare lens. She'd also brought a printed copy of the Percy Warner Park trail map, but she'd done the Mossy Ridge trail before and shouldn't need to consult it.

A last-minute cancellation had left her morning free. After a quick check of the weather, she'd decided not to waste such a perfect day. She stuck close to town, so she could still make her midday check-in with Teddy. Though the sun was getting higher, a slight breeze stirred the canopy overhead, creating wavering shadows on the ground. The shade kept the air cool, but her skin was heated with the effort of the incline she'd just climbed. The four-and-a-half-mile loop had enough ups and downs to give her a workout. But she hadn't been struggling as much as the last time she attempted the trail, so maybe she was in better shape.

She finished her snack and stowed her trash in her pack. As she continued on the trail, she wished she'd brought a pair of earbuds. She didn't normally have any trouble losing herself in her surroundings, but today she hadn't seen any wildlife, and none of the foliage grabbed her eye. In fact, she hadn't pulled out her camera once. Where she normally found peace, today she felt only overwhelming loneliness. She'd invited Nina along once, months ago, mostly out of obligation. But Nina had declined. Since then, she'd enjoyed the solitude.

This morning, she'd apparently carried the rest of her life onto the trail with her. She'd reexamined her recent time with Teddy, trying unsuccessfully to stay objective. He'd been absentminded and a little confused, but not enough to worry yet about dementia. He'd fallen but hadn't been seriously injured. So, maybe her fear of losing her one remaining parental figure had overshadowed her ability to see Teddy as simply an aging man, in decent health for his age, who would have the occasional bad day. But she couldn't control the sick feeling in her stomach.

Since her own parents had died, she'd felt as if she'd been prematurely grieving Jacqueline's parents as well. The death of Jacqueline's mom had been hard, but Teddy—well, that would be excruciating. During Sean's teen years, when he'd become rebellious and sometimes angry, she'd cried on Teddy's shoulder. When he'd secretly tracked down his biological mother on Facebook, only to find she'd gone on to have two children after giving him up, he'd relied on Teddy for comfort and advice. Teddy had been a partner in raising Sean—in ways that Jacqueline never had.

Jacqueline had shut down on her well before the separation—after Elle. She'd buried herself in her work and traveled more than ever. Casey resented Jacqueline's ability to step away from her family and leave her to deal with it all. Jacqueline acted so distant from every part of their relationship that picking a fight seemed the only way Casey could wrestle some kind of reaction from her.

Initially, after the breakup, trying to co-parent had taxed their ability to be civil with each other. They'd struggled to be cordial around Sean, but stuffing those emotions had inevitably led to blowups later.

They'd put all of that behind them and become two people raising a son. Casey had long ago released the thread that connected her to Jacqueline. And while she'd admit to an occasional yearning for the kind of fresh, uncomplicated love they'd once shared, she never expected to feel a tug on that string again. Last week, when Jacqueline had broken down in her arms, Casey had wanted nothing more than to fold into her and comfort her.

But she had a partner, she reminded herself. She had to remind herself, because she was out here stomping around in the woods alone. She didn't want to be attached to the person she dated twenty-four seven. And until today, she'd enjoyed these quiet hikes by herself. But she'd like for Nina to show a bit more interest in her hobbies. Of course, she only begrudgingly went along on the microbrewery tours Nina liked so much. But at least she'd made an effort.

She worried that she could so easily say what she didn't like about their relationship. They were getting ready to move in together. Shouldn't she still be in the blindly happy phase? Almost certainly, if Nina found herself with a morning off, she would have spent her time searching the MLS listings for a house they could share. Casey's first thought had been to escape her life for a few hours.

Jacqueline had heard more than she cared to about the new insurance plan. The representative from the contracted insurance company had spent two hours yesterday on health-reimbursement accounts alone. Someone should have told her she was speaking to a roomful of human-resources professionals, so she wouldn't structure her training as if presenting it to a bunch of new hires in orientation.

Jacqueline's four-hour drive on Monday had taken more than six, due to a rollover accident just before Chattanooga. After spending all day Tuesday in staff meetings, they'd begun the insurance training classes yesterday. Two of the three nights, she'd endured dinner and drinks with Owen and several other coworkers. She'd slipped away from their table between dinner and dessert to call Casey. But even the corner of the restaurant that she tucked herself into was too loud for more than a quick check-in. Her father was good. And since she couldn't hear very well, and Casey had nothing new to report, Jacqueline couldn't find a reason to keep her on the phone.

This morning, she'd called her father while driving in to the regional office for the day's sessions. She'd consumed her first cup of coffee on an empty stomach, and the remaining half of her second cup still sat on the table in front of her.

When the speaker called for a short break, Jacqueline shifted in her chair, thankful for the chance to get up and restore circulation to her legs. She left the room and kept going until she passed through the front door. Once outside, she took a few laps around the yard. Most of the drivers had headed out with full trailers earlier in the day, but the ever-present smell of diesel exhaust tainted the air.

She pulled out her phone, pleased to see a message from Marti asking if she was free for drinks later. She was supposed to drive home after this afternoon's sessions, but she could definitely use a little distraction. If she asked, Casey would check on her father for one more night. She typed out a quick affirmative reply to Marti.

Five minutes later, she'd just poured herself a glass of water from the pitcher on the table at the back of the conference room when her phone rang. She answered on her way to her seat, but seconds later, she knew she needed more privacy. She abandoned her water, scooped up her notebook and a pen, and stepped back out of the room. The rest of her colleagues returned to the meeting, giving her the hallway to herself.

Lena Blackstone, one of the drivers in Knoxville, claimed that management had discriminated against her. She was sketchy on details and insisted that Jacqueline come over there and see for herself. Jacqueline jotted as many notes as she could manage to get. She mentally reviewed her schedule for next week, wishing she had some reason to say she couldn't make it and try to conduct her investigation by phone. Instead, she assured Lena that she'd contact her soon to schedule an in-person interview early next week.

She caught Owen during the next break and filled him in. She'd either arrive in Knoxville Sunday night, or she'd be getting up before the sun Monday to make the drive. She'd have to find some time tonight for a lengthier conversation with Casey to fill her in on next week.

The rest of her day dragged on, and by the time she got back to her hotel room, she collapsed on the bed, wishing she didn't have to dress to go out again. At least she only had to go as far as the hotel bar, but she'd still have to shower and change clothes. She could cancel, Marti would understand. They had no obligation to each other. But she wouldn't. Drinks with Marti would almost certainly lead to sex, and Jacqueline needed the stress relief.

She rolled over and grabbed her phone from the nightstand. She could delay getting up just a bit longer. She scrolled to Casey's contact and connected the call.

"How's Dad?" she asked when Casey answered.

"He's good. We had dinner together, and then he fell asleep in his chair. Are you on the road?"

"Um—no. Listen, I know I said I'd be home tonight, but could you check on him for one more night? My meetings ran late, and I'm too exhausted to think about driving home tonight. I'll be there early tomorrow, so—"

"Sure. It's no problem." Casey's quick acceptance made her feel a little guilty.

"I'm sorry. I don't want to put this on you, but—"

"I'm here, Jacq. Don't worry."

Jacqueline sighed. The soft way Casey's voice caressed the nickname made her chest ache. "There's more. Man, this sucks. You've been so great, I hate to keep imposing."

"Just ask."

"We've had a complaint I have to deal with personally. I have to go to Knoxville next week."

"When?"

"Monday. I don't know how long I'll be. It depends on how involved this thing is."

"Jacq—"

"I know." She cringed, then put on a pleading tone Casey had never been able to say no to. "Please, Casey. I'll owe you, big."

"Yeah, I'll work it out."

Jacqueline sighed, suddenly wishing Casey had offered some resistance, if only to make her feel less like a manipulative shit.

"What's wrong?"

"Nothing."

"You sighed."

"Yeah. I did. Um—" She shook her head and cleared her throat. "Everything's good. I'm just tired. Thanks again. I'll talk to you later."

She lay there for a minute longer, debating whether to take time before she got in the shower to send an email to the legal department informing them of the impending investigation. She glanced at the clock on the bedside table, then rolled off the bed and headed for the bathroom. She'd send that email later. She needed every extra minute for a nice, hot shower.

❖

Casey stood in her bedroom, still looking at the screen of her phone. Something about her whole conversation with Jacqueline had felt off. She'd sensed that Jacqueline was being deceptive but couldn't discern what about. She'd seemed nervous about telling her she'd be out of town next week as well. No, she'd sounded strange before that—when she'd said she wouldn't make it home tonight. But why would she lie? Casey hadn't given her a hard time about adjusting her schedule thus far.

Changing her plans for next week might take some work, but it was actually quite doable. She'd be shooting a wedding this weekend, so she'd blocked out the first part of next week to work in her studio, editing and putting together the final package for that couple.

She walked into the living room, still flipping through the calendar app on her phone.

"That was Jacqueline." Nina scooted forward on the couch as she spoke.

"Yes. She won't be home until tomorrow. I'm going to walk over and check on Teddy once more before bed. Do you want to go?"

Nina stood. "I think I'll head home."

"I won't be gone long." Casey caught her around the waist and pulled her close, but Nina didn't return the embrace. "Stay." She brushed her lips along Nina's jaw in the way Nina found hard to resist. "When I return, I'm all yours."

Nina sighed and stepped away, letting Casey's arms drop away from her. "I have to work early tomorrow. I'll call you."

"Hey—"

"Walk me as far as my car." Nina picked up her purse and headed for the door.

Casey grabbed her keys and cell phone and followed. Nina tended to shut down when she was upset, leaving Casey no choice but to wait until she was ready to talk. At the car, Casey gave her the expected kiss, holding her until Nina pulled away.

Jacqueline slid onto a stool at the bar next to Marti. She signaled the bartender and ordered a drink, probably her only one of the night, and another for Marti.

"Hi, there." Marti leaned close and slipped her hand onto Jacqueline's thigh.

"Buy you a drink?" Jacqueline discreetly kissed her cheek, just in front of her ear.

"I think you just did." Marti straightened but left her hand where it was. "How's your dad?"

"Can we talk about anything else?" She didn't want to discuss her concerns about her father's well-being with Marti. She hadn't come here to delve that far beneath the surface. She hadn't lied to Casey so she could have a therapy session with Marti; she needed sex. She covered Marti's hand and squeezed, seeking the familiar thrill of her touch. "What's new in the world of aviation?"

"Well, I don't want to ruin your next trip for you, but we're no longer giving out peanuts on flights."

"What? The honey-roasted peanuts are the only reason I fly." Jacqueline smiled. When the bartender set their drinks in front of them, Jacqueline handed over cash, declining his offer to open a tab.

"We're not staying long enough." Marti winked at him and his face flushed. He nodded and turned away with a goofy grin.

"You should be ashamed of yourself."

Marti laughed. "He should thank me. He'll be thinking about us together for the rest of the night." She angled closer and pulled Jacqueline's earlobe between her teeth, then whispered, "Especially when he sees us leave together."

Jacqueline downed the rest of her drink and set the glass back on the bar. "Let's go."

Marti looped her arm through Jacqueline's and led her to the lobby. They entered one of the elevators, and Jacqueline selected the button for her floor.

Minutes later, Jacqueline opened the door to her room and let Marti enter ahead of her.

"What, no suite this time?" Marti teased her as she turned around and trapped Jacqueline against the wall by the door. She bracketed her hands on either side of Jacqueline's shoulders.

"Sadly, no." Jacqueline slipped her hand along Marti's hip.

"Disappointing."

"Does that change your mind about coming up?"

Marti turned away and strolled across the room, obviously pretending to be considering her answer.

"You're thinking too hard."

"I have a lot of attractive offers. Lucky for you, you're often at the top of my list." She glanced around her. "But, eh, this room."

"I get upgraded one time, and you get spoiled." The king-sized bed took up most of the space, and the bathroom was small. The décor was outdated, but everything seemed clean, and she'd stayed here so often the staff took good care of her, hence the occasional upgrade.

Marti turned toward her. "Come over here and distract me from my dismal surroundings."

Jacqueline moved closer and let Marti pull her in. Marti kissed along Jacqueline's jawline, sliding her hand beneath the hem of Jacqueline's shirt to stroke her belly. Jacqueline closed her eyes and tried to immerse herself in the sensation. But behind her lids, she saw Casey's face, her expression kind and determined as she'd insisted on helping Jacqueline through these weeks. She jerked and opened her eyes.

Hoping to erase the image, she pushed Marti back on the bed and climbed on top of her. She straddled her, then rose and unbuttoned her own shirt from the bottom. Marti shoved her hands inside the fabric, caressing each exposed inch until she reached Jacqueline's breasts. She paid extra attention to her nipples before moving up to push Jacqueline's shirt down her shoulders.

When Jacqueline tried to shrug out of the garment, it caught around her arms and pinned them to her body. Marti sat up and grabbed the collar. She pulled Jacqueline close and rasped in her ear, "Let me help you with that." After throwing it to the side, Marti pulled her own shirt over her head.

Let me help you. Casey had said those words just before Jacqueline broke down in her arms. She shook her head against the sound and buried her face in the curve of Marti's neck instead. When Marti grabbed her wrist and guided her hand to her breast, she felt Casey's fingers circling her wrist. Casey's arms around her. *Let me be family again.*

Crying out, Jacqueline wrenched free and got off the bed.

"Jacqueline?"

Casey's voice filled her head as she slammed her back against the wall between the bed and the bathroom. She slid to the floor, her elbows on her drawn-up knees, and covered her face.

"Jacqueline, what's wrong, baby?" Strong arms circled her and tried to pull her close. Too strong. They held her too tight. Not like Casey's arms—supporting her without restraining her. *Baby?* Casey didn't call her baby. Not Casey. Marti.

Jacqueline lifted her head and stared into concerned brown eyes. Not Casey's beautiful blues.

"Hey, talk to me?"

"I'm—I'm sorry. I need a minute to clear my head." She held Marti's gaze, trying to seem reassuring. Marti hadn't done anything wrong. She'd been headed down the exact path Jacqueline had led her.

"What's going on?" Marti tightened her arms, maybe hoping the pressure would help, but Jacqueline couldn't breathe.

"I can't—" She pushed her hand against Marti's chest until she managed some separation between them. When Marti released her altogether, she got to her feet and stumbled toward the bed. She scooped up her shirt and held it to her chest, realizing the ridiculous gesture of covering what Marti had already seen countless times, but needing the barrier between them.

"Jacqueline?"

"I'm sorry. I'm just tired. I didn't realize the toll this week has taken."

"That was more than fatigue just now. What's going on?"

She slipped her arms through the sleeves of her shirt and held it closed with one fist. "Suddenly, I have a headache. Can I take a rain check on tonight?"

"A headache?"

Jacqueline met her eyes and nodded, seeing the disbelief reflected there.

"Sure." Marti's smile was forced as she retrieved her own shirt and put it back on. "Get some rest. Call me later, so I'll know you're okay?"

"Of course." Jacqueline followed her to the door, squelching the desire to apologize again. Contrition would be meaningless without an explanation, and she wasn't prepared to offer one.

"Take care of yourself, Jacqueline." Something in Marti's expression hinted that she thought this might be their final good-bye.

"You too." If she received any confirmation from Jacqueline it wouldn't be verbal.

She closed the door behind Marti and rested her forehead against it. *What the hell was that?* Even after her most stressful days, she'd never had trouble letting go for a few hours with a woman. As much as she liked and respected Marti, her feelings for her never ventured beyond friendly—sex was just sex. So why, all of a sudden, were thoughts of Casey intruding? Why had touching Marti felt disloyal to a woman she hadn't had a physical relationship with in eight years—well, six years if she counted that one slipup, but she didn't.

CHAPTER NINE

When Jacqueline stopped next to the curb in front of her father's house on Friday afternoon, she saw Casey's car in the driveway. Her heart kicked in her chest and nearly took her breath away. She almost drove away. Only Sean's Camry parked next to Casey's car made her pause. And her option was taken away completely when Sean opened the front door. She got out before Sean could wonder what was taking so long, but her legs felt shaky as she went up the walk.

He stepped out the door and greeted her with a quick hug. A scruff of hair, a new addition to the landscape of his face, brushed her cheek as his pressed against it briefly.

"Hey, son. What are you doing here?"

"I'm helping Mom with a wedding tomorrow. My afternoon class got cancelled, so I came up early to see Poppa."

"What's going on here?" She grasped his chin and pretended to inspect the scattered growth.

He pulled his head away and shrugged. "It's a beard."

She laughed. "It looks like it's trying to be."

"Very funny."

"How's school?"

"Tougher than last year."

"Not partying too much, are you?"

"No, ma'am."

"Good." She threw an arm around his shoulders. "I know you're trying to help look out for Poppa, but you know he wouldn't want you to let that interfere with your studies."

"I got it all covered." He slipped out from under her arm and tossed her a wink. "I even have a little time left over for the ladies."

"I don't like that at all." She narrowed her eyes at him as she followed him inside the house. Her father and Casey sat on the couch next to each other. Sean's iPad was propped up on the coffee table in front of them, and they both bent forward, looking at something on the screen.

"I learned it from you."

"What?"

"You know, keeping it casual, don't let them get attached." Before she could light into him, he said, "Take it easy, Mama. I'm messing with you."

"Okay, smart-ass." She glanced at Casey. Her attention hadn't left the screen in front of her, but her posture had gone more rigid.

He grinned and sat on the couch on her father's other side.

"Sean's showing us some pictures he took around campus," her father said.

Sean had carried his own SLR camera since he was ten years old. He had a good eye, and though he hadn't been moved to make photography a career, he still enjoyed it as a hobby. Casey encouraged him, praised his work, and engaged him in conversation about techniques. Jacqueline had always loved the way Casey's face shone with pride when he brought her a new collection of photographs.

"Do you want to squeeze in? There's room next to Mom." Sean pointed to the end of the couch opposite him and shuffled over a little.

Jacqueline glanced at the space next to Casey, really no more than half a cushion, then shook her head. She couldn't handle being smashed against Casey from shoulder to knees right now. "After my drive this morning, I don't think I can sit anymore right now. Okay if I look at them later?"

"Sure."

She escaped to the kitchen and grabbed a can of diet soda from the fridge, then leaned against the counter and listened to the murmur of voices from the next room. After a night of restless sleep, she'd driven home today with the radio turned up as loud as she could handle, changing the station every time she heard a song that remotely made her think of Casey, their relationship, or their time apart.

Seeing Casey's car in the drive had completely undone any progress she'd made forgetting what happened last night. She rolled the cool soda can against her forehead.

"Hey," Casey said from the doorway. Jacqueline raised her head, then popped the drink open, trying to look more relaxed than she felt. "Rough week?"

"Yeah, kind of."

"Anything I can do?" Casey moved into the room, closer to her, and she would have backed up if she weren't already pressed against the counter.

Casey's expression was warm and sympathetic. Her words didn't carry even a trace of flirtation, but every response Jacqueline came up with was inappropriate. So she shook her head.

"Are you eating?" Casey rested her back against the counter next to her. Jacqueline imagined she could feel the fabric of Casey's shirt sleeve against hers.

"No more or less than I ever did."

"You look thinner."

"I've been exercising." She knew her tone became more sarcastic in direct correlation to the increasing concern in Casey's, but she couldn't help it.

Casey laughed.

"I'm serious. Nothing strenuous, of course. But I've been walking here in the neighborhood and around my hotels when I travel."

"Please be careful walking around in strange cities."

"I will. I actually enjoy it—helps clear my head. And having a few less lumps and rolls doesn't hurt either." Jacqueline pinched her side.

"I liked your curves," Casey said so quietly that Jacqueline could almost tell herself she'd misheard her.

"I should check on Dad." She turned as she passed Casey to avoid brushing against her.

Sean and her father still sat in front of Sean's iPad, but instead of the pictures, Sean was now explaining something about his current studies.

Casey had followed her from the kitchen, and she touched Jacqueline's lower back. "Sean's with him. Let's get some fresh air. You can show me your route."

"Okay." Jacqueline stepped forward, discreetly terminating the contact between them. To Sean and her father, she said, "Hey, guys. We'll be back in a bit."

They both nodded, and her father waved her off with his hand before returning his attention to Sean's tablet.

As Jacqueline and Casey exited the front door, Jacqueline sucked in a sharp breath at the flash of familiarity. The cool spring air and scent of fresh-cut grass reminded her of the day they'd first looked at their house with the realtor. After spending their first few years together in apartments, the idea of buying a house with Casey had made her feel very grown up.

"What's wrong?" Casey asked as she drew even with her on the sidewalk.

"Nothing." She shook off the nostalgia that had settled around her like a thick cape resting on her shoulders. "The neighborhood has changed." She grasped a safer topic. Many of the smaller homes had disappeared to make room for new duplexes. Though builders used touches of period architecture, the new homes lacked the charm of the previous cottages.

"I hate those places." Casey waved a hand toward one of the newer houses.

"Me too." She wanted to say she missed the old neighborhood, but she was afraid Casey would know she meant she missed the "old them," too. When she walked these streets, she longed for the days when Casey was her best friend. She had to go back quite a few years, before they started arguing all the time—when they were young and it seemed as if they existed only for each other. Then she felt like an unrealistic fool. Of course, everyone yearned for the simpler days of their early courtship, but that wasn't life. Real life tested relationships, and theirs hadn't survived—hadn't been strong enough.

❖

By the time Casey and Jacqueline returned to Teddy's house, he'd retired to his room for a nap. Sean had been waiting for them before he left. He threw a few things into his backpack and slung it over his shoulder.

He gave Jacqueline a hug. "I'm meeting some friends for dinner tonight. I'll probably stay with Mom tonight since we have that wedding tomorrow."

"Sure. Be safe."

"Always." He kissed Casey on the cheek on his way to the door. "See you later."

After he left, Casey and Jacqueline stood in the living room, an awkward silence between them. Casey had sensed something was going on with Jacqueline and had invited her on the walk hoping to get her to open up. Instead, they'd walked mostly in silence, save the occasional comment on how the neighborhood had changed, which only seemed to make Jacqueline more subdued.

Casey picked up her purse. "I should probably go, too."

"Thanks—for everything." Jacqueline glanced toward the hallway leading to Teddy's room.

"Let him sleep, Jacq," Casey said over her shoulder as she headed for the door.

"How did you know?"

She paused with her hand on the knob. "Because you were the same way with Sean when he was sick—always waking him up just to check on him."

Jacqueline lowered her eyes to the floor. "Dad thinks I treat him like a child. Maybe he's right."

"He's okay, you know." She didn't want to venture too far into Jacqueline and Teddy's father/daughter relationship—that was no longer her place. But even after eight years, the lines always blurred a bit for Casey. She'd never stopped caring about Jacqueline—loving her, even, in some ways. She just couldn't be unhappy anymore. And when she'd finally gotten the nerve to ask Jacqueline to go— she had gone. That might have been what hurt the most.

"Has he said something?"

Casey sighed and set her purse on the floor by the door. She crossed to Jacqueline, took her hand, and pulled her down onto the couch. "No. But you're killing yourself to make sure he's watched so closely. He's been better since the soreness from that last fall abated. I mean, I still think he gets confused easily and that does need monitoring, but he's not as fragile as—"

"I don't know how to do this." Jacqueline's brows drew together over suddenly wet eyes.

"I know, sweetheart." She wanted to pull her into her arms again, but she didn't think Jacqueline would allow it. She did seem to tolerate the hand-holding, and when Casey gave hers a little squeeze, she felt the answering pressure from Jacqueline.

"Everything's just such a mess right now." Jacqueline's fingers moved lightly over the inside of Casey's wrist, and she wondered if the caress was intentional. "I don't want you to sell the house."

"Jacq—"

"I know. It's selfish of me. I'm sorry. The house is yours. But a part of me felt like as long as you lived there, I still had a connection to it—and to my memories there."

"I have to live my life."

"I know. And you should." Jacqueline slipped her hand free, and Casey folded hers in her lap. "You and Nina should make a home of your own. Wherever you choose."

"I'm not trying to hurt you."

"I'm not hurt." A note of petulance echoed in Jacqueline's words, but then she took a breath as if resetting her tone. "I truly do want you to be happy."

Casey believed her. "And I want you to, as well." She knew she was about to cross a line, but Sean's words still lingered. Jacqueline seemed open—vulnerable—and she wasn't sure when they would next be in a place when Jacqueline would hear her again. "It's okay to get attached. You don't have to always keep it casual."

Jacqueline flushed and looked away guiltily. Casey hadn't thought Jacqueline had been celibate all this time. But she got an uncomfortable feeling in her stomach when she thought about Jacqueline behaving as Sean had implied she did. Part of her hated that Jacqueline wasn't still the sweet, somewhat shy woman who had first taken her to dinner twenty-one years ago.

At that moment, Jacqueline's phone vibrated and lit up with a text notification. Since she'd left it on the coffee table earlier, she would have to stretch across Casey to get it. Automatically, Casey grabbed it and passed it to her. She hadn't meant to look at the screen, but her eyes fell there almost on their own. She saw the name "Marti" and the words "last night" before Jacqueline pulled it away.

Jacqueline unlocked the screen, read it, then tucked it in her pocket.

"Marti?" Casey asked before she could stop herself.

"A friend in Atlanta."

"A friend you saw last night?"

Jacqueline didn't answer.

"Did you have plans to see her before or after you called and asked me to check on Teddy because you couldn't make it home?" She didn't want to know. She didn't want to hear about what Jacqueline had been doing while Nina was leaving Casey because she didn't want to share her with Teddy.

"It's not what you think—"

"Before or after?" Casey repeated, her words as tight as the knot in her throat.

"Before."

"Seriously?" She shot off the couch, unable to watch the guilt overtaking every feature of Jacqueline's beautiful face.

"Casey, I can explain."

"I'd love to hear it." It seemed like someone else spewed the words. Surely not Casey. Because she most definitely did not want to hear whatever Jacqueline was about to say. "I can't wait to find out how you justify this one to yourself."

"I—um—I actually—"

"Yes?"

"Shit. Give me a minute."

"Sure. You need some time to come up with a suitable lie?"

"No, I—"

"I don't even want to know." Casey grabbed her purse and wrenched open the front door. As she left, she muttered, "Here I was thinking you'd changed. I'm such an idiot. And you're the same selfish—"

"I'm *selfish*?" Jacqueline followed her out of the house, but Casey ignored her, intent only on getting to her car and leaving. "I'm selfish for wanting to take care of my family? For trying to be everything to everyone?"

Casey spun around and came face-to-face with Jacqueline. "Just how exactly does you screwing some woman while I'm here looking after *your father* add up to you taking care of your family?"

Jacqueline gasped and fell back a step, as if Casey had actually struck her.

"I can't—" Casey turned back and quickly covered the distance to her car. "I can't do this now."

"Casey." Jacqueline took a step toward her, but when Casey paused in the open door to her car, she froze.

"I'll check on him next week while you're gone because I said I would. But after that, you're on your own."

CHAPTER TEN

This was a wasted trip," Jacqueline muttered as she rested her elbow on the table in front of her and braced her forehead against her palm. She'd been in Knoxville for two days and had determined that she could have completed this investigation over the phone.

She'd arrived in town late Sunday night and interviewed Lena Blackstone Monday morning. Lena alleged that she was passed up for promotions because she was female. After taking her statement, Jacqueline talked to Lena's manager as well as the center's hiring manager, who didn't even recall Lena having applied for an open promotional position.

Jacqueline logged into the applicant tracking system and pulled the postings for the two promotions she said she'd put in. Lena's name didn't appear on either list. She had to dig a little further to find the issue.

In both cases, preference was given to internal applicants who applied by a specified purge date. If they had a shortage of qualified existing employees, only then would they consider external applicants. In one case, Lena had mistakenly applied as an external applicant, and because they had a number of good internal employees to consider, they didn't add any of the external applications. In the second, she'd applied internally, but after the expiration date, so her paperwork wasn't processed. Not only had she not been purposely discriminated against, but she hadn't actually been in contention for either job through her own fault.

Her next interview with Lena didn't go smoothly. Lena insisted she'd received no direction from her superiors about how to put in for the jobs, probably because she was a woman and they didn't want her to get the promotion. Jacqueline gave her the printouts of the job postings that specified which systems to apply through. None of the other applicants had had trouble following the directions.

After determining Lena's claim was unfounded, Jacqueline just needed to complete and submit her final report. She sat back in her chair, opened the laptop in front of her, and began summarizing the course of her investigation over the past two days.

She couldn't wait to finish and head home, though what she faced there wouldn't be much easier. True to her word, Casey had continued to check on her father for the past two days. She hadn't answered any of Jacqueline's calls since their argument last week. But, since Monday, after Jacqueline had hung up without leaving a voice mail, she'd received a text from Casey with an update on her father. If he knew they'd argued, he hadn't brought it up in any of her phone conversations with him. The one time she'd heard Casey in the background and asked to speak to her, he'd haltingly told her that Casey had just stepped out of the room, then changed the subject. She was too proud to beg him to convince her to get on the phone, so she'd let it go.

"Do you think you'll spend more than a few days at home any time soon?" Kendra asked as she slid into the coffee shop booth across from Jacqueline.

"I sure as hell hope so. I'm running on fumes here." Jacqueline took a sip of her coffee. "I got back from Knoxville a couple of hours ago and have to go into the office this afternoon. But tomorrow, I'm taking a day to work from home. Dad has a follow-up with his doctor."

"It's Friday. Why not?"

"Exactly."

"Here. You look skinny. I got you a muffin." Kendra slid a plate covered with a huge chocolate-chip muffin across the table.

"I'm good. Thanks."

"Fine. I got it for me." She pulled it halfway back to her. "But as my maid of honor, you're obligated to eat half my calories so I'll still fit in my dress."

"I'm your maid of honor?" Jacqueline broke a piece off the top. "Oh, it's still warm."

"Of course you are. You're the only woman I've ever lived with that I didn't want to kill on a regular basis."

"You did have some nightmare roommates after me."

"Yes, but even after you dumped me to room with Casey junior year and left me with an endless string of crazies, here I am still asking you to stand up with me at my wedding."

"Because you're the better person." Jacqueline raised her coffee in a mock salute.

"Speaking of Casey."

"We weren't."

"She called me."

Jacqueline froze with her cup halfway to her mouth. "I assumed you two still spoke." She paused and then added, "What did she say?"

"Nothing about you. Not even after I dropped your name in conversation. She only actively avoids talking about you when she's mad. What happened?"

"You enjoy this, don't you? Being in the middle, calling yourself Switzerland all the time. But I think you get a kick out of listening to us both and knowing even more about what's going on than either of us does."

"Fine. Don't tell me what happened. Have you stopped to consider why, after eight years, there's still something for me to be in the middle of? You're lesbians. Aren't you supposed to be best friends after, like, a year and a half?"

"You're hilarious." Jacqueline tore off another piece of muffin and shoved it in her mouth.

"Are you two going to be able to handle being involved in my wedding together?"

"Of course. I've actually seen more of her in the past month than I have in years. We'll be fine." She wasn't certain where they stood, but the wedding was three months away. If all else failed, she'd stick to the other side of the room. "Oh, I'm throwing you a shower. I think it's one of my official duties."

"Do people even do that anymore?"

"I don't know. But we will."

"I'm not some twenty-something buying my first house with my new husband. Aren't showers only for the first marriage?"

"Okay. Call it an engagement party."

"You know what I'd really like?"

"What's that?"

"Remember the poker parties we used to have?"

Jacqueline laughed. "Sure. I met Casey at one of them. I haven't played poker in years."

"Brush up on your Texas Hold 'Em, my friend. I expect you to help me clean out the guests like we used to."

❖

"Teddy, I brought lunch," Casey called as she opened his front door. She stopped quickly when she entered the living room. Jacqueline sat on the couch with her open laptop resting on her thighs. Fatigue dulled Jacqueline's eyes, and her hair was messed up like she'd had her hands in it all morning. Casey couldn't back out of the room now, and she couldn't give in to her sudden urge to go to her, so instead she offered a somewhat stilted greeting. "I didn't know you were here."

"I took Dad to the doctor this morning. I'm working from here for the afternoon. I should have texted and let you know you didn't need to come today."

"Well, I'm here now and I have enough food for three, so we may as well eat." She forced herself into the kitchen, not in the mood for a confrontation. Maybe they could keep things polite through lunch, and then she could escape unscathed. "Where's Teddy?"

"On the back patio, reading the paper."

"Good. It's a gorgeous fall day. You should join him. You look like you could use some fresh air."

"I've got a million things to do this afternoon if I want to have any semblance of a weekend," Jacqueline said, propped against the doorframe between the kitchen and living room.

"Well, you've already put your laptop aside. And now you're halfway to the patio. I apparently brought enough fried chicken to feed an army." She gestured to the bucket of chicken she'd picked up on her way back from her morning shoot. "So let's go out and have a picnic with Teddy." She looked up and caught Jacqueline staring at her with a mix of fondness and confusion. "What?"

"Nothing." Jacqueline looked away. "You're very good at taking care of all of us." When she glanced back up, her expression grew serious.

"Well." Casey broke eye contact first this time. The mood in the room suddenly felt a bit too domestic. She looked down at the three plates she'd been filling with food. "How was his appointment?"

Jacqueline didn't answer right away, and Casey worried she wouldn't go with the subject change. But then she straightened and came farther into the room. "I think he's finally being honest with his doctor."

"That's good."

"He tells me he's fine. But once the doctor called him out on his shit, he admitted to back and leg pain. The doc prescribed some anti-inflammatories and pain pills."

"If you leave them on the counter, I'll make sure he takes them when I'm here." Casey spoke without thinking, then realized she'd told Jacqueline she wouldn't be coming anymore after this week. She'd just given Jacqueline an opening to bring up their recent argument.

"The doc also thinks he's depressed." Though Jacqueline didn't stray from the previous topic, her tone became more tentative.

Casey nodded.

"You're not surprised."

"Not really. He hasn't been the same since your mom died. But lately, he seems more—I don't know—lonely, maybe."

"I've tried suggesting activities for him. But he seems content to sit in that house and let me bring everything to him."

"What did the doctor suggest?"

"He doesn't want to put him on medication just yet. He says he can suggest a therapist with experience with the elderly."

"God, it's so weird thinking of your dad as elderly." He'd been in his mid-forties when they'd first started dating. She'd been completely intimidated the first time Jacqueline had introduced her. He'd just returned home from a construction site covered in grease from his work as a heavy-machinery mechanic. He'd greeted her gruffly and barely spoke to her at dinner, leaving Jacqueline's mother to do the entertaining. She hadn't known at the time that she was the first girl Jacqueline had brought home to meet them. "I can't imagine him willingly seeing a therapist."

"In the absence of drugs and therapy, he said, as a first step, we should get him out and active. He's lost too much weight and needs to eat better. And more importantly, poor nutrition can lead to bone loss and other health issues."

"Okay. So," she looked down at the fried chicken, potatoes, and gravy, "after this meal, healthy cooking, then. And we have to entice him out of the house."

"I thought you were done after this week," Jacqueline said sarcastically.

"I'm not doing it for you." Just like that, the tension was back between them. She picked up her and Teddy's plates and headed for the patio.

The screened patio had always been Teddy's favorite place to unwind. He and his wife had spent their evenings drinking their after-dinner decaf in the side-by-side lounge chairs that occupied one side of the area. Opposite the loungers, a round patio table and four chairs were perfectly placed to feel the light midday breeze.

"How did you know I wanted fried chicken?" Teddy opened his napkin and laid it across his lap.

"You mentioned it twice last week, and we didn't have it. I took a chance that you were still in the mood."

"Enjoy it. After this it's all grilled chicken and leafy greens," Jacqueline said as she joined them on the patio. She took the chair across from Casey.

Teddy waved a drumstick at her. "Are you doing the cooking?"

"I can follow a recipe." Jacqueline gave Casey a stern look, warning her not to argue.

Teddy didn't seem convinced. He looked at Casey and said, "Maybe you could bring over a pot of that potato-and-kale soup you make. We could live on it for a couple of days."

"Hey, I'll be in town all week. And I should be able to get home for dinner. So I got it covered."

Teddy smiled as if he'd meant to rile Jacqueline up. "Maybe soup for lunch."

"I think you may be getting spoiled by all of this attention, Dad." Jacqueline winked at Casey, then gave her an apologetic look.

Casey turned her attention to her plate. She couldn't deny the way her stomach had fluttered in reaction to the wink, but then again, being the focus of Jacqueline's attention had always affected her that way. Likely, Jacqueline had winked out of habit in the same way that she reacted automatically.

"I have back-to-back shoots on Monday. But I can come for lunch on Tuesday." She'd told Jacqueline she was done helping out. But she'd enjoyed spending time with Teddy these past few weeks. And why should he have to sit here alone all day just so she could spite Jacqueline?

"Soup, then?"

"Let's make a deal, Teddy. I'll bring soup, if you'll go for a walk around the block with me before lunch."

"You'd make an old man walk for his lunch?"

She laughed. "Yes."

"To the corner and back."

Casey pretended to consult Jacqueline, who gave a small nod. "Deal."

Casey ate the rest of her lunch quietly, listening to Teddy and Jacqueline talk about the plight of Teddy's second cousin from Arizona who had just been diagnosed with prostate cancer. Casey had never met the cousin, but the conversation led to a roll call of other distant family members that neither had seen nor thought about in years. Jacqueline recalled a reunion that had brought a good number of them together when she was a teenager, Teddy remarking that since then, no one in the family had taken the initiative to organize such an event.

Once they'd finished lunch, Jacqueline gathered up their dishes and went to the kitchen.

"I'm going to head home." Casey bent and gave Teddy a half hug, urging him back to his seat when he tried to stand to see her off. She kissed his cheek. "I know my way out."

He grabbed her hand. "Don't let her chase you away. You're welcome here."

She teared up immediately, then flushed with embarrassment. His love and acceptance, so freely given, made her uncharacteristically emotional. "Take care. Call me if you need anything. Anytime, okay?" She sniffed and swiped at her eyes as she entered the house.

Chapter Eleven

Jacqueline had just finished packing up the leftover food, when Casey hurried through the kitchen with her head down. She was surprised when Casey didn't stop or speak, and she didn't recover until Casey was well through the room.

"Hey." She caught up to Casey near the front door. But she didn't really know what she'd intended to say when Casey turned with her purse in her hand. "Do you want to take the rest of the food home?"

"No. Keep it here. You two will eat it sooner than I will." Casey turned back toward the door.

"Can we talk?" Why did everything she said sound like she'd blurted it out?

"About?" Casey looked frustrated.

"Okay. You were right. I was a selfish ass." Jacqueline braced one arm on the couch, needing some kind of anchor to keep her from crossing to Casey. "I knew I should have come home. But lately, between Dad and work, I don't have—I just needed—"

"It's clear exactly what you needed."

"No, I—"

"Please don't insult me."

"Marti is—she's a friend." *Friend* was probably a stretch.

"So, you've never slept with her?"

She blushed and looked away. She wasn't ashamed of her behavior. She'd always owned the truth about her relationships. But laying it all out before Casey made her feel embarrassed about what that truth said about her.

"How many times when we were together did you call and say you were sorry but you wouldn't be home that night after all?"

Jacqueline gave a short nod. "More times than I should have. But I wasn't cheating on you. I never—"

"I know. But it didn't seem to bother you much when you couldn't come home either."

"What was I supposed to do, Casey? This is my job. Was I supposed to quit so I could stay home and live a fairy tale with you and Sean? I'd be sacrificing everything I've worked for since college. That's not realistic."

"You don't think I gave things up? You talk about college as if you were the only one there with dreams. God, when I think about that girl I was then—I had plans, too, you know. I was creative and—and imaginative and—"

"You were good—you are—an amazing photographer. I've always told you that."

"Taking portraits—was not my dream, Jacq. But life happens. I made sacrifices, for Sean and for us." Casey's college aspirations to travel, then exhibit photographs of her trips seemed so far away. They'd been only twenty-five when they adopted Sean, and she'd just been getting started making a name for herself.

"Sean is grown now, maybe you could—"

"You don't get it. Sean became my dream. My priorities changed when he came into our lives. I know I could have tried to have it all, lots of women do, but I made my choice. Maybe someday I'll venture into a new aspect of my career, but even if I never accomplish anything more, I don't regret it."

"So, I'm a heartless bitch because I didn't sideline my career?"

"I didn't say that."

"But it's what you think. Have you forgotten who was bringing home the paychecks while you were getting your business going?"

"Jacq—"

"I refuse to let you make me feel guilty for providing for my family. Do you think I don't know what I missed out on while I was sitting in all those hotel rooms?" *What I'm still missing.*

"Well, apparently, you're making up for it with your hotel-room activities now," Casey snapped.

"I didn't have sex with Marti that night." She chose to ignore the reference to any other nights before then.

"That is so not the point. I'm not trying to tell you who you can and can't sleep with."

"Then exactly what are you trying to do?"

Casey shook her head—almost absently—the way she did when she was about to shut down emotionally.

"What?" Jacqueline prompted, desperate to get through before Casey's walls came up.

"Forget it."

She stepped closer and raised her voice, trying to change Casey's course. "What the hell did you want from me?"

"I wanted you to want me," Casey shouted back. Her purse hit the floor and she covered her mouth with a trembling hand. She cleared her throat and went on, softer now. "Back then, I wanted you to *want* to come home. So badly, that you would drive through your exhaustion just to not be away from us for one more night."

Jacqueline stared at her, unable to formulate a single response to that heartbreaking statement. Casey's face flushed and tears filled her eyes.

Casey began talking again, as if trying to find a route away from the tension filling the space between them. "I know it wasn't *realistic*, or safe even. You could have fallen asleep at the wheel and had an accident, and I wouldn't have wanted—"

Jacqueline surged forward, until she'd physically erased the space between them. She cradled Casey's face in her hands and took her mouth in an aggressive kiss. Casey sagged against her, responsive at once, her tongue meeting Jacqueline's in a rhythm they'd perfected two decades ago. She slipped her hands to Casey's neck, gentling her touch against the soft skin and the feather-light ends of her hair. The feel of Casey's lips moving against hers exploded against her every nerve ending, bathing her in the taste, texture, and scent of Casey.

Before she could figure out how this could be both a familiar kiss and a first kiss at once, Casey's hands pushed against her chest, weakly at first, then stronger until she broke the connection.

"What are you doing?" Casey backed up until she hit the wall behind her. She held two fingers against her lips, and Jacqueline recognized the haze of arousal in her eyes.

"Oh God, I'm sorry." Jacqueline sucked in a quick breath, unable to get enough oxygen to recover.

"Damn it, Jacq."

"I know."

"You can't just—"

"I know. I'm so sorry. I don't know what happened. I couldn't stop pushing you, and then—I didn't think. I just couldn't think." She'd been swamped with the need to erase past pain and felt helpless to do so.

"I should go."

Jacqueline nodded and bent to pick up Casey's purse at the same moment Casey did. They nearly butted heads, and their hands clashed on the handle. Casey jerked it away, pulled open the door, and practically fell through it.

Jacqueline caught the door as it swung open and slowly closed it behind her. With her hand still on the doorknob, she rested her forehead against the door. She'd meant to apologize and erase the uneasiness between them. But she'd only made things worse. Casey had kissed her back—she'd responded almost immediately. And she'd probably beat herself up over that. She was the most loyal person Jacqueline knew, and she'd feel guilty. Hell, she might even confess to Nina. "Shit."

"You okay, Jacq?" Her father stood in the doorway from the kitchen.

"Yeah. I'm good." She didn't ask him how long he'd been there.

"Casey left?"

"Yep."

"Do you want to talk about it?"

She laughed, a harsh bark that hurt her throat. "Not really."

"What's going on with you two?"

"Nothing." She turned and rested against the door, staring at him across the room.

"I should pretend I couldn't hear you shouting from outside?"

"If you don't mind."

"I can't help but feel like I'm adding to the stress between you." He eased into his favorite chair, moving a little stiffly, and gestured to the couch.

"It's not about you." She perched on the edge of the couch, bracing her elbows on her widespread knees.

"You've managed to be civil for years until recently."

"Maybe that's been the problem. We've stopped being civil. But you aren't making it harder. If anything, looking out for you has kept us from totally losing it. Until today, I guess."

"What happened?"

"Some old issues. Some new." Jacqueline stared at the floor between her feet. "This carpet needs to be replaced. Have you ever thought about hardwoods in here?"

"Like I need another reason to slip and fall."

"Good point." She smiled. "Do you think she's happy with Nina?" She didn't look up, unable to handle it if he looked at her with pity in his eyes.

"You know, this kind of stuff was always your mother's department."

She nodded, swallowing tears. "I know."

"She loved Casey. She once said she'd never seen you happier. After you split up, she didn't think you'd ever give your heart to anyone like that again."

"She was right."

"Be careful, baby."

She raised her head and found his eyes as wet as hers.

"That's what she'd say if she were here." He looked at the framed photograph on the bookcase in the corner. In it, a ten-year old Jacqueline was squished in between her parents. They'd been on vacation in Myrtle Beach.

"Yes. That sounds like her." Jacqueline stretched across the space between them and squeezed his forearm. He covered her hand with his. At moments like these she could convince herself that his signs of confusion were not aging but rather her imagination.

She could get lost in staring at that photo and wishing that she and Casey had what her parents had had. She could wallow in the fact that she'd never have the happily-ever-after they'd had. But she didn't think she could stand to watch Casey find it with Nina or anyone else. If that meant distancing herself from Casey, she'd find a way to do it.

❖

"…for better or for worse, for richer, for poorer, in sickness and in health, to love and to cherish; from this day forward until death do us part."

Casey watched through the viewfinder of her Nikon as the two women standing under the arbor stated their vows. She snapped a series of shots as each of them slid a ring on the other's finger. She lifted her head long enough to confirm that Sean was at the other end of the aisle capturing another angle.

As the couple shared their first kiss, then joined hands and turned toward their guests, their smiles radiated pure joy. They made their way down the aisle, which was barely wide enough for them anymore as their friends and family crushed in around them. She didn't follow them, trusting Sean to get the necessary images. She didn't want him to worry about keeping her out of the periphery of his frame.

Casey had photographed enough weddings to do the ceremony almost on autopilot. And this wasn't even her first same-sex wedding since the federal law had changed. But for some reason, hearing their laughter and witnessing their happiness and the celebration of their guests made her throat ache with the effort of containing her own emotions. After taking several pictures of the retreating couple, she lowered her camera and realized she now stood close to the arbor herself.

For a long time, a wedding hadn't been in Casey's plans. And she had a ready-list of reasons why. She didn't need a piece of paper. She wouldn't do it until it was legal in Tennessee. Weddings weren't magical for her. They were work. If pressed, now that it was legal, she would concede that maybe someday she'd be married, but she didn't need more than a courthouse ceremony.

But today, she envied the happy couple. They clearly loved each other to the exclusion of all else. And no matter what else happened to them in life, they would have this day, when everything could be as simple as two words: I do.

As the ceremony gave way to the reception, Casey captured the shots all couples desired, cutting the cake, the first dance, two separate father/daughter moments. She also managed to get a number of photos of family and friends and some candid moments of the brides together. They were beautiful, the venue was gorgeous, and the lighting was perfect. She wouldn't be bogged down with tons of extra editing on this one.

Casey took a break to congratulate the brides, eat the small piece of cake they foisted upon her, and chat with the mother of one of the women, who had been a persistent presence during the planning. She looked up at one point and saw the brides dancing together, and the love between them left her breathless. As she shifted her gaze away, she met Sean's eyes across the room. He stared at her as if trying to solve a puzzle. His attention shifted to the two women, then back to her. Then he raised his camera and panned back to the dance floor.

Casey looked down at her own camera and pretended she was fiddling with some settings. Hopefully, Sean had gotten the shot she'd been too distracted to focus on. She knew she was romanticizing the scene before her. They were a real couple who likely had their issues just like everyone else. But today the complications in Casey's life felt enormous in comparison. She touched her fingertips to her lips. She had kissed Jacqueline countless times in so many ways in her life. And that, she told herself, was why even now, a day later, she could still feel the pressure of Jacqueline's lips against hers. Her body didn't need much urging to recall the imprint of years spent with Jacqueline.

She hadn't stopped the kiss right away. And, honestly, she hadn't really wanted to stop it when she did. The guilt of that lapse weighed heavily in her chest. They'd gotten caught up in a moment, lost themselves to the charge of emotions. It wasn't as if it had never happened before. But not since she'd been seeing Nina. If not for Nina, Casey could have chalked the kiss up to a momentary indiscretion. She would need to avoid being alone with Jacqueline until she had her reactions under control, but they could get past it.

But now, she grappled with whether she needed to confess. Nina would be hurt. Was it worth assuaging her own guilt, given that she and Nina had experienced their own tensions lately? Nina already resented the time she spent with the Knight family, and telling her about this kiss would only make things worse. She didn't think she would come clean, and that worried her. If she could bury this transgression, what did that say about her future with Nina?

❖

"Jacqueline Knight." Jacqueline answered her cell phone without looking at the display. She'd been fielding calls all day from employees with questions about the new insurance plans. She didn't mind explaining the various components, even when the calls came from employees in centers where she'd already conducted education.

Owen's baritone vibrated through the phone. "I'm looking over your report from Knoxville, but I don't see the P&C letter. Would you email that to me?"

Jacqueline opened her file on the Lena Blackstone investigation and scanned through the documents. "Owen, can I call you right back?" She waited only long enough for him to acknowledge her before she disconnected.

She hadn't included the privileged and confidential letter in her email to Owen because she didn't have one. More specifically, she hadn't obtained one. Usually, when she received a complaint, she first emailed the legal department so they could draft a P&C letter and open a case on it. The document, sent by a company attorney, contained a bunch of legalese that declared any work-product generated from that point forward in the course of the investigation to be confidential due to the attorney-client relationship. In the case of future litigation, the fact that they'd opened an investigation would be discoverable by the other side, but the company could not be compelled to turn over any paperwork, emails, interviews, or anything else associated with the investigation.

Lena Blackstone had called her while she was in Atlanta. She remembered thinking that she needed to notify legal, then putting it off to go meet Marti. Somewhere in the middle of her failed liaison with Marti and the disagreement with Casey, she'd completely forgotten to send that email.

"Shit." She picked up her office phone, and dialed Owen's number. She didn't see any point in delaying the inevitable. When he answered she blurted out her admission. "I didn't get a P&C letter. It was a complete oversight on my part and I don't have an explanation—not a good one, anyway."

He sighed. "Jacqueline—"

"I screwed up. Do you want me to call legal?" She copied both Owen and the legal department on her final report and was actually surprised she hadn't received a call from someone over there first.

"I'll take care of it. They'll probably want to talk to you later."

"Sure."

"This could be a big deal, Jacqueline. This case was unfounded, but if it hadn't been—if a lawsuit was filed, we'd have to hand everything over to the plaintiff."

"I know." She cut off the rest of her response—*I'm not an idiot*—because, clearly, she was. He was within his right to talk to her like an unseasoned intern, since she'd acted like one.

"I'll call you back after I've talked to legal."

She hung up and dropped her head onto her desk, not even bothering to cushion the blow with her arm. If this was the shape of her Monday, the rest of the week could only get better. She couldn't even fix her mistake. Since she'd already completed the investigation, she'd gain nothing from getting the letter now. Only the work done after the dated letter was protected.

As screwups went, this one shouldn't cost the company in the long run. But Owen didn't like mistakes. She didn't either, even more so since she'd made this one because she'd been distracted by her personal life. Legal wouldn't recommend more than a stern lecture, but she'd just have to wait and see how Owen weighed the situation.

Chapter Twelve

How did I let you talk me into this," Kendra said for the fourth time in the two blocks since they'd left the house.

"You're a good friend." Jacqueline glanced at Kendra. For someone who professed to hate exercise, she'd thrown together a well-coordinated outfit. Her neon-pink T-shirt matched the stripe down each leg of her capri-length spandex pants. She even had pink laces and a brand insignia on her cross-trainers.

"I'm so damn out of shape." With Kendra's long legs, she had no problem keeping up with Jacqueline's pace.

"I needed this. It's been a hell of a week," Jacqueline said.

"What happened?"

Without going into too much detail, she filled Kendra in on her screwup at work. She'd heard back from Owen within two days. He'd made it clear that a critical letter in her file could keep her from moving up in the company and that he'd done her a favor by not taking her disciplinary action to that level. He didn't want to waste all of the time he'd spent grooming her over one mistake. But he'd told her this was a one-time pass from him.

"So you're supposed to feel beholden to him?"

"Beholden?" Jacqueline laughed. "I wouldn't have put it exactly that way, but yes, I guess so."

"That's bullshit. Was this really a big deal?"

"Not this time. But it could have been."

"But it wasn't."

"I couldn't have known that when I didn't ask for the letter. I have to grovel to him a little. It's politics. Don't tell me you music-industry people don't have any of that."

"You're right. I'm lucky to have a solid group around me. And a good-enough reputation to say screw you and move on if I don't like the way of things."

Jacqueline shook her head. "It's different for me. I've put in a lot of time and I'm almost there."

"And you still want it? The big chair? Your boss's job?"

"Sure. Why wouldn't I?" They'd reached the end of the block, and Jacqueline stopped and faced Kendra.

"I'm just saying that it's okay to change your mind. Maybe you want different things now than you did when you were a hot, young, twenty-something."

Jacqueline turned away and headed down the next street, assuming Kendra would follow. "You're not suddenly wise just because you're getting married, you know."

"Maybe I am."

"That reminds me. Everything's all set for your bridal shower next month."

"I wish you'd stop calling it that. Are you sure you're okay having it at Casey's house?" Kendra swung her arms, one hand tapping Jacqueline's in a casual touch that, if she didn't know Kendra better, she might believe was accidental.

"Sure. It makes sense. Her house is bigger than both of ours, and this way I'll be close if Dad needs anything." She'd had mixed feelings when Kendra told her Casey had volunteered her house—their old house—for the party. She smothered a sarcastic comment about taking advantage of the house before Casey sold it. The locale made sense, for all the reasons she'd just given Kendra, so she'd just have to get over any weirdness.

She'd told Kendra to let Casey know she'd take care of the planning. Running with Kendra's idea for a poker theme, she'd found a company that rented an authentic poker table and the services of a dealer. She'd even hired a company to cater a mini-buffet designed to emulate the kind found in casinos. She'd texted the details to Casey but asked that they keep everything from Kendra until that day.

When she followed Kendra around the next corner, she realized they'd be going right by Casey's house. As they drew closer, Kendra craned her neck like she was trying to see if Casey was home. Jacqueline's hope that they could pass without incident disappeared when she saw Casey sitting on the porch. She'd been avoiding Casey for five days. Given her work schedule, it hadn't been too difficult. When she hadn't accidentally run into Casey at her father's even once, she'd wondered if Casey might also be staying away from her. Casey had responded to her texts about the party with short, to-the-point answers.

They hadn't talked about the kiss, yet. Knowing Casey, she'd eventually want to. Jacqueline couldn't forget about it. In fact, as time went on it seemed like she remembered parts of it that she hadn't noticed at the time. Like Casey's small, sexy moan when their mouths came together. Or the way Casey had grasped desperately at her waist before wedging her hands between them to break their embrace. Or how Casey's lips tasted like peppermint and felt just a little sticky. She didn't wear lipstick, so it must have been lip balm.

"Are you up there drinking beer while this bitch has me out sweating?" Kendra's voice jerked her away from her memories of the kiss. Kendra had stopped at the end of the walk leading up to the house, and Jacqueline almost ran into her. Her heart was racing and she couldn't look at Casey. She was certain her nipples were pushing out through her sports bra and T-shirt, but she didn't dare check, with Kendra staring at her like she was an idiot.

"Absolutely." Casey lifted her bottle. "Want one?"

"Yes, yes, yes." As Kendra grabbed Jacqueline's elbow and started dragging her up the walk, Casey went into the house.

Once Casey was out of sight, Jacqueline pulled her arm free. "I'll meet you back at Dad's house."

"What? Come on." Kendra reached for her again, but she backed up a step.

"I'm not done walking yet."

Kendra gave her a look that said she knew there was more going on, then said, "Well, I'm having a beer."

Jacqueline didn't wait for her to get all the way up the walk before she stepped onto the sidewalk again and resumed her route. She didn't look back when she heard Casey come back to the porch.

She picked up the pace, practically power-walking to her house. She would have to get her shit under control before the party. She hadn't even asked if Kendra had invited Nina, but since Casey was hosting, it would be rude not to have, so she had to assume Nina would be there. Apparently, avoidance worked only until she couldn't help being in Casey's company. She would have to figure out some other way to distract herself during the party.

The kiss was a very vivid memory, but she had another one she could draw on that would surely remind her of why she should stay away from Casey. She'd been trying not to go back to such a place of anger, but maybe she had no choice. She called up her memory of the day she'd known her relationship with Casey was over—their last big fight. It didn't even matter what they'd been arguing about at first. Things had escalated until they'd been screaming at each other, and then they'd heard Sean's bedroom door slam and both realized he'd been in the hallway listening.

Casey had gotten very quiet when she said, "I'm tired of fighting."

"I know it's exhausting, Casey. We're going through a rough patch and it's hard, but we'll get through it." Jacqueline was relieved that Casey might be calling a truce, but she had been mistaken.

"I don't know if we will. I think I need some time."

"Time for what?"

"Time. Space."

"What are you—you're saying we're done?" Exasperated, she threw out the most ridiculous scenario she could think of, but when she saw the devastation on Casey's face, her chest ached and a flash of nausea hit her.

"Jacq, I'm sorry, I—"

"No. No, no." She shook her head vigorously and backed away, but distance didn't ease the iron fist around her stomach.

"Is this about you wanting more kids? We'll find a donor or use a sperm bank. We can have a baby of our own. That's ours to keep." Jacqueline moved toward her, but she pulled out of the circle of Jacqueline's arms.

"It's not about just any kid. It's about them. The children in the system who need something stable, who need love—we can give them that."

"For how long? Until someone else decides our time is up? I can't do it. I don't want to fall in love with another child only to have her torn away from me."

"I know it was difficult. Letting Elle go hurt me, too. But now we know what to expect, and we just have to tell ourselves it's for the kids. We can help each other through anything."

"Please, Casey, I can't."

Casey clenched her jaw. *"You can. You just won't."*

"You're right—I won't." Tears spilled unrestrained down Jacqueline's cheeks. *"Losing Elle—I won't survive something like that again."*

By the time Jacqueline reached her father's house, fresh tears followed the tracks of her memories. She hadn't completely replaced the ghost of their most recent kiss, but she had succeeded in resurrecting the sick feeling that had been ever-present in her stomach after their breakup. Tendrils of anger, resentment, and pain curled around her heart, like a rogue vine of kudzu, threatening to smother every other emotion. Mission accomplished.

Casey returned to the porch carrying three beers, only to find Kendra standing there by herself. Jacqueline strode away from them on the sidewalk like a woman on a mission.

"She's been acting strange lately," Kendra said.

"Huh, maybe work stress?" Casey didn't think Kendra picked up on the false, overly high tone of her voice.

She handed Kendra one of the beers and gestured to the rocking chairs. After setting the spare drink on the small table between them, she pushed the balls of her bare feet against the floor to set her rocker in motion.

"Maybe. I think it's more than that. She's handled work stuff before, though this latest snafu was a big one. But she's been distracted and kind of—sad."

Casey didn't say anything, though she was dying to ask about Jacqueline's work problem. Kendra had gone on as if she'd assumed Jacqueline had told her about it, so she must not have confided in her about their most recent issues. Casey had visited Teddy twice in the past week and even gotten him to walk to the corner and back as he'd promised. But she hadn't seen Jacqueline at all. Avoidance was Jacqueline's modus operandi in the face of conflict. But this time, Casey wasn't too eager to confront their mistake either. She'd been short with Nina all week, but even through two apologies, she hadn't confessed about the kiss. Now, it seemed like too much time had passed. The sin of omission would be nearly as great as the original transgression.

Kendra shifted to her favorite topic lately. "I've picked out the bridesmaid dresses, and I think you're going to love them."

Casey grimaced. "I wanted to talk to you about that. I'm so flattered that you asked me to stand up with you, but—would you be terribly hurt if I declined?"

"What? Are you afraid of the dresses? Because, I swear, I didn't pick something ugly just to make me look prettier." She feigned flipping her hair. "Frankly, I don't need to do that. I'm going to be radiant."

"I was thinking that maybe I could do your pictures." Casey loved Kendra and Gavin and was thrilled to see them take the next step together. But being a bridesmaid just wasn't her thing. She didn't want the attention, and she certainly didn't want to stand next to Jacqueline during a wedding. She could just imagine the looks she'd be getting from Nina, whom she'd informed that attendance was not optional. She refused to go stag to the wedding because Nina wanted to be a baby about Casey's history with Jacqueline.

They were two forty-year-old women, for God's sake; they both had a past. Now she wasn't sure it was a good idea, but she'd made such a big deal that she couldn't change her mind.

"I'm not inviting you to my wedding and then making you work. You'll be a guest."

"Or a bridesmaid." Which, to her, felt like work.

"You're going to look gorgeous in this dress. Nina will thank me, I promise."

"I don't even think of it as work. Do you really want to spend all that money to hire the second-best wedding photographer in town when you could have me, for free?"

"When you put it that way..."

"Consider it my wedding gift. I'd really love to do this for you two."

"Okay. You're relieved of bridesmaid duty."

"Thank you." Casey faked an exaggerated sigh. Nina wouldn't be thrilled that Casey wouldn't be sitting next to her during the ceremony. But Casey really did want to give Kendra and Gavin some great photos to remember their day.

❖

"I've got good news and bad news," Casey said as soon as Nina walked through the door to her office that afternoon. She looked away from the photos she'd been editing. She'd been trying to finish them before Nina came to take her to dinner.

"Well, it's all going to have to wait, because I have the best news." Nina curled over the back of Casey's desk chair and wrapped her arms around her neck. She kissed Casey's cheek, and then Casey turned to meet her lips. "No distracting me. I got a call from our realtor today. And she found the perfect house for us."

"Perfect?" Casey turned back to her computer screen, clicking to the next photo.

"This place is amazing. Four bedrooms, two-and-a-half baths, a huge kitchen."

"Sounds big." They'd disagreed from the beginning on exactly what they were looking for. Every listing Nina brought her seemed larger than the last. When Casey questioned whether they should spend that much money, Nina assured her that she could afford it. But Casey didn't want to be a kept woman.

"It is. It's so spacious. And the realtor says it's going to go quick, so we need to look at it tomorrow morning or we could miss it." Nina grabbed the back of Casey's chair and spun her around to face her.

"I can't tomorrow. I have a shoot scheduled." She unlocked her phone and flipped through her schedule for the next couple of days. "What about Sunday? I'm free all day."

"Can't you just change it?"

"No. It's all set up."

"What's the big deal? You call the client and tell them you had an emergency, push the appointment back, and come with me to look at this house." Nina's voice took on a whiny edge that annoyed Casey.

"It's an engagement session, and they're waiting on the photos to make the official announcement. I'm not going to flake out on them at the last minute."

Nina huffed and practically stomped across the room. "If I'm not taking a backseat to Jacqueline's family, it's your job."

"That's not fair."

"You're right. It's not fair to me."

"You know how much of my business depends on word of mouth. If one client isn't happy with me it can cost me future business. You can't seriously think it's okay for me to call them tonight and cancel their session in the morning."

"What's really going on, Casey? You're barely able to make time to look at houses—"

"I can't always change my schedule to accommodate you—"

"Why not? You've managed to change it more times than I can count this past month in order to accommodate Jacqueline and Teddy. And when you do agree to look at listings with me, you find something wrong with every one. Do you even *want* to move in with me?" Nina planted her hands on her hips, her eyes flashing with anger.

Casey stared at her, her brain screaming at her to answer, but she couldn't force out the words she knew Nina wanted to hear. She couldn't summon the energy to argue. She'd spent the last several hours staring at a computer screen and had been looking forward to a nice, relaxing dinner. The guilt chewing up her stomach urged her to placate Nina—that maybe she owed her that. But the realization that remorse might be her only motivator stopped the words from coming. "Can we not do this now? I'm exhausted."

"Yes, because every minute that you're not working, you're taking care of Teddy. He's not even your father."

"Wow."

"Oh, don't be so sensitive. You know what I mean."

"He's still my family." As Nina came back across the room, Casey surged out of her chair and maintained some distance between them.

"No. He's Sean's family. Sean is a grown man."

"I don't expect you to understand."

"Here we go again. Because I haven't raised a child, I can't understand your family dynamic. Maybe the problem is not that I *don't* understand, but that I do—a little too well."

"What does that mean?"

"Teddy is also Jacqueline's family. And as long as he's in your life, you're still connected to her."

"That's what you think?" She tried to shove aside the little voice calling her a hypocrite. Jacqueline had kissed *her*. She'd stopped it. She hadn't betrayed her relationship with Nina—exactly.

"Yes. And more than that, I think you want it that way."

Casey drew in a deep breath, fighting her instinctive biting response to Nina's statement. She pinched the bridge of her nose. "I said I don't want to do this now. If you want to talk about this again later—"

"No. I don't think I do." Nina's voice was flat and Casey looked up at her, surprised that she might let this argument go so easily.

"Good. Because it's silly to think that—"

"You don't understand. I don't want to talk about this, or anything else, again."

"What?" Casey let her irritation lace her voice.

"God, I can't believe this. I've just wasted a year and a half on someone who was never planning to commit."

The impact of her words flipped a switch in Casey, injecting her fatigue with anger instead. "Is this where you manipulate me into begging you to stay with me? Because if that's your plan, you're going to be disappointed in where this goes." She was being a bitch—she knew that. But she couldn't find the compassion she knew Nina wanted.

"We're supposed to be moving in together. Is it so wrong that I want to know that you would choose me over them?" Her expression of shock confirmed that she'd expected Casey to protest when she issued her threat. But, like Casey, she seemed unable to back down now.

"It's wrong that you would ask me to choose you over my son."

"You know that's not what I meant."

"I think it was. You've never wanted to share me with my family."

"Teddy is not—"

"Please, do not say that again."

"I want to be in a relationship where I come first for the person I'm with."

"Sean will always come first. I've never made a secret of that." Ironically, she knew how Nina felt. She knew how crushing it was to hand your heart to someone who could never make you their first priority.

"And I could deal with that. But now I'm taking a backseat to Teddy. And Jacqueline—for God's sake, Teddy is a grown-up. Why do you have to report in to Jacqueline every night?"

"I haven't—"

"I think you still have feelings for her."

Casey laughed harshly. The only feelings she'd had for Jacqueline lately were frustration and anger. Even as she thought it, she knew it was a lie. But she owed Nina a bigger truth, anyway.

"We were together for thirteen years. I will always care about her." She took Nina's hands in hers, searching for the emotions she thought she'd been certain of before this argument. "But I'm in love with you."

"Are you?"

"Of course."

"Then why can you find time to take care of Teddy and have lunch over there every day, but you won't make time to see a house with me? The woman you're in love with and supposedly want to live with." Nina's voice rose incrementally both in volume and pitch, and she yanked her hands away at the end as if emphasizing her point.

Casey didn't reach for her again.

Nina nodded, seeming defeated. "I'll come back later for the things out of my *drawer.*" She drove home the truth with that one word. Casey hadn't really been able to commit to her for more than a drawer in her dresser.

After Nina stormed out, Casey played the conversation back in her head. Nina's ultimatum felt vaguely like the one Casey had given Jacqueline all those years ago. She'd pushed Jacqueline, expecting her to cave and draw closer, and had been surprised when Jacqueline had seemed able to walk away. But she'd just given Nina the same response—because she'd been lying. She wasn't in love with her.

Was that how Jacqueline had felt, too? Had she walked away because, like Casey today, she hadn't been compelled to stay? Some part of Casey had always wondered if they'd given up too soon on a great love. But maybe Jacqueline had never felt that way. Maybe their fights over her schedule, their finances, even Elle, had just been a convenient reason to end what wasn't going to work anyway.

CHAPTER THIRTEEN

Casey flipped through the on-screen guide on the television, searching for her next block of mindless entertainment. She settled on a show about people who move into ridiculously small homes. She might like that—downsizing, de-cluttering. But then she'd have to have a separate studio. She glanced at the door to her current workspace. No, she liked it only steps away. Maybe she should just go through the rest of the house and throw away some junk. She'd planned to do that when she and Nina moved but now had lost some of her motivation.

She'd lost the drive to do a lot of things in the three weeks since she and Nina broke up. Other than work, she tended to go a bit hermit after a split. She'd still visited Teddy several times a week, but only during the day when she knew she'd be the only one. He'd worked up to walking around the block with her and seemed to be doing much better physically, though she still worried about his moments of confusion.

When Sean came home one of the weekends, she put on a good front and didn't think he'd suspected a thing. He was used to Nina being absent when he was around, and they didn't talk much about her. In fact, she'd discovered, her friends and family didn't ask about Nina, and if she simply didn't volunteer anything, they weren't curious.

Nina had come and picked up her stuff. They'd made another attempt at conversation that turned into an argument. When Casey had really examined their relationship, she realized they'd been headed toward this impasse for some time. She supposed she'd rather they have figured it out now before they moved in together.

She hadn't seen Jacqueline at all. They still hadn't talked about the kiss and probably wouldn't, since so much time had passed. If she didn't see her before then, Jacqueline would be here for Kendra's party next week. She glanced around the house, noting the changes she'd made after Jacqueline moved out. How did she feel when she came back here?

Maybe she should do some of that de-cluttering before she had a house full of guests next week. Maybe she'd do that tomorrow. She eyed a photo of her and Nina taken on their trip to Boston and decided that's where she'd start. She grabbed a handful of popcorn from the bowl in her lap. Today, she'd take a much-needed day off.

She'd barely moved from her spot two hours later when the front door opened. Sean loped into the room and stopped, obviously not expecting her to be there. Or perhaps he just didn't think she'd be wrapped in a blanket, vegging out on a Saturday evening.

"Hey. I figured you'd be out with Nina." He flopped down on the couch next to her.

"Not tonight."

He nodded, then bit his lower lip like he did when he was trying to figure something out. "Everything okay with you two?"

Casey shook her head. "We broke up."

"Oh, Mom, I'm sorry."

She glanced at him. "You never liked her."

"Eh, maybe not." He gave her the puppy-dog eyes that always coaxed a reaction from her when he was a kid, and then his expression turned serious. "But you haven't liked all of my girlfriends. And I want you to be happy."

"But you knew it wouldn't be with her." She flipped one side of her blanket over his legs and passed him the popcorn bowl, encouraging him to settle in with her.

"I suspected."

"How?"

"She's too much like Mama."

"What does that mean?"

He shrugged. "She wanted you to support her, not financially, but at home. Like everything you do should come second to her."

"Mama's not like that," she said, more for his benefit than because it was true. She didn't want him to have a bad impression of Jacqueline. She might have given up a part of herself for Jacqueline, but she'd done it willingly at the time.

"That's why you're changing your schedule to look after Poppa."

"I do that because I love him." His words touched a wound still fresh from her confrontation with Nina.

"I know. He's like your second father." His casual acknowledgement of her connection to Teddy almost tipped her over the emotional edge she'd been riding lately. "Nah. I just mean, you've been putting everyone else first all your life—Mama, me, Elle, the boys."

Her heart clenched at the mention of the sibling boys, ages six and eight, she'd fostered a few years after she and Jacqueline broke up. They were eventually placed with their maternal grandmother, who'd been resisting raising her daughter's kids because she thought she was too old. But she couldn't handle seeing them in foster care, so she took them in. Casey kept in touch with their grandmother and received periodic updates and photos as the boys aged. She'd shared the photos with Sean so he'd feel less disconnected from the brothers he'd bonded with.

"It's about time you got to come first. And now that I'm out of the house—"

"You don't look very out of the house." She nudged him with her knee. "You didn't tell me you were coming home this weekend. Did you bring me your laundry?"

"I mean, while I'm here…" He glanced guiltily toward the door, where he'd dropped his duffle bag. He lifted his hands palm up and shrugged.

She touched his shoulder, turning their conversation serious once more. "Don't worry about me. I'll be fine. Nina and I weren't meant to be."

"She didn't deserve you anyway."

She smiled. "When did my baby boy grow up?"

He bent his head in a halfhearted attempt to avoid her ruffling his hair.

"In fact, you're so grown up, you should do your own laundry this weekend."

He burrowed closer into the couch, pulled more of the blanket off her, and nodded at the television. "After this episode."

❖

Jacqueline knocked on the door of Casey's house thirty minutes before the guests were scheduled to arrive. The white SUV in the driveway bore the logo of the company she'd hired to cater the party. She was relieved to see Kendra's car beside it, since she'd be less likely to be alone with Casey.

But when the door opened, Casey stood in the threshold. Jacqueline swept a glance over Casey's tight jeans, black tuxedo-style vest, and white button-down shirt but didn't let her gaze linger.

"Sorry, I'm a little late. And I know I said I'd help you get things ready. So put me to work." She followed Casey in, looking at the gentle waves of her casually styled hair instead of the way her jeans hugged her ass. Damn it, even after so many years, Jacqueline didn't have to think very hard to recall the way that ass felt in her hands. She shook her head, chastising her idiot brain, which had apparently lost a purposely constructed filter or two in the midst of that kiss several weeks ago.

Casey turned around and caught her shaking her head. "What's wrong?"

"Hmm? Nothing."

Casey led her to her studio. "I figured we'd play poker in here because it required the least amount of rearranging to make room for the poker table. I told the caterers to set up over there." She pointed to the far wall, where two long tables already held a row of chafing dishes. "They're in the kitchen, and I'm trying to stay out of the way. Kendra's in my bedroom touching up her face."

Casey turned quickly, and Jacqueline stopped right in front of her. This close, she could tell that Casey had put on a little bit of eye makeup, and her lips shone with lip gloss. Jacqueline managed to stifle the urge to ask if it was peppermint-flavored.

"Casey, I—"

"Kendra's so excited about this party." Casey's tone sounded forced, but her intention was clear—distance.

"I prefer to think of it as a wedding shower." Jacqueline went along, thinking avoidance was probably better than bringing up their kiss right before being forced to spend several hours with each other.

"I told you to stop calling it that," Kendra said as she entered the room. The atmosphere between them lightened just a little with the introduction of a neutral party. "A van with a party-rental logo is in the driveway."

Jacqueline grinned at Casey, and they wordlessly agreed to let Kendra in on the plan for the party. "That'll be the poker table and the dealer we hired."

"No way!" Kendra flung an arm around each of them and yanked them close. "You two rock."

Casey reached out to steady herself and grasped Jacqueline's forearm. Without meaning to, Jacqueline, off-balance herself, had grabbed Casey's hip. Jacqueline looked at her own hand, then met Casey's eyes and found confusion and panic. No doubt she worried Nina would come in and see them like this.

Jacqueline jerked free of Kendra and stepped back. "I'll go show them in here."

She reached the driveway just as an older woman pulled a large aluminum briefcase from the van. The woman couldn't have been more than five feet tall, and that included her salon-set, snow-white hair.

"Hey, let me get that for you." Jacqueline reached for the case.

"Oh, it's no problem." She set it on the ground and extended a handle. "It's got wheels." She left the case near the van door. "But you can help me wrestle out this table." She indicated a folded poker table stowed in the back of the vehicle.

"No problem."

"I'm Mabel. I'll be your dealer."

"I'm Jacqueline, the host of the party." She grasped Mabel's hand, finding a strong, sure grip. "Let's get this inside and I'll introduce you to the guest of honor."

Together they managed to carry the table into the studio. After she introduced Mabel to Casey and Kendra, they offered to help. Mabel sent them out to the van for folding chairs while she and Jacqueline set up the table. Then, while Mabel directed the placement of the chairs, Jacqueline ran back out for the aluminum case.

She brought Mabel the case and hovered for a moment, awaiting further instructions. Mabel opened it and unpacked a deck of cards and a dealer button. She started removing chips of varying denominations and colors.

Mabel waved her away. "I'm all set until you girls are ready to start playing."

"Thanks. I'll let you know when the rest of the guests arrive." Jacqueline found Casey and Kendra in the living room. Casey, her back to Jacqueline, lit a candle on one end of the mantle.

"Where's Nina?" Kendra asked at the exact moment Jacqueline approached. Jacqueline almost turned around and walked away, but Casey's response stopped her.

"She's not coming."

"Really? She's taking this jealousy thing a bit too far, isn't she?" Kendra propped her hands on her hips.

Casey turned toward Kendra and her eyes met Jacqueline's instead. Something flashed in them, but before Jacqueline could figure out what it was, she'd jerked her gaze back to Kendra's face. "That's not—"

"Today's not really about her. You'd think she could just suck it up and—"

"We broke up." Casey cut off the tirade that Jacqueline knew Kendra was winding up for. Casey's abrupt statement kicked Jacqueline in the chest, and she might have gasped out loud.

"Oh, honey, I'm sorry." Kendra pulled Casey into a hug so tight that her chin rested on Kendra's shoulder and she physically couldn't turn away from Jacqueline.

Jacqueline looked at the floor, wishing now that she'd walked away at the beginning of this conversation. She hated the look of unhappiness on Casey's face and felt guilty for the part of her that was glad Nina was out of Casey's life.

Kendra released Casey so quickly that she practically stumbled forward. "I'm going to get us some drinks. We'll have more fun without her anyway."

"Hey, I'm sorry about Nina." Jacqueline filled the awkward silence left by Kendra's departure.

"You looked surprised. I thought Sean would have told you."

Jacqueline shook her head. "You didn't break up because we—"

"No."

"Because it was my fault, and if she couldn't forgive you for something you had no—"

"I didn't tell her."

"Oh. Do we need to talk about—"

"I'd really rather not."

"Okay."

"Anyway, that wasn't the reason."

"Okay. Was it recent?"

Casey shrugged. "A few weeks ago."

"Are you—"

"I'm okay."

"I know we're not really friends, but if you need to talk, I'm here."

Casey laughed. "Talk to my ex about another ex. Sure. Maybe you guys can form a little support group or something."

"I'm just trying to—"

"I said I'm fine. It was basically mutual and long overdue."

"All right. Got it." Jacqueline held up her hands and took a step back, physically representing her retreat from the conversation. But her mind was still spinning with this new piece of information. She'd been beating herself up for weeks over kissing an unavailable woman—not that being single made Casey more attainable.

"I found tequila." Kendra held up a bottle and a salt shaker. "No limes. We'll have to rough it."

"Oh, me, please." Jacqueline raised her hand, then took one of the shot glasses from Kendra.

"Are you sure that's a good idea?" Casey was well aware that Jacqueline tended to get in trouble with copious amounts of tequila. In fact, she'd practically carried her home on more than one occasion during their time together.

Eager to put the previous awkwardness behind them, Jacqueline grinned and winked at her. "Just one shot."

"I've heard that before." Casey took the shot Kendra offered. She licked the back of her hand at the base of her thumb and said, "Salt me."

Jacqueline watched as Kendra shook salt onto that spot, unable to pull her eyes away even as Casey swiped her tongue over her skin and tossed back the shot. She licked her own hand and did the same. As the numbing warmth spread through her chest, she thought Casey might have been right that this wasn't a good idea.

Casey fiddled with her poker chips, separating them into two small towers, then shuffling them back together, only to do it all over again. She hadn't played poker in years, but her fingers seemed to remember the motions ingrained through hours spent sitting at a table with most of the women around her now. In fact, several of them had gone on weekend trips to Tunica and one big vacation to Las Vegas together. The group had changed some over the years, but Kendra was very good at keeping her friends in her life—not everyone did that.

Casey's own social group had changed with her lifestyle. When Sean was younger, she'd gravitated toward parents with children the same age. But Kendra had never let her drift away completely, even when she'd split with Jacqueline. Some of their mutual friends had seemed to think they had to choose sides. Kendra had known Jacqueline first and had roomed with her in college, so

Casey wouldn't have been surprised to lose her. Yet over the years, Kendra had remained impressively neutral no matter how Casey and Jacqueline related to each other.

Casey continued to toy with her chips, waiting her turn to bet on the two sevens she'd been dealt. She glanced up and caught Jacqueline watching her hand. Her fingers slipped, throwing the chips off balance, but she recovered in time to keep them from toppling. Watching Jacqueline's face, she continued to manipulate them. She lifted one off the top of the pile. They were actually good chips, casino-quality, nice clay-weight and feel, not like the cheap plastic ones they used to play with. She flipped it across the back of her knuckles and pulled it back into her palm. Jacqueline's eyes changed, and even from across the table Casey recognized the build-up of arousal in them. She used to love witnessing the slow burn of Jacqueline's reaction almost as much as the times when Jacqueline flashed-over, hot and fast.

When the two players before Casey folded, she placed a stack of chips in front of her, indicating a moderate bet. Kendra folded, as did the woman to her right. Jacqueline and three other players called her, staying in the hand. Mabel counted out three cards in a neat stack, then turned it faceup on the table. She slid the cards out side by side, revealing all three. Casey liked to watch a good dealer work, finding beauty in the fluidity of the motions. She'd study the details of their hands—manicures and nail color, rings, scars—and try to imagine the stories behind them.

The cards—a queen, a ten, and a seven—included two hearts and a diamond. When her turn came, Casey pushed forward another bet on her three-of-a-kind, and two more players folded. The next card, the nine of clubs, didn't change Casey's hand, but it did put a straight draw on the board. There were now several other combinations of cards that could beat her sevens. By the time the dealer turned the last card, the four of hearts, only Casey and Jacqueline remained. Careful of both the straight and flush draws now on the board, Casey checked her hand, putting the play in Jacqueline's hands.

Jacqueline cupped a hand over her cards and lifted the corners just far enough to see the faces. She stared across the table, obviously trying to read Casey. She lifted one side of her mouth in a lazy grin that Casey had never been able to resist, but Casey kept her expression neutral. "Your poker face has improved."

"Yours hasn't. Same old tricks." Casey smiled, hoping to take any sting out of her words.

Jacqueline glanced once more at the cards faceup on the table between them. "Were you chasing?" she murmured.

This kind of across-the-table talk used to fluster Casey into giving away her hand. With the cards showing, Jacqueline would also be worried Casey might have the flush or straight as well. Unless she had king/jack or a couple of high hearts, then she'd know she had Casey dominated.

"I'm all in." Jacqueline pushed her three stacks of chips toward the center of the table. She had Casey covered, so if Casey called her bet and lost, she'd be out of the game.

Casey met her eyes and Jacqueline didn't look away. In the past, Jacqueline might have made a small bet or even checked it down and let them both get away from the hand still in good shape. So was this a bluff? Or was she pushing today only because she'd had a little too much to drink? Or did she have the cards and want to knock Casey out of the game that badly?

Casey checked her cards again, considering her options. She'd always had a hard time folding trips, but if Jacqueline caught either of the draws, she had Casey beat. Casey flashed back to their very first time meeting—playing poker, when she'd so brazenly made the bet to obtain Jacqueline's phone number. God, she'd been so incredibly attracted to Jacqueline right away—every sarcastic, expressive, beautiful inch of her. And when Jacqueline had grown flustered by Casey's attention, she'd been even more interested.

She met Jacqueline's eyes one more time and slid her cards into the center, conceding defeat. Jacqueline looked surprised, and a flicker of disappointment gave away her hand. She'd had the cards to win and had wanted Casey to call.

"Can I see one?" Casey asked because she knew Jacqueline didn't like to show her cards.

Jacqueline narrowed her eyes and hesitated. Casey gave her the sweet smile that used to get her whatever she wanted. Jacqueline flipped over the king of hearts, letting Casey know she'd probably made a good choice in her fold. But a part of her wondered what would have happened if she'd pushed her stack in and made another bold side bet. She glanced around the table and knew she'd never have done that in front of the others. Apparently nineteen-year-old Casey had possessed way more guts than the contemporary version of herself. And probably more stupidity, too. Flirting with Jacqueline wasn't a good idea. She glanced at the beer bottle next to Jacqueline's elbow. Especially not tipsy-Jacqueline.

CHAPTER FOURTEEN

"What are you doing?" Kendra whispered as she hurried around the kitchen counter, holding a stack of plates. She glanced at the door to Casey's studio as if making sure none of the guests followed her out.

"Hey, the guest of honor does not clean up." Casey took the plates and set them on the counter.

"Don't change the subject. I don't want to be saying this because I love you both, and I've tried to be Switzerland when it comes to you two—"

"We're getting along. Isn't that what you've been hounding us for all these years? All of us being able to hang out together?"

Kendra pointed a finger at her. "No. I know better. The tequila—"

"You brought out the tequila." Casey grabbed Kendra's finger and gently pulled her hand out of her face.

"And the flirting. I've played enough cards with you to know it's like damn foreplay to the two of you."

"Poker party was your idea."

Kendra yanked her hand free. "You and Nina broke up. And you've been spending a lot of time with Jacqueline these last couple of months."

"I haven't seen her in weeks. I helped with Teddy, that's all."

"I don't want her to get the wrong idea."

Casey started to respond then stopped. At first she'd thought Kendra was looking out for both of them. But now, she suspected Kendra wanted to protect Jacqueline. She hadn't told Kendra about the kiss and assumed Jacqueline hadn't either, but maybe she'd been wrong. Kendra must have some reason to think Casey would hurt Jacqueline.

"The wrong idea about what?"

"About why you and Nina didn't work out."

"Not that it's either of your business—"

"Casey—"

"No, don't *Casey* me." She didn't know why Kendra's warning made her angry. She was a little embarrassed that Kendra had called her out on her behavior, but she had no reason to be mad when Kendra was clearly only concerned about them.

"Just be careful, please." Kendra raised her hands, palms out in surrender. "I won't say anything more about it." She headed back toward the studio and left Casey standing there contemplating their conversation.

She *had* danced dangerously close to a line in the boundaries of her relationship with Jacqueline today. She'd caught Jacqueline looking at her a couple of times, and instead of realizing that alcohol and familiar surroundings probably fueled the heated glances, she'd basked in the attention. And she didn't want to admit that one of the reasons she and Nina hadn't worked out was because Nina's passionate stare had never inspired even half the reaction in her that Jacqueline's did.

❖

"Thanks again, Mabel, you were great," Casey called through the open doorway, then closed the door.

Jacqueline slumped on the couch next to Kendra. The rest of the guests had already left. Jacqueline had stopped drinking tequila in plenty of time to avoid complete embarrassment. But she'd continued to maintain a healthy buzz with beer throughout the night. She'd downed a glass of water after every third drink in an effort to stave off a hangover tomorrow.

Casey glanced at them, then walked into her studio. Jacqueline wanted to get up and follow her, but she couldn't make her muscles obey. They might know better than her brain or her heart what was best for her, but if that were true they'd be propelling her out of this house right now. She'd spent more time in her old home tonight than she had in years, and she might have reached her limit without turning into a sappy mess.

"Come on, Jacq. I'll drive your drunk ass home." Kendra tapped Jacqueline's thigh and stood up.

She looked toward the studio and found Casey propped against the doorframe staring at her across the darkened room. "That's okay. I'm staying at Dad's tonight. I'll walk."

Kendra glanced at Casey, back at Jacqueline, then threw her hands up. "Suit yourself." She bent to hug Jacqueline and whispered in her ear, "Be careful, sweetie."

She hugged Casey on her way to the door. "Thank you for hosting. This was great." She glanced back at Jacqueline before she left, her expression indicating she thought Jacqueline was an idiot.

"Yep. I am," Jacqueline mumbled as the door closed behind Kendra.

"What?" Casey asked as she moved farther into the room, picking up discarded plastic cups as she went.

"Nothing."

"Tonight was fun." Casey rounded the counter into the kitchen and threw away the trash.

"Yeah. Best bridal shower ever." Jacqueline rested her head against the back of the couch and closed her pleasantly heavy eyelids.

Casey laughed, and the low throaty sound felt too familiar. They used to do this—unwind after a dinner party, talking and laughing about their evening. Then they'd secure the house and go to bed together. Jacqueline vividly recalled watching Casey across the span of the bed while each of them undressed in only the moonlight, then sliding under the covers with her.

"I should go." Jacqueline heaved herself off the couch way too fast for her still-fuzzy head. She took a quick step to her right to correct for the sudden motion.

"Hey. Hold on." Casey rushed over and grabbed her arm.

"I'm good." She pulled her arm free. "I'm okay." She was, except for a tiny bit of slurring, but she'd get a handle on that in just a minute.

"I'm not letting you walk. You can stay here."

"S'only a few blocks." Jacqueline patted the pocket of her jeans, making sure she had her phone before she left.

Casey grasped her chin and turned her face until Jacqueline met her eyes. "You're staying. Or I'll drive you to Teddy's."

"You can't drive. You did shots." Jacqueline jerked her face free from Casey's soft fingers. She didn't want to see the dark-blue flares that ringed Casey's pupils and feathered into lighter blue around the edges. Even more, she didn't want to know that those subtle color changes were there without even looking. But she did.

"Hours ago." Casey captured her chin again, but instead of holding on, she slipped her hand against her cheek. "Please, stay. I'll worry if you don't."

Jacqueline relaxed into her hand. She needed Casey so badly that she couldn't keep it all inside. "How do you still wreck me?"

"I think that's the tequila." Despite Casey's even tone, something in her eyes indicated she hadn't been unaffected by Jacqueline's words.

"No." The drinking had dulled her inhibitions. She struggled to regain control before she embarrassed herself further. "I should go."

"Please. Stay in Sean's room."

Jacqueline nodded. But she wouldn't get any rest just down the hall from their bedroom—their former bedroom. Casey took her hand and led her to Sean's room. Neither of them turned on the light.

"Are you really okay?" Jacqueline didn't release her hand as they stopped next to the bed. She tugged Casey closer and rested her hand on Casey's hip.

"Because I lost at poker?" Casey flattened her palm against the center of Jacqueline's chest. She didn't push her away, but she exerted enough pressure to keep her from getting too close.

"About Nina."

"Yes. It's been a few weeks. I'm okay."

"Good." Jacqueline took a step back, letting Casey know she was serious and sober enough to not be a threat. "You've been there for me with Dad. I don't know how I would have handled it all without you. So, if you need anything—I know with, well, everything else, it may not always be comfortable, but I'm here for you."

"I know." Before Jacqueline could react, Casey stepped close and wrapped her arms around her.

"Casey." Jacqueline encircled her waist and rested her hands in the hollow of her lower back.

"Shh, just let me hold you for a second." Casey stroked down the back of Jacqueline's head and cupped her neck.

Jacqueline closed her eyes, desperate to absorb the feel of Casey, her scent, the dance of her fingers across the base of her neck, and the soft brush of her hair against her cheek.

Far too soon, Casey released her. She looked like she wanted to say something serious. But, seeming to make some private decision, she shook her head once and said, "I'll bring you something to sleep in."

Jacqueline rolled onto her back and sighed. She untangled the sheet from around her legs. After a night of restless dozing, which she attributed only partly to the alcohol, she'd finally fallen into a deep sleep, only to be awakened by a sound somewhere in the house. She listened intently, trying to determine if she'd heard Casey in the kitchen or if she was still in her bedroom.

She sat up, still not sure exactly what woke her. Maybe she could sneak out without saying anything to Casey. She hadn't done anything wrong. She'd maybe been too flirty and a bit more vulnerable than she wanted to be. But Casey had, too. And she was the one who was most recently single. She got out of bed and, hearing noise from the kitchen, headed downstairs. She'd face Casey, not because she was brave, but because she was willing to endure the awkwardness in order to spend a little more time with her.

"I hope you have some strong coffee," Jacqueline said as she rounded the corner into the kitchen. But she stopped short and gasped when she saw Sean standing in front of the stove instead of Casey. "Geez, Sean, you scared me."

"What? You didn't expect me to be here to witness your walk of shame?" He sprinkled cheese, mushrooms, and spinach into a pan of cooked eggs.

"Watch your mouth." She shoved him to the side as she angled close to the Keurig machine. As she waited for her coffee, she looked over his shoulder. "Are you going to share that?"

"Sure. Bacon's already on the counter." He gestured behind him with the spatula. "It's turkey bacon. Mom doesn't have any real pig in the house."

"That can't be right. She loves bacon."

"Nope. She gave up pork ever since she saw some video on the Internet about how badly pigs are treated on corporate pig farms."

"Cows are, too." Jacqueline took a bite of a strip of meat that barely resembled bacon and shook her head. "She giving up red meat too? And chickens?"

"Please, don't get her started. Once we got passed on the interstate by a truck hauling a bunch of chickens in crates, and she was a vegetarian for almost six months. But she'll never give up steak." He held up the frying pan. "Plate?"

She grabbed a plate and he tilted the pan over it, simultaneously sliding out and folding the omelet. "Want half?"

"I'll make another." He poured some more beaten eggs into the hot pan. "What's going on?"

"Nothing." She rested against the counter and forked a bite of egg into her mouth.

"Then what are you doing here? Other than sleeping in my room."

She shrugged. "Drank too much at Kendra's thing last night, so Mom made me crash here."

He gave her a look of disbelief. "Be careful. She's vulnerable right now."

She smiled. He was always more protective over Casey. "Don't worry about it."

She might have laughed at his stern stare if he didn't seem to be trying so hard at it. "I'm not a kid anymore."

"What do you mean?"

"You guys tried to hide your problems from me back then. But I heard you fighting. I felt the tension, even if I didn't understand it. Now—something's different again." He kept his eyes on the eggs, working the edges in so the uncooked liquid could fill in around them. Omelets had been his specialty since Casey first taught him the technique when he was nine. He would set his alarm on Sunday mornings and get up early to surprise them with breakfast in bed. As he grew up, the omelet remained the same, but the fillings got more sophisticated—graduating from shredded cheese to the gourmet creation she currently enjoyed.

"My relationship with your mom is between the two of us. It has no impact on how much we love you."

"Your relationship does impact me. It always has." He removed the second omelet from the pan but looked at it like he'd lost his appetite. "I heard you tell her you wished you'd never gotten Elle."

Jacqueline knew right away which argument he referred to. She remembered saying it, weeks before they finally broke up, as clearly as she recalled the stricken expression on Casey's face. She'd hated herself for inflicting that pain, and knowing Sean had heard it brought a new wave of self-loathing. "I didn't mean that. I was hurting and I didn't handle it well."

"I used to wonder if you'd ever felt that way about me, but you were stuck with me because you adopted me and couldn't give me back." Having clearly lost his interest in breakfast, he set his plate on the counter next to the turkey bacon.

"Oh, Sean." Her heart ached for the twelve year-old version of her son. "We didn't give Elle back because we didn't want her. We did, so much. Just like we wanted you. We didn't have a choice. It tore me up to let her go, and I said some things I shouldn't have. I took my grief out on your mom."

He stared at his hands and bent his fingers back one by one until his knuckles popped. "I wasn't always easy."

"You were ours. And we loved every bit of you."

"It doesn't matter now, anyway."

"It does—" She grappled for what to say, but he was gone before she got a chance. She set down her own plate and went after him, but as she rounded the corner she ran into Casey lurking in the hallway. The door to Sean's bedroom slammed.

❖

Casey let Sean pass by her without a word. Like Jacqueline, when he was hurt or angry he needed space. She was debating whether to enter the kitchen when Jacqueline barreled into her. She caught Jacqueline by the shoulders when it seemed like she wanted to run over her to follow Sean. She gave a little squeeze, but Jacqueline still tried to force her way past her. She pivoted and pushed Jacqueline against the wall to get her attention. But when Jacqueline's pain-filled eyes found her, she almost wished she'd let her go. They'd had too many of these emotionally charged moments lately, and given the conversation she just overheard, she didn't think she had the armor for where this was about to go.

"How much of that did you hear?" Jacqueline's voice was rough. She grasped Casey's waist, her hands flexing as if trying to imprint her anguish into Casey.

"Only enough to break my heart." She'd heard Sean's warning about the status of her current relationship with Jacqueline. But her worry about that was eclipsed as soon as he started talking about Elle.

Jacqueline shook her head. "I thought he understood at the time why we couldn't keep Elle. To find out he carried that around with him all these years shakes me up."

"I know." Casey fought the urge to embrace her as she had the night before.

Jacqueline looked down at her own hands, then deliberately opened them. Casey stepped back, giving her room to escape.

"I should go." Jacqueline brushed past her.

"Wait. Let's talk about this." Casey grimaced as the words came out. She didn't want to talk about it any more than Jacqueline did. But if Jacqueline felt half as torn apart by Sean's words as Casey did, she didn't want to let her go, alone and upset.

"I can't, Casey," Jacqueline said, halfway to the front door.

"Of course not." Jacqueline's predictable reaction—flight— had always angered her. She'd never been able to get over the sense of rejection at knowing that when she was hurting, Jacqueline wanted to be anywhere but with her.

"What?"

"Nothing. Forget it." Casey turned toward the kitchen. She should let Jacqueline go, but she couldn't watch her leave.

"What did you say?" Jacqueline came back across the room, now following Casey.

"You haven't changed. You still want to walk away when things get hard." Casey had struck low and dirty with that one, but she couldn't help herself.

Sean's bedroom door opened, and he strode down the hall carrying his backpack. He kept his head down, but the fringe of his hair didn't hide his red eyes and flushed cheeks.

"Sean, hey, I wanted to talk to you about—"

"Not now, Mama. I'm going to meet some friends." He didn't quite carry off a casual tone, but the message was clear.

When the door closed behind him, Jacqueline glared at Casey. "Go ahead, say it." She jabbed a finger toward the door. "That's my fault, too."

Casey sighed and sat down on the couch. Moments ago she'd been itching for a confrontation with Jacqueline. Arguing with Jacqueline felt much more comfortable than the other emotions she'd been experiencing around her lately. Anger, she could handle. Compassion, tenderness, arousal—they were more difficult.

"We had to give her back."

Jacqueline's tortured words sent a bolt of agony through Casey's chest. Her response was a machine gun of clipped words because she didn't have the breath for more. "I was there."

Jacqueline shook her head and continued talking. "The social worker took her from my arms, and she might as well have ripped a piece of my heart out." Her eyes welled up.

"Don't you think I felt it, too?" Casey sagged against the back of the couch. She'd always been quick to judge Jacqueline's emotional availability. And while she'd been an open book compared to Jacqueline, now, she had to admit, she'd held some things back as well. "I felt guilty," she whispered.

"Why?" Jacqueline sat down next to her.

"We had so much to give. A good home, money, security. I was blessed. I really thought I had it all." She barked out a sarcastic laugh. What a joke her perfect life had turned out to be.

"Casey—" Jacqueline touched her arm, but Casey shook her off.

"I felt guilty and selfish—so many kids desperately needed those basic comforts, and we could have—I resented you for making that decision for both of us. I blamed you."

"Yeah, that part I figured out." Jacqueline angled to face her more fully. "So we blamed each other and it blew us apart. But you went on to foster again, so you can't really regret it."

"It's more complicated than regret or not. I didn't want to lose you—"

"You told me to go."

Casey nodded. "And you did."

"What if I'd stayed? What if I'd fought for us?"

"I don't know."

"Do you think we could have made it? Found our way back to happy?"

"Maybe." She really didn't know. Elle hadn't been their only problem. If it hadn't been her, they might have eventually come to a breaking point over Jacqueline's job, her travel, or some other issue. "Maybe not. Does it matter now? Those years are gone, and we can't be anywhere but here."

Jacqueline nodded. "Wherever this is." Her words clearly defined Casey's confusion about the recent changes in the way they related to each other as well. Jacqueline stood. "I want to check on Dad on my way home. Are you okay?"

"Yes." Casey answered as simply as possible, though she couldn't help but wonder if the larger question wasn't, *are we okay?* She didn't know how to answer that one.

CHAPTER FIFTEEN

Do I need to be concerned?" Owen asked as soon as she walked into the Chattanooga office Monday afternoon. He'd been waiting for her near the front desk.

"About what?" She smiled at the receptionist on her way by. He followed her down the hall to the conference room she'd be using for an employee meeting in less than an hour. She dropped her bag in a chair near the head of the table, worrying a little when he closed the door behind them.

"You omitted the Blackstone letter." He held up his hands to stop her protest. "And now the operations manager in Louisville said you snapped at him."

"He called you?" Yes, she'd lost her temper and could have handled things better. Since she'd argued with him within earshot of the dock, she'd known there was a chance he'd complain. But when two weeks passed without incident, she thought maybe he'd blown it off. She certainly had. But she wasn't surprised to learn he'd reported her. He was a whiny baby who had no people skills and even less professional knowledge. She had no idea how he'd gotten his job.

"I phoned him about an unrelated issue. But your name came up."

"The guy's an idiot, Owen." She circled the outside of the room, pausing near a table along the back wall to grab a bottle of water and a banana.

"He said you called him a dumbass."

"Actually, I said he made *us all* look like dumbasses. He withheld important information and then expected me to help him out of a jam."

"I can't have my HR manager implying an ops manager in this company is a dumbass."

"Well, make up your mind, Owen. Did I call him a dumbass, or did I just *imply* it?" She tried to lighten the mood. His nod and small smile indicated she'd succeeded. She sat and rested her elbows on the table. "So, what? Do I need to apologize?"

"That's a start."

"What does that mean?"

"If you apologize, I can probably talk him out of filing a formal complaint."

"A formal—seriously?"

"If he does, I can't go to bat for you with legal. Their collective memories aren't that short."

She bit back a curse. That damn P&C letter would end up screwing her after all. "I'll fix it."

"Make it a sincere apology. And do it in person."

She nodded. Once he'd left the room, she let her head fall forward until her forehead rested on the table. When would she have time to squeeze in an unplanned trip to Louisville? If she'd thought she could get away with delaying, she'd wait a couple of weeks—put off seeing his smug face. But Owen would expect an update when she smoothed things over. Besides, if this incident could jeopardize her future advancement, as Owen had implied, then she wanted to deal with it sooner rather than later. She'd arrive home Wednesday afternoon, only to leave again Thursday morning for Louisville.

She lifted her head and began unpacking the training literature she'd had delivered to the center last week. She needed to focus on her task for the day. Trying to work through distraction was how she'd gotten herself to this point, and continuing to do so certainly wouldn't solve her problems. Later tonight, in her hotel room, she'd have a drink and wallow in self-pity over the current state of her career.

❖

Casey grabbed the loaf of French bread she'd picked up at the grocery store the day before and headed out to her car. She'd been running behind since her first consultation of the day had gone long, and she'd never recovered. Ten minutes ago, she'd finished uploading a set of proofs with just enough time to freshen up before going to Teddy's for dinner. He wouldn't care if she was a bit late, but she opted for the short drive instead of her usual walk.

Several minutes later, she parked at the curb in front of Teddy's house just as Jacqueline got out of her own car in the driveway. Jacqueline circled her car and met Casey halfway up the driveway.

"Hey, I know this is your night with him, but I was hoping you had room for one more?"

"Sure." Casey engaged her vehicle locks and slipped the fob into her jeans pocket. Jacqueline's keys jangled in her hand. She didn't have any pockets marring the lines of the brown skirt that hugged her hips and ended just above her knees. As Jacqueline turned toward the house, Casey followed, noting the creases in the back of Jacqueline's ivory drape-necked blouse. *Even wrinkled she's gorgeous.* Casey acknowledged the observation easily. Jacqueline's beauty had always reached her, even through their most disconnected times.

Tendrils of Jacqueline's upswept hair had worked their way free around her face and at the back of her neck. She sported ballet flats instead of the heels that accentuated her calves, giving one more hint to what she'd been doing just before she arrived.

"How was your drive?" Casey asked.

"Boring. Chattanooga." Jacqueline slipped off her sunglasses and tucked them into her purse. She'd always shown fatigue in her eyes first, and today her weariness was evident. "I have to go to Louisville first thing tomorrow, so the fun isn't over yet."

"From one end of your region to the other? I thought you'd gotten more efficient at plotting your travel."

"I have. This one's out of my control." Jacqueline used her key, swung open the door, and called, "Dad."

Though Casey didn't hear a response, they found him in the living room staring at the television. The sound had been muted, so he should have heard her.

"Hey, Dad."

His eyes snapped to Jacqueline's face, then tracked to Casey's, and a moment of recognition was followed by confusion.

"I hope you don't mind me crashing your dinner party." Despite Jacqueline's casual statement, the tension in her voice indicated she'd sensed something was off with Teddy as well.

"Dinner party?"

"It's Wednesday." Casey held up her loaf of bread as if that might jog his memory. When they'd talked earlier in the week, he said he'd put one of the lasagnas she'd stocked his freezer with into the oven for tonight. Since she didn't smell the spicy tomato and garlic aroma, he'd apparently forgotten about dinner.

"What are we having?" He clearly didn't remember their plans but seemed to be putting the pieces together and was maybe hoping her answer would give him a hint.

"Not lasagna, I guess." Casey said as she went into the kitchen to confirm her suspicions. When she opened the freezer door and saw the pasta dish still in there, Jacqueline looked over her shoulder.

"New plan?" Jacqueline's mouth was close enough for Casey to feel her breath on her ear. She shivered and wondered if she imagined that she could feel the vibration of her words in the press of Jacqueline's chest against her back.

"Yes." She cleared her throat to get rid of the tremor in her voice.

"I'll go pick something up from that Italian place you like." Jacqueline stepped back so Casey could close the freezer door.

"No." Casey turned around. Jacqueline still stood close. Before she could stop herself, she touched Jacqueline's cheek. "You're already spending too much time in your car lately."

"Casey." Jacqueline tilted her head into Casey's palm.

She dropped her hand and moved back against the refrigerator. "Let me see what I can come up with. You deserve some comfort food."

"Okay. But nothing too complicated. Otherwise, we'll order pizza or something. From the looks of that freezer, you already spend enough time cooking for him."

"I enjoy it." She opened the pantry, hoping she could throw together something that still utilized the French bread. She grabbed a couple of cans and turned around. "The soup will be canned, but I'll make up for it with amazing grilled-cheese sandwiches."

"Sounds perfect."

If they left it to Teddy he'd have only a stack of processed American slices in the fridge. But since Jacqueline had been doing his grocery shopping and cheese was one of her vices, Casey was certain she'd find a better selection.

She grabbed Swiss, cheddar, and Monterey jack and put together three sandwiches. Jacqueline kept her company while she toasted both sides on a stovetop griddle pan. She let Jacqueline lead the conversation and noticed that she kept it light and steered away from both her work and Teddy. Actually, Jacqueline seemed more content to listen than to talk, asking Casey about where she'd been hiking and if she'd taken any interesting photos lately. Casey launched into a detailed description of a new location she'd gotten access to in the future, which would be perfect for her fall sessions. The owner of the farm was the grandmother of one of her clients, and Casey had shot her granddaughter's school pictures there. The woman had been so impressed that she'd given Casey her number and told her to call whenever she wanted to take pictures there. She'd even refused to charge Casey any rental fees.

"You should see it, Jacq. There's this old weathered barn and, a couple hundred yards away, a newly painted red one so it covers whichever mood I'm going for. Then, of course, there's all this rustic farm stuff to play with. And the stream that runs through the property passes by both barns. I say stream, but it's as wide as a street and waist deep in the middle. And when the leaves are changing, the colors reflect off the water brilliantly. The afternoon light there is amazing." She stopped, realizing she'd been waving her spatula around like a crazy woman. "Sorry, I'm babbling. And I'm sure you don't care about—"

"I do." Jacqueline smiled, her eyes warm with affection that Casey would have sworn Jacqueline couldn't feel for her anymore. "I've always liked how passionate you get about your work."

Casey held her gaze for a moment longer, basking in the glow before she made herself look away. She pulled the pan off the burner. "I'm almost ready here. So go round up Teddy."

As she plated their dinner, Jacqueline herded Teddy to the table. He and Casey chatted while they ate. Jacqueline grew increasingly quiet, though she did moan her approval of the grilled cheese.

Casey hadn't seen Jacqueline since their emotionally charged conversation about kids the previous weekend. She'd felt unsettled about where exactly they'd left things. But when Jacqueline had showed up today looking a little beat-up and clearly not wanting to discuss the causes, she'd decided to play along. Other than that awkward and too-familiar moment in the kitchen, they'd engaged in polite conversation that left her no closer to understanding the new ebbs and flows of their relationship.

Something else was bothering Jacqueline, but Casey waited until they were alone in the kitchen again to ask about it. Jacqueline insisted on cleaning up since Casey had cooked. Teddy didn't have a dishwasher, so she filled the sink to wash their few dishes. Casey grabbed a towel and said she'd dry them. She waited until Jacqueline was up to her forearms in soapy water and couldn't escape before she made an attempt.

"What's really going on? You look exhausted."

Jacqueline shook her head, her expression beginning to shut down.

"Is it just Teddy? Or—Kendra mentioned you had a problem at work."

Jacqueline scoffed. "Problems, actually."

"Do you want to talk about it?"

"I just need to get through this week." Jacqueline passed her a plate.

"Okay." She smothered her desire to convince Jacqueline to confide in her, telling herself that wasn't her job anymore—if it had ever been. Sometimes she felt like she'd spent their whole relationship asking Jacqueline for more.

"Don't do that."

"What?" She affected a casual tone.

"Don't act like I've disappointed you. I can't handle that, too."

"To be disappointed, I'd have to have some expectations of you."

"Ouch."

She laid the towel down on the counter next to the sink. "You know, suddenly, I'm tired as well. I think I'll say good-bye to Teddy and head home."

She'd taken two steps toward the living room when Jacqueline's voice stopped her. "I screwed up. A couple of times."

Casey folded her arms, waiting to see if Jacqueline was just tossing her a tidbit to placate her.

"I missed a crucial step in an investigation a while back. I got through that one relatively unscathed. But I lost my temper a couple of weeks ago, said something stupid, and now I have to go to Louisville and apologize." Jacqueline picked up the towel and dried her hands, then turned toward Casey.

"You're driving all the way up there for an apology."

Jacqueline nodded. "Owen's orders. I was wrong, I admit that. But I'm not looking forward to this. I can practically see the smug look on the manager's face." She sighed. "And then there's Dad. Is this just a symptom of aging? Or something more?"

"Aging, I think. But if you continue to have concerns, we can encourage him to go back to his doctor for further tests. I'll support whatever you decide and help in any way I can."

"I appreciate that." Jacqueline closed her eyes and pinched the bridge of her nose. "You've been so great, Casey. I can't thank you enough. And I haven't even asked how you're doing since you and Nina split up. Are you okay?"

"Sure." Casey waved a hand dismissively. "In a lot of ways, the breakup has made my life simpler."

"How so?"

"Just—you know, there's only so much of me to go around. And this time of year tests my patience."

"I remember." Jacqueline grimaced as if recalling how Casey's temper shortened as the fall wedding season bled into the holidays.

"Okay. I wasn't that bad."

"I bet my asking for help added to the stress."

"Honestly?"

"Of course."

"Maybe a little. But I never considered any other option. Whomever I date just has to understand that sometimes my family needs me."

Jacqueline gave her a grateful, if lazy, smile, almost as if she didn't have the energy for anything more.

Casey resisted the urge to reach out to her. "You're barely going to have any time to relax. You should have gone home and rested before your drive tomorrow."

"I'm away so much, I need to check on him when I'm around."

"You could have called. He would have understood you not driving down here."

Jacqueline twisted the towel in her hands, her eyes downcast. "I wanted to see Dad. But you're right. He'd have been okay. I needed to see you."

"Jacq—"

"Please, don't say it. I know. But," when she lifted her gaze, Casey's breath caught at the uncharacteristic vulnerability in her eyes, "I couldn't bear the thought of sitting alone in my apartment tonight."

"Come home with me." She didn't know why she'd said it, but she didn't want to take it back.

"You don't have to do that. I'll be fine. I can just stay here."

"I know. But I—thinking about you—just come with me." Jacqueline needed company and, yes, she could have left her with her father, but for whatever reason, she wanted to be what Jacqueline needed.

CHAPTER SIXTEEN

Jacqueline paced around Casey's living room, wondering if she'd made a mistake accepting Casey's offer to spend the night. She'd been exhausted and didn't want to drive back downtown. But, as she'd admitted, she didn't want to be alone. And even more than that, she wanted to be with Casey. Spending the evening with her had felt so good. She could easily lose herself in the domesticity of it all. For one night, she could pretend that her trip tomorrow wouldn't feel so long and draining because she might have something to come home to.

But those kinds of thoughts would get her in trouble. Casey had turned her away years ago, and though Jacqueline had herself convinced she'd detected hints that Casey wanted to let her back in, a part of her still knew it wasn't a good idea. Even if they could somehow find the courage to put themselves back on the roller coaster that had been their relationship, they had no right to force Sean to come along.

When they'd arrived, Casey had left her alone in the living room while she went to get something for her to sleep in. Jacqueline had ignored her suggestion to make herself comfortable and instead had spent the last several minutes wandering around the room.

She paused by a bookcase, made to look like a ladder angled against the wall. On the shelf at eye-level, three frames held photos of Sean, two with Casey and one with her father. The placement looked uneven, as if there had been a fourth one that was now missing. Had there been a picture of Nina that Casey had removed? She felt guilty for how good that idea made her feel. She probably shouldn't have brought Nina up; it was none of her business. She'd structured the question around her concern for Casey, but a part of her had been afraid Casey would say how much she missed her and regretted their split.

"You don't look like you're relaxing," Casey said as she came back into the room. She'd changed into one of her old college T-shirts and flannel boxer shorts. Jacqueline had seen a lot of versions of Casey in sleepwear, from the current one to her forays into sexy lingerie. But this one had always taken her back to their early days, when they'd skip class and spend hours in their dorm room making love, only putting on clothes to open the door for the pizza guy. "Is something wrong?"

Jacqueline blinked and realized she'd been staring. Casey glanced down at the stack of clothes, similar to her own, that she'd been holding out for who knew how long, then back up at Jacqueline.

"No. I'm good. Thank you." Jacqueline took the clothes. She turned back to the bookcase to distract herself from sexy-college-coed Casey. She skimmed over the blank space on the picture shelf and spotted one of Casey's old cameras on display. The Pentax had been an early favorite of Casey's and a go-to SLR for many years.

"Do you ever shoot with this anymore?"

"Not so much."

"Why not?"

"I'm strictly digital now, I guess." Casey shrugged. "I still have the darkroom we built in the studio, but 35mm doesn't work for the kind of stuff I'm doing professionally. All my proofs are digital and so are a lot of my package choices. Lately, I've been making time to shoot for pleasure again. I guess I shouldn't complain about having too much work, should I?"

"There are definitely worse problems to have."

Casey glanced at the clock on the wall. "You should get some sleep."

Jacqueline nodded. They moved together down the hallway, and she paused outside Sean's room.

"Thank you, for this." She indicated the sleepwear, but her gratitude extended to the company as well. "Good night."

"Don't stay in Sean's room," Casey blurted, and her expression changed as if the words had escaped without her consent.

"I guess I could sleep on the couch but—"

"Sleep with me. I mean, in my room. If you want to. There's plenty of—never mind."

"Okay," Jacqueline said too loudly for the soft atmosphere between them. "I'd like that."

She followed Casey into her bedroom. But once inside she stood awkwardly in the space she used to feel so comfortable in. Casey had painted the walls, transforming them from the sunny yellow they'd chosen years ago to soft gray. The king-sized mahogany panel bed they'd shared remained, but the charcoal-and-blue comforter covered in a simple leaf-and-vine pattern was new. The overall effect was clean and soothing.

"I like what you've done in here. It's nice."

Casey circled to the far side of the bed and pulled back the covers. "It was time for an update."

Jacqueline nodded. She looked down at the clothes in her hand, then at the bed between them. Why had she thought she could do this?

"Right. So the bathroom is still through there." Casey nodded toward the open door.

"Good to know you haven't moved it."

Once inside the bathroom, Jacqueline stripped down. She laughed when she caught herself modestly tucking her bra and underwear inside the folded pile of her own clothes—as if Casey hadn't seen everything already. As she pulled Casey's T-shirt over her head she breathed in the foreign scent of her fabric softener, grateful for anything that distracted her from the all-too-familiar fragrance of Casey's favorite cherry-blossom-scented lotion. She could probably stay strong against a hint of it, but immersed in it in the small room, she couldn't stop the memory of Casey smoothing it on her heated post-shower skin.

By the time she returned to the bedroom, Casey had already snuggled under the comforter, her eyes closed. While Jacqueline typically needed at least thirty minutes propped against the headboard making notes on her agenda for the next day in order to unwind, Casey possessed the irritating ability to fall asleep almost immediately after getting into bed. Casey also tended to take a bit more than her share of the bed, sleeping close to dead center of the mattress, and tonight was no exception as her golden waves threatened to spill onto Jacqueline's pillow. The lamp on her nightstand cast the only glow in the room, and the whole scenario suddenly felt very intimate.

She couldn't get in that bed next to Casey and pretend she was okay. She curled her hands into fists against the urge to touch Casey, and she wasn't even within range of her yet. If she opted to sleep in Sean's room, or even to leave altogether, she'd have to give Casey some kind of explanation. *Just get in the bed.* She'd slept next to Casey thousands of times without losing her shit; she could do it one more time. She'd pretend this was like any other night they'd gone to bed together—to sleep, any night they'd gone to sleep together.

❖

Casey closed her eyes when she heard the bathroom-door hinge squeak. But when Jacqueline didn't come to the bed right away, Casey struggled not to peek. Was Jacqueline having second thoughts about staying? Casey had questioned the wisdom of her invitation as soon as they'd stepped inside the bedroom. So she'd climbed into bed and shut her eyes so she could fake sleep and hope the awkwardness was gone by morning.

Finally, the bed dipped under Jacqueline's weight, and the sheet pulled against Casey as Jacqueline got settled underneath it. Though Jacqueline seemed to be trying to stay as close to the edge of the bed as possible, Casey could feel her warmth.

"I know you're not sleeping," Jacqueline said, poking her in the side.

Casey rolled onto her back, bringing her closer to Jacqueline. "How?"

Jacqueline shrugged, her shoulder rubbing Casey's. "I just do."

"This is weird, right?"

"Yeah."

"I never thought we'd be in bed together again. I mean—not that we're—we, uh—I'm going to shut up now and go back to faking sleep."

Jacqueline laughed. "I know what you meant. A lot has happened recently that I never thought would." She turned on her side, bent her elbow, and propped her head on her hand. "Sometimes it feels like we could be friends again."

"I'd like to think I never stopped being a friend when you needed one." Casey tried to steer them away from dangerous territory. She couldn't handle a trip down memory lane with Jacqueline so close.

Jacqueline brushed a lock of hair off Casey's forehead, then ghosted her fingers over Casey's jaw. "When I first met you—"

"We're not those girls." Casey couldn't turn her head away, but she considered it a victory when she managed not to angle into the caress.

"I know that."

"Do you?"

"Yes." Jacqueline touched her chin, but when her fingers drifted upward, Casey grabbed her wrist before she reached her lips. "When I look at you right now, I don't see that college coed. I see the woman who selflessly cared for my father, the woman who's been there for me when I thought I'd break, neither of which you have any obligation to do."

"Do you also see the woman you can barely go two weeks without arguing with? Because that's also been true these last couple of months." She squeezed Jacqueline's wrist, then started to release her. But as soon as they separated, Jacqueline turned her hand and captured Casey's fingers.

"We've always kind of had that, too. Haven't we?"

Casey nodded, staring at their linked hands. They'd never lacked for chemistry, whether they were heating each other up or burning down their relationship. "We were so full of feelings back then."

"You were full of yourself." Jacqueline tucked their hands against her chest.

"I'm serious."

"So am I."

Casey elbowed her playfully. "I was emotional and inspired."

"You were the biggest flirt I'd ever met. I never stood a chance."

"Most women didn't."

Jacqueline seemed to be considering her response. Casey recognized first her impulse to volley back with a joke of her own, but then her expression turned serious. "You were pretty amazing. Fearless. Are—you are amazing."

"Nice save." Casey grinned. "But lately, it seems, I go through my days feeling numb—detached—like I'm watching my life happen to someone else."

"What can we do about that?"

Casey shrugged.

"I'm serious. You've been a rock for me with Dad. Let me do something for you."

"It's fine—I'm fine."

"Okay. I have an idea. Are you free Sunday morning?"

She shook her head. "I have a shoot scheduled. But Saturday could work." She'd have to get some billing and editing done on Friday in order to justify some playtime. Even without knowing what they'd be doing, she couldn't resist the offer to spend a day with Jacqueline. During their relationship she'd grown to resent the part of herself that seemed to sit around waiting for Jacqueline to have time for her.

"Okay. I'll pick you up."

"What are we doing?"

"You'll see."

"How will I know how to dress?"

"Wear comfortable shoes. Bring your camera and your longest lens. I'll take care of everything else."

"You're really not going to tell me."

"Nope." Jacqueline kissed Casey's temple, then released her hand and rolled onto her side. "Now, go to sleep. I didn't come over here for you to keep me up all night."

❖

Casey stepped out of Jacqueline's car in the lot beside the park office at Bledsoe Creek State Park. She'd been here once before but hadn't recognized the route until she saw the sign as they turned off the main road. Jacqueline had refused to divulge their destination, even when she'd called last night on her drive home from Louisville. She'd been pulled into a meeting late yesterday in Louisville and had gotten a very late start on her drive back. So she'd phoned and asked Casey to talk for a few minutes to wake her up behind the wheel.

Now, she suspected Jacqueline hadn't wanted to tell her where they were going for fear Casey might not come along. Though the park was known for having several nice trails and lots of wildlife, Casey had avoided it when she'd started hiking recently. She hadn't wanted to resurrect her disastrous first visit.

"It's such a gorgeous day." Jacqueline rounded the car and opened the trunk.

Casey pulled her hair through the back of a baseball cap and settled it on her head. The sun was rising quickly in the sapphire sky, and she'd need the shade before long.

She tilted her head, looking up at the trees around her. But her attention drifted again to Jacqueline, who provided much more beautiful scenery. Jacqueline wore a long-sleeved thermal shirt and dark jeans that looked almost new. In fact, they probably were. She'd always gone from business to totally casual, skipping almost everything in between. As soon as she got home from work, she'd strip off her suit and put on sweats and a T-shirt. She'd said she spent way too many hours of her day in uncomfortable clothes to do so when she didn't absolutely have to. Today, she'd left her hair unrestrained but pushed a pair of sunglasses up on her head to act as a hair accessory, which Casey found unexplainably sexy.

"I know these trails probably aren't up to your normal workout." Jacqueline pulled two bottles of water from a cooler and shoved them into her backpack. She fidgeted with the zipper and didn't meet Casey's eyes. Was she nervous about Casey's reaction to coming here?

"It's not so much about the exercise as it is clearing my mind." She decided to keep her answers neutral until she figured out Jacqueline's plan for choosing this particular place.

Though she'd had a busy week, she'd looked forward to the weekend. Given that she'd shared a bed with Jacqueline Wednesday night, she expected to be a bit more conflicted about spending the day with her. The alarm on Jacqueline's phone woke them both too early Thursday morning, but there'd been something comforting about feeling Jacqueline's weight against her side as she opened her eyes. Jacqueline had thrown on her clothes from the night before and headed home to get ready for her trip. Casey had walked her to the door, and Jacqueline had hugged her and thanked her for putting up with her the night before. Maybe they were both far too good at pretending they weren't crossing any lines, but the entire exchange had felt civil—perhaps even friendly.

"Sure. But you're used to more challenging hikes."

"I've been working my way up, yes." Casey slipped one of her light sling bags containing her camera over her head and around her body.

"I can tell." Jacqueline glanced down at Casey's legs.

"Why here?" If she had any hope of enjoying this day, she might as well get this conversation out of the way first.

Jacqueline shrugged. "My way of turning back time."

"What does that mean?"

"Last time we were here, I screwed it up."

When he was about nine years old, Sean had begged them to take him camping. One of his friends had gone several times with his father and bragged about what a great time he had. Jacqueline wanted to rent an RV, but Casey had insisted that in order to get an authentic experience they had to rough it in a tent. It poured down rain for most of the weekend, and instead of making the best of it, Jacqueline spent two days telling Casey how much better their trip would be if she'd listened to her about the RV. Eventually, Casey gave up on salvaging the trip for Sean, and they'd packed up and left a day early.

"I think we find enough to disagree on without rehashing old arguments, so if that's what you brought me out here to do—"

"It's not." Jacqueline grabbed Casey's hands. "I remembered there were trails here. And we didn't exactly get to explore them last time."

"I don't want to do this." Casey pulled her hands free. She'd forgotten how angry she'd been at Jacqueline after that weekend. She turned back toward the car, intending to insist Jacqueline take her home.

"Wait." Jacqueline caught her hand as she tried to spin away. "When the weather didn't cooperate, I handled things badly. But there was a lot of pressure on that trip, and I couldn't stand to see you so disappointed."

"Me? I was worried about Sean. He had a tough beginning. I was trying to give him everything he'd never had."

"That's just it." Jacqueline stroked her thumb over the back of Casey's hand. "You needed it to be perfect. And when it wasn't, you got mad at me. And, yes, I made you feel bad for not having done things my way in the first place. That was wrong. But I got tired of trying to overcompensate for his crappy biological family."

"What?"

"Do you know what I remember about that weekend?"

Casey shook her head.

"I remember how cute you looked when we got caught in that first rainstorm while we were setting up the tent. Your hair got wet and your T-shirt clung in all the right places." She winked. "And when I laughed at you, you kissed me. Then there was that big clap of thunder, and—"

"And I bit your lip."

Jacqueline nodded. "Hard." She touched Casey's cheek. "When we pulled apart, Sean was laughing at us. He had this big grin on his face. I guarantee he wasn't thinking about his shitty start in life."

"You remember all that?"

Jacqueline's lips pulled into a small smile, but deep sadness reflected in her eyes. "Like it was yesterday."

The silence between them echoed with ancient wounds. Jacqueline stayed quiet, clearly leaving the next move in Casey's hands. The openness in Jacqueline's expression helped Casey make her decision. Jacqueline had brought her here with good intentions. They could move past their mistakes or they could wallow in them.

Casey stepped back, but she kept hold of Jacqueline's hand. She glanced at the sky again. "There's no rain in the forecast today. So, let's go check out these trails."

Jacqueline smiled and followed her toward the sign marking the beginning of the longest section of trail.

Jacqueline seemed to be taking the relaxation aspect of the hike just as seriously as she did. For the next thirty minutes, they walked mostly in silence. Occasionally, one of them would point out a bit of scenery—a glimpse of the lake, an especially bright cluster of foliage, or the remains of a hand-stacked stone fence left over from when the bordering clearing used to be farmland. Casey stopped a few times to take some quick shots.

They kept a steady pace, and by the time they crested the steepest climb, they were both breathing heavier.

"Do you want to go down and come back up?" Jacqueline paused at the top and bent to catch her breath.

"I wouldn't do that to you."

"I wasn't volunteering to go with you. I'd wait here while you did it, if you need the challenge."

"Ah, okay. No thanks." Casey pointed at the trail ahead. "Let's just keep going." She started off again.

"Hey, I'm working on breathing here."

Casey glanced over her shoulder. Jacqueline stood with her hands on her hips. "Come on. You aren't going to get calves like mine standing around." She smiled when she heard Jacqueline's menacing growl in response. Jacqueline was a leg woman. Though Casey wouldn't admit it aloud, she'd dressed with that thought in mind. Despite the cool weather, she'd chosen her favorite cropped workout pants, which hugged her thighs and ended just below her knee, leaving her lower legs bare. She told herself she'd picked them because she didn't like heavy clothes on her legs when she walked. Usually, as long as she kept her upper body warm, she didn't feel the chill, so she'd layered a flannel shirt over a long-sleeved T-shirt.

"Hey," Jacqueline whispered. She grabbed the strap of Casey's camera bag and tugged her to a halt.

Startled, Casey didn't adjust for the sudden change in direction, and she fell back against Jacqueline. She glanced around, trying to figure out what Jacqueline had seen that she'd missed while fantasizing about teasing Jacqueline with her exposed calves like she was some kind of Victorian maiden.

"Over there." Jacqueline pointed to their right, while her other arm slipped around Casey's waist. She kept her voice down and spoke so close that Casey thought she felt Jacqueline's lips move against her ear.

Through the trees, about fifty yards away, a family of deer stared back at them. A fawn, the faint dusting of spots still visible on its back, nuzzled close to its mother, who seemed poised to run off with her youngster at the first sign of danger. Another doe and a buck with a small set of antlers had frozen in place as well.

Moving slowly, Casey raised her camera and focused. The skittish mother flinched as she released the shutter several times. She angled to look over her shoulder and found Jacqueline's face still close.

"Look at that baby. He's so cute."

"Did you get the shot?" Jacqueline's eyes flickered down to her camera, then returned immediately to her face. Was Jacqueline looking at her mouth? Casey nodded mutely. "Good. Let's keep going." With her hands bracketing Casey's hips, she guided her forward slowly.

The deer bolted as soon as the next bunch of leaves crunched under their feet. Casey took another picture as their white tails swished and bounced through the trees. When she resumed their previous pace, she slipped away from Jacqueline and immediately missed the pressure of her hands on her.

Chapter Seventeen

Jacqueline followed Casey along the Shoreline Trail, a section that, befitting its description, traced the edge of the lake near part of the campground. As they neared a wooden dock that stretched into the water, she said, "How about a rest?"

"What's wrong? Can't keep up?"

"No, I can't." While she hadn't had too much trouble keeping pace with Casey, she could definitely use a break from watching Casey's backside sway in front of her.

Casey glanced at her in surprise.

"What? You don't think I can admit you're in better shape than I am?" She nodded toward the dock. "Let's go sit for a minute." At the far end, a slightly larger platform had a roof and some built-in benches.

As they reached the end of the dock, Casey rested her forearms on the railing. "Look at all the birds." When Casey glanced over her shoulder, her smile captivated Jacqueline. She'd so rarely seen this expression of pure happiness from Casey in recent years. Instead, she'd gotten used to Casey's smile being cautiously polite when directed at her.

"Let's sit for a while." Jacqueline dropped her backpack on the floor and settled on the bench.

"Are you sure? We can finish the walk." Casey paused with her camera half-raised.

"This is why we're here. I did some more current research on the place, and we didn't get to see much of it last time, but I read they have good wildlife here."

Casey laughed. "They have good wildlife?"

"And now you're laughing at me." Jacqueline stood, but Casey rushed over and guided her back down with a hand on her shoulder.

"No. I'm sorry. It's sweet that you looked it up online. Thank you."

"*And* I tromped through the woods with you. I want credit for that, too." When they'd first met, she had followed Casey into a wide range of locations and climates. Casey, in all her creative-glory, had been captivating. And seeing her today, intense and focused as she snapped away, Jacqueline was just as seduced by her. Instead of letting that thought freak her out, she settled back against the bench and enjoyed Casey in her element. She moved confidently from one side of the dock to the other, expertly adjusting her settings before taking another series of photos.

Casey cradled her camera in one hand, the fingers of her other hand twisting the focus ring on the long lens. Jacqueline didn't have to strain to remember the feel of those fingers against her skin. She also didn't have to work too hard to conjure up the image of Casey in college. Her blond waves were the softest Jacqueline had ever touched, and it broke Jacqueline's heart when she restrained them in a ponytail so they wouldn't blow into her face while she was shooting. When she talked about her art, passion lit her blue eyes from the inside. Jacqueline had fallen in love first watching those beautiful hands work a camera, then feeling them on her own body.

"Look at him." Casey pointed near the opposite shore at the bird she'd just photographed. It had just slipped into the lake and was gliding toward them. It dipped its head in the water, either bathing or hunting for food. "He's gorgeous."

Jacqueline stuck her hand inside the zipper of her backpack, then joined Casey at the railing that circled the dock. "Gorgeous? It's ugly." It was a duck or a goose of some kind; Jacqueline had never been sure of the difference. Its head was mottled with patches of white that stood out against its dark-colored body. Red, warty growths clustered around its beak. "What is it?"

"I don't know."

"Do you think he's in here?" Jacqueline pulled a book from behind her back. The cover was worn and creased next to the binding from being folded back too many times.

"My bird guide." Casey grabbed the book and immediately started flipping through it. "Where did you get this?"

"It was mixed in with some of my books. I must have taken it by accident—when I moved out." Jacqueline felt silly admitting that she'd held on to this piece of Casey. Just talking about the day she'd packed her things and left their home made her stomach churn with nausea. "I'm sorry."

Casey shrugged. "Clearly I didn't miss it."

She hadn't been talking about the book. "No, I—"

"Hey, it's okay. It's just a book. I'd have bought another one if I was that into birds." Casey touched her cheek and she closed her eyes.

She wanted to move into her, to grab her waist and pull her close. Instead, she stepped back and said, "Well, get your aviary fill now, because I'm not sitting out here all day." She smiled to soften the sarcasm in her words.

"You would if I asked you to." Casey's broad grin and the cocky edge to her voice felt familiar.

They'd lost this. In the last years of their relationship, they'd stopped making time for these days for the two of them to just hang out together. Jacqueline had been working too much. Sean had been young and needed so much of them. And by the time they could even think about focusing on each other, they were too exhausted.

She'd tuned out the clicking of Casey's shutter, until she realized the camera was now pointed at her.

"What are you doing?" She half turned away.

"What were you thinking about just now?" Casey took several steps forward, circling her to take a couple more shots.

"Why?"

"You looked so—distant, yet beautiful. I couldn't help myself."

"Yeah, well, stop it." She held a hand up between her face and the lens.

Casey pulled her arm down and held it out of the way. She tapped the shutter release two more times. "I love the way your face changes with your moods. I can see them all, from distracted to embarrassed to irritated."

"Casey." Jacqueline grappled with Casey's wrist and hand, trying to get hers back in front of the camera.

"You never used to mind being one of my models." Casey set her camera on the bench and turned to Jacqueline again. She stepped close, her hands coming to rest on the front of Jacqueline's shoulders.

Jacqueline flashed on a memory that brought a rush of heat to her face. Casey had awakened her one morning with her camera in hand. She'd said their bedroom had the perfect morning light. She'd pushed back the sheet to expose Jacqueline's bare skin and taken a series of shots. Jacqueline had posed for a bit, putting on a bit of a show for her before she grabbed her and pulled her back into bed. The camera lay forgotten on the nightstand for the rest of the morning.

"Hmm, from irritated to aroused." Casey moved in and spoke close to her ear. "That was always one of my favorites."

Jacqueline stood very still, not trusting herself to move. Casey slid her hands up to the sides of Jacqueline's neck, and Jacqueline grabbed her hips, intending to push her away, but when she felt Casey's lips against her cheek, she froze.

"Casey," she whispered on a pleading breath. *Kiss me or let me go.*

Those words didn't make it out of her head, but Casey's next move felt like a response to them just the same. She brushed her lips over the corner of Jacqueline's mouth, then claimed it fully. They angled their heads and slanted their mouths together as if they'd been waiting—Jacqueline had—she'd been waiting so long for Casey to kiss her, to not feel as if she were the only desperate fool fighting her feelings.

She pulled Casey flush against her, reveling in the solid pressure from breasts to thighs. *They fit—they'd always fit like this.* That thought hit her as Casey's tongue slid along her lower lip, and Jacqueline tried to push away the reminder that they didn't really. Casey was no longer hers. She returned the kiss for a moment longer, taking her own mental snapshot to catalog along with the rest of her memories.

Sooner than she wanted to, she squeezed Casey's hips and eased her back. "You can't do that again."

"I didn't plan it that time, Jacq." Casey hands slid to Jacqueline's chest, and she flexed her fingers in Jacqueline's shirt.

"You know what it does to me when you say my name like that." Jacqueline released her and took a step back. "I'm trying to respect our boundaries."

"What if I don't want us to have boundaries?"

"I have to have them."

"Why?"

"You sent me away. I vowed that if you wanted me back, you'd have to come begging."

"You always did like it when I begged," Casey drawled.

Jacqueline reacted viscerally to Casey's words. Her knees almost buckled, yet somehow she managed to stay upright. Her heart thudded, pounding blood into her pulse points so heavy she could feel the rhythm.

"Why, Miss Casey, are you flirting with me?" She forced a light tone, hoping to hide how affected she'd been.

"Maybe. I'm not sure I'd recognize it. Do you know how long it's been since we flirted?" Casey laughed. "At least eight years, right?"

Jacqueline shook her head. "Longer than that. You stopped awhile before we split up. And I was too dumb to realize how much I missed it."

Casey's expression grew serious. "It's not all on you. I let some important things fall to the wayside as well."

"Well, the past is the past. Today is for relaxation and recharging your creative batteries." Jacqueline drew back as well, determined to restore the space between them, both physically and emotionally. She'd already risked ruining the day by letting that kiss go on too long. And Casey seemed as eager as she to write it off to a moment of weakness. "So," she waved toward the water behind Casey, "back to the birds."

❖

Casey replayed their interaction while Jacqueline drove her home. The conversation they'd started their day with had left her with something to think about. Despite the arguing and frustration Casey associated with that trip, Jacqueline had managed to hold onto a moment that she'd forgotten. When she really thought about it, the passion, the love, and the humor in that memory represented the best of them. She'd never have thought Jacqueline would be so sentimental about something that happened so long ago. So much so that she'd planned this day in an effort to create better memories of Bledsoe Creek. And she really had. The rest of their day had been exactly what she'd needed, a day to decompress—to breathe fresh air and take some photos that had absolutely nothing riding on them professionally.

While they were out on the dock, she'd turned toward Jacqueline and stopped short for a moment. Jacqueline had been staring out across the water, but clearly she wasn't focused wherever her gaze landed.

Was she thinking about work? Or Sean? Or another woman? What had captured Jacqueline's attention so fully while she was with Casey? She'd reacted quickly to a surge of jealousy in the one way she knew she'd gain Jacqueline's attention. She'd flirted, then touched, then kissed. She'd given in to what her heart wanted instead of what she knew to be prudent. And it had felt so good, even when Jacqueline tried to ease away—*if you wanted me back, you'd have to come begging.* Jacqueline's words fueled the competitive fire in her. She imagined any number of the women Jacqueline had slept with over the years would beg in an instant. So she'd pushed.

But Jacqueline's response had slowed her down. *I was too dumb to realize how much I missed it.*

In the time that they'd been apart, Jacqueline had never given any real indication that she'd changed or that she'd wanted to. But those words were spoken softly and with more humility than she'd heard from Jacqueline in years. None of the many apologies and pleas to try again that Jacqueline had issued in those first months after their split had felt nearly as genuine as this one sentence.

Now, stealing glances at Jacqueline across the cabin of the Lexus, Casey couldn't shut down the part of her that still cared for her. *Cared for?* Those words didn't feel strong enough, but she hesitated to say that she still loved Jacqueline. She had at one time—fiercely. Of course she did. But she didn't want to admit that Nina had been right. She'd never stopped, but she'd learned that love wasn't the only thing she required. And Jacqueline hadn't been willing to try to give her what she needed.

So what was all that back at the park? Jacqueline pulled the car into Casey's driveway and turned off the engine.

Casey angled toward Jacqueline and met her uncertain gaze. "Thank you for today. It was—"

"I'm sorry. It was weird, I know."

"I was going to say perfect."

"Yeah?"

"Yes. It was exactly what I needed." She didn't want to analyze things. The way she felt now—looking at Jacqueline and the happiness shining in her eyes—were enough for the moment.

"Sometimes I can't believe how much time has gone by." Jacqueline glanced at the house.

Casey looked too, seeing the hedge that had been only waist high when they moved in and now blocked the view of the neighboring house, and the shutters that had been deep green and were now in need of painting. Their son had become a man. Yet, Casey didn't feel that far removed from the woman who fell in love with this house and optimistically planned to grow her family here.

"Can I come in for a minute?" Jacqueline asked.

Casey stared straight ahead, not making eye contact with Jacqueline. She didn't want to tell her no, but she wasn't sure she trusted herself in her current nostalgic state.

"Please. I just want to talk."

She nodded, then turned away quickly and got out of the car. She let them into the house and headed straight for the kitchen, thinking it offered the least-intimate environment.

"Can I get you something to drink?"

"No. I'm good."

Casey leaned against the counter. Trying to appear more casual than she felt, she resisted the urge to fold her arms over her chest. "What did you want to talk about?"

Jacqueline stood opposite her, just a couple of feet of travertine between them. "I don't know what's going on with us lately. Those kisses…" She took a breath. "My first instinct is to not bring it up, and I get the feeling yours is too."

Casey nodded.

"Because that's how we communicate with each other. But ignoring our issues has never worked for us before. I'd like to try something different. Okay?"

"Okay."

"So, I own the first kiss. We were arguing. I got emotional. But you were with Nina, and it wasn't fair of me to put you in that position. But today—I'm not sure what happened there."

Casey inhaled slowly, gathering her thoughts. Jacqueline was really trying here and she supposed she should, too. "Today was my fault. You planned this whole day just for me—trying to give me the relaxing time I needed. It was a sweet gesture, and I got caught up in the moment."

"So, it would have happened with anyone who took you out for the day?" Jacqueline stood a little straighter, as if she preparing to flee if her feelings got hurt.

"Of course not. But given our history, is it really a surprise?"

"I suppose not."

"I didn't stop wanting to kiss you just because we decided not to stay together."

Jacqueline's expression changed, and Casey felt her shift into an offensive mode. "We didn't decide. You did."

"You didn't put up much of a fight."

"We'd been fighting for so long, I was exhausted. I was heartbroken over Elle, and instead of trying to understand, you just kept pushing. Like you always did. You had to control everything in our lives."

"That's not true." Casey straightened, now, prepared to defend herself.

"It is. From day one. You decided I should ask for your number that day. You decided we would foster Sean—"

"And I've never regretted—"

"I haven't either. I wouldn't trade him for anything. But can you really say I could have talked you out of it?"

Casey didn't say anything.

"You determined when our relationship was over."

"That's not fair. Okay, I made the final call, but we were on that road—"

"You decided. And, you're right. I didn't fight. I was hurting so badly that I convinced myself letting you go couldn't feel any worse than holding on." Jacqueline took a step toward her, the anguish in her eyes ripping a hole in Casey's soul. "But I was wrong. Being without you was a hundred times more painful."

Casey closed the space between them in the time it took Jacqueline to draw another breath. She wrapped one hand around the back of Jacqueline's neck and pulled her in, her other hand catching her around the waist as their lips met. She poured all of the emotions she couldn't voice into this kiss—the sadness, the regrets, and her grief. Jacqueline's hands slipped under the hem of her shirt, and she ran her hands possessively up Casey's back, urging her closer, as she deepened the kiss.

Jacqueline surged against her, and the edge of the countertop bit into her lower back. Casey pushed her hands into Jacqueline's hair and raked her nails against her scalp. Her need to get closer—to feel more—quickly outpaced her common sense. She'd had only a taste of Jacqueline in these past eight years, and those encounters were laced with remorse. *Being without you was a hundred times more painful.* Jacqueline's suffering, laid bare in those words, had paralleled her own so perfectly. And, she'd felt, touching her— kissing her—was the only way to soothe them both.

Wait. The word echoed in Casey's practical mind, but it never reached her lips. As Jacqueline's mouth moved to her neck, Casey dropped her head back, and the word that escaped her was very different. "Bed."

CHAPTER EIGHTEEN

B ed."
Jacqueline shook her head in the hollow of Casey's neck. She lifted Casey onto the counter and moved between her thighs. "Here."

Casey wrapped her legs around Jacqueline's waist. Jacqueline's hands blazed under her shirt, leaving a trail of goose bumps across her stomach. Jacqueline shoved the flannel shirt off her shoulders and pulled her T-shirt over her head. She removed her own shirt, dropped it on the floor behind her, and pressed close to Casey.

Casey trembled. Jacqueline's arms around her—her breath against her skin as she kissed her collarbone—felt like coming home. She cradled Jacqueline's jaw and guided their mouths back together. When Jacqueline slipped her hands beneath the waistband of her spandex pants, Casey planted her hands against Jacqueline's chest and shoved her backward.

Jacqueline stared at her, her expression a mix of desire and confusion. "I'm sorry."

Casey slid off the counter and grabbed Jacqueline's hands, keeping her close. "You've been with enough women to know that apologizing isn't a turn-on."

"You're not just another—"

"I wasn't stopping." Casey closed her teeth on Jacqueline's earlobe, knowing Jacqueline's weaknesses better than her own. "We just need a little more room to move."

Keeping hold of Jacqueline's hand, she headed toward her bedroom. She glanced at the bed as they entered, having intended to shove Jacqueline down and have her way with her. But feeling Jacqueline's hands in the tight band of her workout pants reminded her that she'd been hiking less than an hour ago. She needed Jacqueline's hands on every inch of her, and she didn't want to be self-conscious. So, instead, she led Jacqueline into the master bathroom and turned on the shower.

"Take off your pants." She shucked off her own and kicked them to the side, letting her panties go with them. Since Jacqueline made no move to undress further, Casey reached for the waistband of her jeans.

"Should we slow this down?" Jacqueline covered her hands, stilling them.

Casey fisted her hands in denim and met Jacqueline's eyes. "Do you want to?"

"I don't think I'm in any condition to make that call right now."

Casey was a grown woman—certainly too old to be losing control over a woman, let alone one with whom she had a complicated history. The practical side of her—the one that knew better—was quickly being overtaken by the part that craved Jacqueline's touch.

Casey dragged her gaze deliberately over Jacqueline's body. Her breasts were fuller than the last time Casey had seen them, but still so familiar that, just looking at them, Casey could feel their weight in her hands, taste the texture of her nipples on her tongue. "Well, then we have a problem, because we're the only two people here. And I can't look at you like this and say no. But if you ask me to, I'll try like hell."

Jacqueline shoved her jeans down and pulled them off, hopping on one foot, then the other.

Casey laughed. "I haven't seen you undress that fast since the days when we had to try to squeeze one in before Sean got home from school."

Jacqueline laughed with her. "Get in that shower before I remember that you're the mother of a twenty-year-old."

"Oh, did you just call me old?" Casey acted offended, but it felt good to be with Jacqueline. She hadn't imagined a moment like this between them in so many years, but she'd have thought she'd be freaked out by the possible fallout. She didn't know what she was doing—probably inviting heartache. But when Jacqueline looked at her like she'd give anything to touch her, it might be worth it.

She stepped into the shower stall and remembered when they'd replaced the old characterless fiberglass shell with tile. They'd spent the day together in here, fumbling their way through their first major rehab project. She turned to find Jacqueline glancing around the shower and wondered if she was having the same thoughts. But she didn't ask. They seemed to be walking a line between a conscious choice and convincing themselves that this moment was out of their control. And Casey was okay with pretending, if it meant Jacqueline wouldn't stop touching her.

"You're forgetting that you're a month older." She pushed Jacqueline under the spray. "Let's see if you can still keep up with me."

Jacqueline's eyes flashed predictably in response to the challenge. When Jacqueline reached out, Casey let herself be caught. Jacqueline grabbed a handful of Casey's hair, wringing water down her back as she squeezed. Casey moaned as the sensation sizzled from her scalp to settle into a throb between her legs.

"You like that?" Jacqueline stroked a finger against Casey's erect nipple.

Casey smiled when it hardened even more. "Nope. The water's just cold."

"Well, then let me warm you up." Jacqueline bent and took her nipple in her mouth.

"Oh, God." She clung to Jacqueline, needing help staying upright as Jacqueline's tongue and teeth did amazing things.

Casey fumbled for the body wash and squeezed some into her palm. "We're going to have to get out of here soon before someone gets hurt." She smoothed her hands over Jacqueline's body, rising and dipping along her curves.

Jacqueline grabbed the bottle and returned the favor. She kissed Casey while trailing bubbles down her back and over her buttocks. As she slipped her tongue into Casey's mouth, she cupped her ass and angled their pelvises together.

They washed each other quickly, moaning as they stroked sensitive flesh but not lingering too long. After they'd rinsed and efficiently toweled dry, they came together again in bed.

Casey immediately sought Jacqueline's mouth as they reached for each other. She didn't want slow. She didn't want time to think. She needed only to revel in the feel of Jacqueline under her fingertips. They fumbled for control, but eventually Casey rose over Jacqueline, straddling her. Only then did she gentle the pace. Jacqueline's eyes turned hazy. She'd always loved when Casey took control—always responded to Casey's weight on top of her.

She ground her hips into Jacqueline, teasing them both with not quite enough friction. But before long, she'd gone too far, testing the edge of her own self-control. Jacqueline wrapped her legs around the outside of Casey's thighs, pulling her in stroke after stroke. Jacqueline reached between them, cupping her breast.

"God, you have great breasts." Jacqueline squeezed her nipple.

Casey arched, giving Jacqueline better access and increasing the pressure between her legs.

"I need you to touch me, soon."

Casey lifted herself up enough to get her hand between them and slipped her fingers into Jacqueline's drenched folds. She toyed with her for only a second before she had to have more of her. Sliding down, she left a trail of kisses across Jacqueline's stomach. When she pressed her tongue against Jacqueline's clit, Jacqueline sighed as if she'd been waiting for that touch.

Casey sank into her, tasting her thoroughly. Jacqueline pushed her fingers into Casey's hair and tugged, indicating she wanted Casey to speed up the pace. Thrilled that she could still read her, Casey somehow managed to keep her strokes long and slow, though every part of her body screamed to give Jacqueline release and then seek out her own.

"Please, Casey, God, that feels so good." The desperation in Jacqueline's voice broke Casey's resolve.

She slid one hand under Jacqueline's ass, lifting her hips, and sucked her harder. She brought Jacqueline right to the edge, then slipped two fingers inside her and pushed firmly, knowing the intensity would be exactly what she needed. Jacqueline cried out and grasped at the back of Casey's neck and her shoulders. Casey continued to play her tongue over Jacqueline's clit, gentling in proportion to the ebb of Jacqueline's climax.

Casey moved up to lie next to Jacqueline, but as she aligned their bodies, Jacqueline wrapped her arms around her. She kissed her hard, stroking her tongue into Casey's mouth. She caressed her hands down Casey's back. When she cupped Casey's ass and pulled her closer, her intentions were clear.

"Hey, just enjoy yours for a minute." Casey kissed the corner of Jacqueline's mouth softly, trying to convince them both that she didn't need some attention right then.

"I want you." Before Casey could argue, Jacqueline reached between her legs.

"Oh, God, I want to tell you that you don't have to do that, but shit, I really want you to." Casey dropped her head back and Jacqueline bit her neck. Casey smiled at the jolt of pleasure. She loved Jacqueline's teeth against her skin.

When Jacqueline entered her, her body was still so primed from touching Jacqueline that Casey lost the ability to form a conscious thought. She became a quivering mess of sensation, registering Jacqueline's skin against hers and the panting breaths that might be hers or might be Jacqueline's—she wasn't sure which. Every time Jacqueline drew back, Casey's nerve endings revolted at the vacancy, until she pushed home again, and Casey nearly sobbed at the completeness.

"Don't stop." She wasn't above begging for the release she desperately needed. Jacqueline didn't stop, and Casey knew with certainty that she wouldn't until Casey had shattered around her fingers. She pressed her face into Jacqueline's neck and surrendered.

She convulsed and cried out, desperately riding Jacqueline's hand over her peak.

"I've got you, baby," Jacqueline soothed her as she rolled down the other side of her climax. Jacqueline eased out of her and held Casey close to her side. She stroked her hair and whispered endearments against her forehead.

❖

Jacqueline stared at Casey's ceiling and wondered when she'd last felt so completely drained after sex. She'd had some marathon sessions over the years, but none had left her feeling like this—like she'd left every piece of herself inside another person. Maybe she had. Maybe she'd left herself with Casey eight years ago, and that's why no else had touched her this way since.

Casey stirred, mumbling softly as she dozed. She'd drifted off only moments ago with her head on Jacqueline's chest and her arm draped across Jacqueline's stomach.

"We're still really good at that." The soft edges of Casey's words hinted at lingering drowsiness. "I guess some things don't change."

Jacqueline nodded, but Casey's words replayed in her head. *Some things don't change.* Then Jacqueline's own thoughts twisted the idea and taunted her. *Nothing has changed. I haven't changed. My job still needs so much of me, and there'll never be enough left for Casey.*

What had she done? She'd so easily fallen into the flirtation and convinced herself that the consequences didn't matter. She loved Casey—with all her heart. But she'd been stupid enough to think that was enough once before. She'd been young and naive enough to think she would never lose Casey, but she had and she could again. She'd had it all and she'd let it slip away, and now she wasn't sure she deserved to get it back. Until she figured that out, she had no business being here—risking hurting Casey and Sean.

Her burgeoning panic left her limbs weak and jacked up her pulse rate. She worried Casey could hear her heart pounding, and that fear didn't improve her condition. Telling herself to relax only made her tense more.

"Jacq?" Casey lifted her head slowly.

Jacqueline couldn't meet her eyes. Casey would know—as soon as she looked at her, she'd know. She needed just a second before she fractured the fantasy of what they'd just done together. She slipped her arm from under Casey's neck and sat up, but Casey rose beside her.

"Sweetheart?"

Sweetheart.

Over the years Casey had used the word countless times—in varying ways. She'd caressed the endearment with passion, she'd teased it with flirtation, and she'd even twisted it with derision in the midst of an argument, but none had touched Jacqueline more deeply than at this moment. The concern in that one word made Jacqueline's throat ache with emotion.

She turned and forced herself to look at Casey. She owed her eye contact—didn't she? But when she lifted her gaze and saw the trust in her eyes warring with apprehension, she nearly chickened out. If she let Casey get invested in her again, she'd only hurt worse later, when Jacqueline let her down again. "I will always love you. But this—"

"Please, don't," Casey whispered.

Jacqueline couldn't let herself be deterred. She shouldn't have gotten into bed with Casey, and she had to own that. The only way she could do that was to force herself to face it head-on. It might hurt Casey for a minute, but in the long run, she'd be better off. "This was a mistake."

Casey let out a sound somewhere between a gasp and a sob, as if the words physically hurt her. Her face was a slide show of emotions: hurt, disbelief, then anger.

"Get out."

"Casey, I'm—"

"I said, get out. Of my bedroom. Of my house. And of my life."

Jacqueline wanted to apologize, to somehow take back the pain she'd caused. But she'd have to go back so much further than just this evening. So, instead, she grabbed her jeans from the bathroom floor and tugged them on as quickly as she could. She didn't remember where she'd left her shirt, so she took one of Casey's button-down shirts off the chair nearby. Casey scooted out the other side of the bed, clutching the sheet in front of her.

"God, I can't believe I let—I have to be the biggest idiot—" When Casey reached a certain level of anger, she had trouble finishing a sentence. "I just allowed myself—thinking you'd changed—and I slept with you." She whipped the sheet tighter around herself and glared at Jacqueline. "A mistake? A mistake! So, it's okay for you to have a slut in every city, but sleeping with *me* is where you draw your moral line?"

Jacqueline staggered back a step, fumbling with the buttons of the shirt. She had little defense against Casey's words. She deserved the lancing pain in her chest. Giving up on the buttons, she clutched the edges of the shirt together and fled the room.

She made it as far as the living room, but something stopped her. She sat down on the couch, propped her elbows on her knees, and cradled her head in her hands. She'd screwed up pretty big this time. While she suspected Casey's parting shot was calculated to draw the most blood, it wasn't inaccurate. She'd given Casey every reason to believe she could screw her and leave, and that's the thing that hurt the most. But what should she do now?

"What are you doing out here?" Casey stood in the archway between the hall and living room, her expression full of anger and confusion.

"I only made it this far." Despite being at a loss a moment ago, she suddenly knew what to do—be honest. Casey deserved nothing less. "You said I leave when things get tough. I thought I'd try staying this time—see how that works for me."

"And?" Casey raised a cautious brow, but Jacqueline thought she detected a softening in her tone.

Jacqueline gave her a wry smile. "It's too early to tell."

"If I give you credit for staying, will you leave?"

Jacqueline stood. Though her instinct was to go to Casey rather than to the door, she didn't make a move in either direction. "If that's what you want."

"It is."

She nodded. A part of her expected Casey to crumble in the face of her gesture—at least she could have seemed to consider it for a second before she outright rejected her. She skirted around the coffee table as opposed to crossing closer to Casey, but she stopped again before she left.

"I don't want to lose you," she said to the closed door in front of her.

"Jacq—"

"Please, let me say this." She turned, then wished she hadn't. The anguish in Casey's eyes gutted her. "We are Sean's—" She stopped. This moment had nothing to do with Sean, and to pretend otherwise was a cop-out. "I picked a fight back there." She nodded toward the bedroom. "Because I'm scared. We've been amicable for years, but lately—something's changing. Even if it only leads to us being friends again, it matters to me. You matter—so much. And that scares the shit out of me."

"I don't know what I'm supposed to do with all of that. I want to believe you. I know we took a risk, but, for once, I let go of logic and went with my emotions. Yet instead of being there with me, while I was basking in what had just happened between us, you were trying to figure out how to tell me you regretted it."

"I don't—"

"You called it a mistake." Casey shook her head and lifted her hands in a hopeless gesture.

"I don't regret the connection, both physical and emotional, that I felt with you today. But that means the whole day, not just the sex. If the sex jeopardizes my chance to have any kind of relationship with you, maybe it was a mistake. But it's one we've already made, so if we can move past it and still have something substantial, it will have been worth it."

"What does substantial mean? What are you asking me for?"

"I don't know." Jacqueline shrugged, at a loss herself. "The truth is, we don't have just ourselves to consider."

"I need time to think." Casey folded her arms across her chest gently, as if protecting herself rather than in anger.

"Can we talk in a couple of days?" She wanted a timeline.

"I'll call you."

Jacqueline nodded, then slipped through the door and down the walk to her car. During the drive back to her condo, she rolled the windows down, turned on the radio, and did her best to drown out her own thoughts. She would spend plenty of time analyzing this night, but she didn't need to rush that process. For now, she hoped that sticking around and baring her emotions would be enough to keep from losing Casey altogether.

CHAPTER NINETEEN

Sunday morning, Jacqueline sipped a heavenly Bloody Mary, perfectly crafted with just the right amount of heat. She relaxed in a wrought-iron chair, soaking in the warmth of the sun on her arms and neck. Instead of scooting into the shade of the umbrella overhead, she slipped on her sunglasses.

"Does Gavin know we're here? Won't he be jealous?" She'd been surprised when Kendra suggested they check out the brunch at the new spot in SoBro that boasted a James Beard award-winning chef.

"I'm just assessing the competition. I'll report back to him and we'll call it research."

"Well, tell him the Bloody Marys get two thumbs up." Jacqueline raised her glass. "And I made that plural because I fully intend to drink more than one."

"Any particular reason?"

"Um, because they're delicious." She took another sip to demonstrate her point and to keep from giving a more detailed answer. After yesterday, she shouldn't have accepted Kendra's invitation to brunch. Overindulging in alcohol was also a very bad idea in her current state of mind. "We had this amazing day together yesterday."

"We did?" Kendra smirked at her.

"Casey and I."

"Yeah, I figured." Kendra lifted her mimosa, but instead of taking a drink, she gave Jacqueline a contemplative look. "So why, after this *amazing* day, are you so miserable?"

"We argued."

"That's not new. What happened?"

"Order whatever you want to try, and we'll share." Jacqueline waved away the menu when Kendra tried to pass it to her.

Kendra gave their order to the young waiter. Jacqueline raised her nearly empty glass, silently asking for another, and he nodded. When he'd left, Kendra turned back to Jacqueline.

"We slept together, and then I told her it was a mistake."

Kendra coughed, then set her glass down and stared at Jacqueline. "What are you doing?"

"I really don't know."

"If you needed a punch in the gut, you could have called me."

Jacqueline chuckled. "You'd punch me?"

"I wouldn't enjoy it." Kendra propped her elbow on the table and leaned forward, studying Jacqueline with far too much intensity. "How's Casey today?"

"I don't—she sort of kicked me out."

"So you had sex with her, then left? Your usual MO then?" Kendra's voice dripped with sarcasm and more bitterness than Jacqueline expected.

"That's not fair."

"What were you thinking?"

"Clearly, I wasn't." Jacqueline set her glass down, suddenly too nauseated to drink. "You're the one who's always pushing me to move things forward with her."

"Yeah, I said talk to her. Not screw her and desert her."

Though she'd been berating herself since yesterday afternoon, now she felt compelled to defend herself. She rubbed her finger between her eyebrows. "I did try. After she asked me to leave, I stayed and we talked, a little."

"Damn, I can't imagine how she's feeling today. I need to call her."

"Can you care for just a second about what I'm experiencing? You know how I feel about her, Kendra. And yesterday—I wasn't exaggerating—it was one of the best days I've had in so long. And I'm not just talking about the sex. We were hanging out, just the two of us, and it was so relaxing and really a good time."

"Then tell me what happened." Kendra still looked skeptical.

"You want to make me the villain here. But she kissed me. Then I backed off. But when I dropped her off at her house, I asked her if I could come in to talk."

"I'm sure you were only interested in talking."

"Come on, Kendra, stop looking at me like that. She came on to me. I couldn't—" Jacqueline's phone buzzed a text notification. She glanced at the screen, then set it down with a sigh.

"Casey?"

She shook her head. "Marti. I'm going to Atlanta next week to meet with Owen about some recent issues, and she wants to get together."

"Are you still sleeping with her?"

"No."

"Does Marti know that?"

"Yes. Well, maybe. We left it in a weird place last time. But I haven't slept with anyone in a while."

"Until last night."

"Yeah."

"So are you meeting Marti?"

"Probably."

"And you think that's a good idea?"

"I owe her a conversation."

"I thought they were just hookups. No attachment."

"They are. Were. But Marti—"

"Do you have feelings for her?" Kendra's expression grew fierce, protective, but not of Jacqueline. Apparently everyone in Jacqueline's life felt they needed to protect Casey from her.

"Yes. But not like you mean. I care about her. If circumstances were different, I think we could be friends. But I love Casey."

Jacqueline sat back and waited while the waiter deposited plates in front of each of them. She stared at the fried-egg sandwich with bacon and avocado. Kendra had actually called her order pretty well. It looked like the kind of thing she'd normally choose. But today, she had no appetite. Kendra's pulled-pork omelet looked even less appealing.

"You've probably blown any second chances with Casey." Kendra laid her napkin across her lap and picked up her fork. "How did you two leave it?"

"I told her I didn't want to lose her, even if we only have friendship. She asked for time to think." Jacqueline shrugged, though she felt anything but ambivalent. "I'll go to Atlanta and get my own head straight. Hopefully when I get back we can talk. We've been in such a good place lately."

"A really good place, it sounds like." Kendra gave her a cheeky smile and sipped her drink.

Jacqueline laughed. She could always count on Kendra for a welcoming shoulder and a bad joke.

❖

"What's up, dude?" Casey called to Sean as she walked into the living room with one of her larger camera bags slung over her shoulder. She'd returned from an outdoor shoot, surprised to find his car in her driveway on a Tuesday afternoon. Since she apparently had some muscle waiting, she'd left the bulk of her gear in the car for him to fetch later. He sat half-reclined on the couch with a bowl of popcorn in his lap.

He gave her a look that said she was too old to say *dude*. "Cable's out in the dorms."

"God forbid you study instead."

"Exactly." He grinned at her. "Besides, I needed to do laundry."

"You usually wait until the weekend. Have you got a hot date or something?"

He suddenly found something very interesting in his popcorn bowl.

"You do!" She'd been teasing, but she knew his guilty look. She plopped down next to him, purposely sitting closer than he would prefer. "Who is she?"

She could practically see him weighing the idea of stonewalling before he spoke. "A girl in my Intro to Ag Engineering class."

She raised her brows, prompting him to go on.

"Mom, she's just a girl. I barely know her."

"What's her name?"

"Gemma."

"So you met her in class and asked her out?" He'd had one serious girlfriend in high school, but after they'd broken up, he'd only dated occasionally. She always required him to tell her who he was hanging out with, friends or girlfriends. She'd known his closest friends, but he didn't share more than he had to about girls.

"Something like that." He glanced up. "We're just going to a movie. Don't make a big deal."

She stifled her urge to question him further. He genuinely seemed nervous. "Do you need any money—for the movie or dinner?"

He shook his head. "I'm a grown man. I don't need my mom to pay for my dates."

"You're a college student. Don't be too proud."

"I'm good. But thanks."

"Okay. Have you talked to Mama?" She shouldn't use her son to get information about her ex. That wasn't good parenting. She hadn't been brave enough to call Jacqueline yet. She hadn't made any decisions in the three days since she'd last seen her. Every time she tried to sort out what she wanted, or where they might end up, her mind teased her with images of their afternoon in bed. She couldn't possibly be objective about the future when she could only focus on the feeling of being in Jacqueline's arms.

"Nope." He shoved another handful of popcorn in his mouth. And she thought that might be all she'd get out of him. "She's in Atlanta."

Atlanta. Marti. "She said she'd be out of town, but I don't think she said where."

"Yeah, until Thursday. Meetings or something. You know, important stuff."

That certainly sounded better than saying she'd run off to Atlanta for some no-strings sex to chase what they'd done out of her head. She couldn't even wait long enough for Casey to come to her before she went looking for a diversion.

"What's going on with you two anyway?" He glanced at her, but his gaze seemed sharper, as if he was forcing nonchalance.

"Nothing." Did he hear her voice waver? "What do you mean?"

"You've been spending a lot of time with her lately. Are you getting back together?"

"It sounds like you don't want us to."

"It's not that simple. I did. When I was a kid, for a long time I wanted you guys to make up. But what kid doesn't want their parents together? Being adopted and having two moms already made me different. Having two moms who are also dating other women—" He stopped, seemingly at a loss as to how to explain.

"Wasn't easy, huh?"

"So maybe there's a part of me that will always want that." He turned toward her, fully engaging. "Nina and I were never going to be best friends. But it seemed like you were happy with her. If it's not her, there must be someone else out there for you."

"Just not Mama."

"I don't know. Maybe Mama isn't so good at being with one person for a long time."

"Actually, she was pretty good at it. We spent thirteen years with each other." Casey's throat ached and tears burned her eyes. She brushed the fringe of his hair back off his face, surprised that he didn't pull away. "I know it's hard to remember past those last few years, but there was a time—your mama and I were very good to each other."

"Until me?"

"Oh, baby—"

"You know what, just forget it." He turned back toward the television and pulled the popcorn bowl into his lap.

She'd heard him try to shut down after a similar discussion with Jacqueline, and she wouldn't let him do it again. "Sean, look at me." His jaw tightened in resistance, and when he yielded to her mom-voice and turned his head, his eyes flashed with a lingering trace of defiance. "Our problems weren't simple. I don't think any couple's are. But you were not the cause of them." She squeezed his shoulder.

"Do you still love her?"

"Of course. Always will. But being together takes more than just love."

He tilted his head and she waited, despite the urge to fill the silence. Finally, he nodded and lifted his chin toward the bag she'd dropped by the end of the couch. "Since that's all you brought in, I'm guessing you have stuff in the car I need to grab."

"You're such a great son."

"Yeah, yeah."

"Maybe I'll call Poppa and see if he wants company for dinner. Do you want to go with me?"

He shrugged. "Sure." He grabbed another handful of popcorn as he stood up.

"Are you even going to be hungry?"

He gave her the smart-ass look he'd learned from Jacqueline when he was six. "Have you met me?" He stuck out his stomach and slapped his hand against it, grinning at the hollow-watermelon sound.

While he unloaded the car, Casey grabbed her camera bag and went into her studio. At her desk, she woke up her computer. She'd intended to start working on the photos from today's shoot, but when her screen illuminated, the pictures she'd taken at Bledsoe Creek came up in her editing software. She'd transferred them over Sunday afternoon, but then, still confused about her argument with Jacqueline, she hadn't had the heart to look at them.

She scanned several thumbnails, dismissing images that didn't stand out. When one grabbed her eye, she enlarged it. She remembered taking a series of shots featuring the small grouping of ducks. Their dark-brown heads faded down their necks into light-tan bodies mottled with variegated brown feathers. Their monochromatic nature, further enhanced when placed against the drab tones of bare trees and dry leaves at the waters' edge, had interested her. The one male of the group stood out, with his yellow beak and darker feathers.

"Nice." Sean looked over her shoulder.

"Right? There's something about it."

"Definitely. You expect autumn shots to have these brilliant reds and oranges, but this captures another side of the season."

She smiled with pride. "Why couldn't you have been a photographer?"

"I know. Instead, I'll be wasting my life in veterinary school."

"It's not too late to change your mind." She raised her eyebrows with false optimism. "I need a good apprentice."

"I actually agree. You do." He pulled a stool over and sat down next to her, his expression turning serious. "I still want to help you with Kendra's wedding. But I was thinking next semester I might get a job at an animal hospital."

"Oh, of course." She tried to hide her disappointment.

"It's not that I don't want to work with you. But you know how much competition there is for post-grad openings. I need all the experience I can get."

"I know."

"You should reach out to the art school and find an actual photography student to help out. Maybe talk to the program director and see if they could offer course credit or something."

"I'll think about it." He had a good idea. But she'd never worked with anyone else. In the beginning, she couldn't afford to. By the time she'd built the business up enough to justify an average wage for an assistant, Sean had been happy to fill the spot. Now, the idea of bringing in someone else would be a big adjustment.

"You're not just saying that?"

"Why are you so ready to shove me off on someone else?"

"Mom." She'd used that same chastising tone on him numerous times. "You're talented and passionate. A student who's just as excited about the work as you are could really learn a lot from you. And maybe you'd get something out of it, too."

"I'll consider it."

"Great. I'm going to finish my movie."

Casey went back to flipping through the pictures from last weekend. When she reached the series she'd taken of Jacqueline, she stopped. She'd said at the time that Jacqueline looked distant, but now she saw that it was more than that. She appeared almost sad. She tried to remember what they'd been talking about right before that moment. Jacqueline had handed over Casey's bird book. The mood had been light and familiar—one of their more stress-free interactions. And when she turned around, Jacqueline had taken her breath away. She stared out over the water, not moving even when the wind swept a strand of hair across her face.

She'd been taken by Jacqueline's beauty and the simplicity of the moment. But looking at the photo now, she couldn't recapture that feeling. The day had been colored by what happened after. She should have said no when Jacqueline asked to come in, especially since she still felt weak from that kiss at the park. But Jacqueline's assertion that they should try something other than their usual communication pattern had caught her off guard.

Then, she had a whole list of "should-haves" in regard to sleeping with her. She should have stopped it after the kiss, before the shower, after the shower—any one of those times, really. She'd been angry when Jacqueline said having sex was a mistake, but actually, the comment hadn't been so out of character for her. Jacqueline panicked—and when she did, she tried to back out of a situation as quickly as possible. Casey had acted predictably as well. She knew what to say to cut Jacqueline the deepest, and when they argued, she'd never hesitated to inflict pain.

Finding Jacqueline still in the living room afterward had been the surprise. The openness and naked honesty of that exchange was what had Casey reeling. Though Jacqueline had agreed to give her time to think, she'd made it clear that she both wanted to talk further and to maintain some kind of relationship. But Casey couldn't have another conversation until she knew for certain what she wanted from Jacqueline.

She was becoming more and more convinced that she wanted another chance at a relationship, but she worried that they would put the feelings of their family on the line along with their own. They both needed to have changed, or the outcome would likely be the same. And even if she could figure her own self out, she didn't know if one brave stand in the living room was enough to convince her that Jacqueline had.

CHAPTER TWENTY

Jacqueline poured a splash of rum into a glass, topped it with Coke, and dropped in a few ice cubes. As soon as she'd returned to her room, she'd grabbed the ice bucket and made a quick trip to the vending area down the hall. She didn't usually indulge in anything from the minibar, but she didn't feel like going to the hotel bar.

She'd just finished making her drink when she heard a knock at the door. After she answered it, she wished she'd insisted she and Marti meet downstairs. She'd thought they needed a little privacy for this conversation. But Marti had shown up in her flight-attendant uniform, and Jacqueline was kind of a sucker for the high-waisted skirt and that scarf tied around her neck.

"Hey, come on in." She stepped back, then closed the door behind her. She lifted her glass. "Rum and Coke. Can I make you a drink?"

"No, thanks." Marti sat on the edge of the bed and crossed her legs. Jacqueline's eyes followed as if they had no choice, and when she jerked them back to Marti's face she found a look of satisfaction. "I didn't think I'd be hearing from you again." Marti patted the bed beside her.

"I didn't either." Jacqueline chose the chair across the room instead. "I need to apologize for the last time we saw each other."

"You really don't." Marti's gaze flickered as if searching Jacqueline's expression. "It's Casey, isn't it?"

"No. Yes. Kind of." Ending a previously satisfying casual sexual relationship over a woman she had little chance at getting back with could go down as the stupidest thing she'd ever done.

Marti uncrossed, then recrossed her legs. "I hope you're not expecting me to be honorable and tell you that you should be with her."

"I'm not."

"Good. Because I'm not that woman. I know you guys were together for a while, but that was ages ago and it didn't work out for a reason, right?"

Jacqueline nodded.

"This—what we have—it works for me. It's easy, and we both know what it is. I'm not looking for more. But I don't want to give it up either."

Though she thought she knew the answer, she let herself consider whether she could continue to sleep with Marti. They'd never had any expectation of commitment, and Marti said she didn't want one now. Unfortunately, Jacqueline did. And not with Marti. "I think I have to."

"For her?"

She shook her head. "For me."

"And when she doesn't take you back, will you be calling me again?"

"No. I respect you too much to do that."

Marti raised her brows. "And if I'm not looking for your respect?"

Jacqueline stood and paced to the window. Shit, Marti didn't play fair with that sexy little growl. She could try to lose herself in sex with Marti, but she'd be lying if she said she wouldn't think about Casey. "This isn't about you. It's about what I need."

"We've never been monogamous. Why does anything have to change?"

"Maybe you're right. It is about her—a little bit, at least. Casey and I may not be together, but I'm realizing that nothing less is acceptable to me." Before Marti could respond, Jacqueline's phone vibrated against the nightstand. Jacqueline grabbed it and read the display. "I'm sorry. I need to call Sean. He says it's important."

"Of course."

She dialed and stepped over by the window. Sean answered right away. "What's up?" she asked.

"Don't freak out. Everyone's okay."

A jolt of fear jumped into her throat. "What's going on?"

"I'm at the hospital with Mom—"

"What happened? Is she okay?" The alarm grew, nearly taking her breath away.

"Yes. It's Poppa. He burned himself pretty bad, and Mom, too." He spoke quickly and started to sound panicky himself.

"Slow down. Tell me what happened." She forced herself to stay silent while he explained that he and Casey had been at her father's for dinner. Her father was trying to move a pot of boiling water from the stove to the sink when he spilled it, splashing his arms and chest.

Before Jacqueline could ask why Sean and Casey had let him tend to boiling water, he said, "Mom said she only turned her back for a second before he grabbed the pot. She's pretty upset. And when he got burned he dropped it, and water splashed on Mom's legs. She's got some burns, too. The doctor said hers are minor."

Jacqueline paced across the room. "Okay, I'm still in Atlanta. I'll make a few calls and see if someone can cover my meeting tomorrow, and then—"

"Don't worry about it, Mama." Sean sounded more confident. "I just wanted to let you know about Poppa. They'll probably be released before you can get here anyway. I'll take them home, and if they need someone with them tomorrow, I can skip class."

Numbly, Jacqueline mumbled a response that Sean seemed satisfied with, since he then said good-bye and hung up. Jacqueline lowered her phone and sank onto the edge of the bed.

"Is everything okay?" Marti scooted closer and rubbed her back.

"Yeah." Sean hadn't even hesitated. They didn't need her. Her family *expected* to handle things without her. Casey had covered for her for years, and now apparently Sean was taking responsibility, too. "I have to go."

"Now?" Marti reached for her hand, but Jacqueline jerked it away and stood. "I'd hoped at least for a chance to change your mind."

"I'm sorry. That's not going to happen."

"You said everything was okay. Maybe you should stay for the night and drive in the morning."

"I have to go now." She finally looked at Marti and felt badly for how she'd treated her. They'd said again and again that they didn't expect anything from their relationship, but she could see from Marti's disappointment that she'd thought they would at least continue as they were. "I really am sorry."

Marti seemed to understand her apology wasn't about today's departure. She shook her head stiffly. "I have no regrets. And hey, just because we're not sleeping together doesn't mean we can't have dinner when you're in town. I wasn't just using you for your body, you know."

Jacqueline laughed. "Of course. I'll keep in touch."

"Okay. You have some packing to do. I'll get out of your way."

After she'd seen Marti out, Jacqueline hastily got ready and headed for her car. Thankfully, she'd taken only a couple sips from her drink and could make the trip with a clear head. She'd call Owen while she drove and explain that she'd be unavailable for her meetings tomorrow.

❖

Jacqueline pulled into her father's driveway just after midnight. She hadn't gone to her condo first, instead driving straight from the hotel. The house was dark, so she tried to be as quiet as possible as she let herself in the front door. The groan of the hinges and the slide of the deadbolt as she locked it behind her echoed through the silence.

She turned toward the living room and found Sean stretched out on the couch across the darkened room. She slipped out of her shoes before she walked farther in. Sean stirred and lifted his head.

"Hey, sorry if I woke you," she whispered.

"That's okay. Poppa's couch sucks anyway." He sat up and made room for her next to him, his legs bridging the space from the couch to the coffee table.

"Why aren't you in the guest room?"

"Mom's in there. I told her to go home, but she insisted on staying with Poppa."

Jacqueline nodded. Casey wouldn't leave her father's care all on Sean. But she apparently didn't need Jacqueline either. She hadn't even called her.

"I told her I talked to you." Apparently, Sean could read her better than she thought. "But I didn't think you'd come home early."

She bit her lip, stifling comments born of hurt feelings. Maybe she should be happy that her family helped each other so readily and that Sean took his responsibility to their family seriously. But a part of her wanted them to need her. Sean yawned and pushed back into the couch as if trying to get comfortable again.

"Okay. Let's get some sleep." She stood and tapped him on the foot.

"You're staying?"

"I'm here. No sense driving back to my condo now. I want to check on them tonight and again in the morning."

He pulled the other blanket off the back of the couch and tossed it to her. She dropped it on the recliner, where she'd catch a couple hours of sleep. Sean rolled over and faced the back of the couch, demonstrating an ability to fall back into sleep that Jacqueline hadn't had since she was a worry-free teenager.

As she stood there listening to his snores, she replayed the last several hours. She'd driven home as quickly as she could, hearing her father's and Casey's warnings in her head as she traversed over Monteagle Mountain faster than was probably safe at that time of night. She knew they were fine. Sean had told her as much on the phone. Neither would even be admitted to the hospital. But still she worried all the way home that something had gone wrong since she last spoke to him. She struggled sometimes, knowing that someday she would go off on a trip and her father wouldn't be there to tell her to be safe. Hearing Sean tell her that her father was at the hospital had reminded her that she wasn't ready for that day. But it would come whether she was ready or not. And she'd be left with only the memories of how she spent this time—right now. She'd made some poor decisions in that regard lately, and she wasn't quite sure how she would fix the situation, but she was determined to try. For now, she needed to see him—to see them—and to know they were okay.

She eased open the door to her father's room first, relieved when she saw him. She'd take a closer look at his burns tomorrow, but Sean had said most of the water had missed him and splashed on the floor. He'd been left with some blisters and reddened skin. Casey and Sean had taken him to the hospital to be safe.

She paused outside the guest room—her childhood bedroom. She didn't hear any noise from within and shouldn't risk waking Casey. But she pushed the door open a crack anyway. Casey lay sprawled out across the bed. She'd stripped the bed of all but the sheet, and even it was folded and rumpled, as if she'd been restless. Her right leg stuck out, but a bandage obscured her calf. Jacqueline's chest clenched at the thought of even minor burns marring the skin beneath. Casey began to roll over, but when her left leg lay against her right, she whimpered and flipped onto her back.

A bottle of pills, probably for pain, sat on the nightstand next to the lamp. Jacqueline didn't want to disturb her, but she didn't seem to be getting restful sleep anyway. She headed back to the kitchen for a glass of water.

❖

"Sweetie."

Casey felt Jacqueline's hand on her forehead, heard her soft whisper. She fought her way through the fog and opened her eyes. She thought she'd been dreaming, but Jacqueline sat on the edge of the bed next to her.

"Jacqueline?"

"I'm here. You looked like you were having trouble sleeping. Is it time for another one of those?" She nodded toward the pills.

"Probably. I need some—"

"Water." Jacqueline lifted a glass Casey hadn't noticed she'd been holding. She set it on the nightstand and picked up the painkillers. Casey sat up while Jacqueline shook a pill into her palm. "More?"

"No. Just one. I'm trying not to overdo it."

"The bottle says two."

"One."

"Stubborn." Jacqueline gave her the water.

"Yes." Casey smiled, then tossed back her medicine. "What are you doing here, anyway? Sean said he told you we were okay."

"My family is here." Jacqueline shrugged. "Besides, I was thinking I've never slept in Dad's recliner, and he always seems to really enjoy it."

"Jacq—"

"Don't bother. I'm staying."

Casey could spend half the night arguing with her or just accept that they would have a full house and get some rest. She took Jacqueline's hand and tried to pull her into bed. "Come on. You can sleep with me."

Jacqueline resisted. "Casey—"

"You're not sleeping in that recliner all night. Please, don't argue with me. I'm too exhausted, and from the looks of you, so are you. It's not like either of us has the energy for anything but sleep."

Jacqueline nodded and stood. She took the glass from Casey and set it back on the nightstand, then circled to the other side of the bed, straightening the sheet as she went.

Casey scooted back down, being careful as she adjusted her injured leg under the covers. As soon as the painkillers kicked in, she'd be comfortable enough to drift off again. She lay on her back, in deference to her leg, and rolled her head to the side, coming face-to-face with Jacqueline as she stretched out next to her.

"Are you okay?" Jacqueline glanced toward Casey's legs.

"I'm fine."

"God, if anything happened to you." Jacqueline's voice sounded as if she'd forced the words through broken glass. She closed her eyes and Casey touched her cheek, wanting them open again—needing to see what those beautiful eyes gave away. When they did, she found a depth of pain that surprised her.

"Hey, I'm fine. It's a minor burn." She stroked her thumb along Jacqueline's cheekbone and curled her fingers against her jaw.

Jacqueline covered her hand and held it in place. "I know I said I'd give you space to think and we would talk later, but tonight—getting that call from Sean—only made me realize what I probably should have already known. I can't do any of this without you in my life."

A traitorous bubble of hope clogged Casey's throat. She shouldn't do this now. She'd had a stressful day and would likely react too emotionally to anything Jacqueline said. She pulled her hand back, depending on mere inches of mattress to be a good-enough barrier between them. "Can we talk in the morning?"

"Yes. But I need you to know something. Dad's problems aren't going away. He'll probably get worse in the coming years. You're as much his family as Sean and I are. So that means we're going to be working together to take care of him, at the very least."

"I agree. We'll figure it out in the morning." She rolled over, facing away from Jacqueline. Her speech was starting to sound like one of those "let's just be friends" moments. And Casey wasn't sure if she was more afraid it would be or that it wouldn't. Before tonight, she might have welcomed smoothing their tension back into a friendly place. But waking to find Jacqueline in her room had thrown her. Sean had assured her that he'd relayed their minor injuries and told Jacqueline she didn't need to come home. But she had. She'd chosen them.

Casey closed her eyes and shut out her own analysis of what that might mean for the two of them. She'd said they would talk tomorrow. Tonight, she'd fall asleep to the sound of Jacqueline's breathing and the wonderfully radiant heat of another person next to her in bed.

She still hovered at the edge of consciousness when she felt a light touch at her waist.

"Casey?"

For some reason, Casey didn't respond. And when Jacqueline spoke again, she suspected Jacqueline thought she was asleep.

"I love you." After a few quiet seconds, Jacqueline inched closer, sliding her arm more fully around Casey's waist. Jacqueline curved her body around Casey's, just touching her but not fully cuddling into her. Casey held still for as long as she could. When she heard Jacqueline's breathing begin to even out, she took her hand, eased it even more around her, and held it between her breasts. She closed her eyes and let Jacqueline's breath against the back of her neck lull her into unconsciousness.

CHAPTER TWENTY-ONE

Casey opened her eyes to the distant sound of a cell phone ringing in another room. The ringtone wasn't hers, so she was surprised she'd even heard it. A board creaked in the hallway, and she suspected Jacqueline leaving the bed had actually awakened her.

She threw her hands over her head, enjoying a deep stretch before getting up. She wished she could say waking this way felt unusual, but finding Jacqueline gone to answer her phone had been pretty common. She'd been running in circles trying to figure out if they'd changed enough to take another chance. Maybe this phone call, whoever it was, was the universe's way of telling her things remained the same. Jacqueline might have driven home the night before, worried about their safety, but the moment she knew they were okay, work took the front seat again.

She was both sad and a little relieved that it appeared her decision was made. They should just go back to the way things were—cordial, responsible co-parenting, maybe even someday—friends.

She didn't hear any movement from Teddy's room yet, so she headed for the kitchen to make some coffee. As she approached, she could hear Jacqueline's voice. She probably should have returned to the bedroom or at least backed away to give her some privacy, but she could hear the stress in Jacqueline's tone, and curiosity got the better of her. She stood close to the entryway to the kitchen, angled so she wasn't noticeable but could see Jacqueline. Jacqueline had her back to Casey, looking through the window at the backyard. She clutched her cell phone in one hand, her other one braced against the countertop.

"Owen, I can't—" Jacqueline clenched her fist and shook her head. "Can't anyone else cover it for me? Yes, I know other people had to come in from out of town. It's not like I planned to have an emergency." She pantomimed slamming her hand down on the counter in front of her, stopping just short of making contact. "Yes, everyone's fine. But I can't just turn around and leave them again."

Casey could hear Owen's rapid speech through the phone but couldn't make out what he said.

"I know it's my job, but this is my family." Whatever Owen said next pissed Jacqueline off. She straightened and shoved her shoulders back. "Yes. You've always been able to count on me." Her voice was ice cold. She tilted her head to the left as if coming to a decision. "The problem is, you're the only one who's been able to."

Casey's sharply indrawn breath filled the silence that followed Jacqueline's words. She grabbed the doorframe beside her. Jacqueline spun around, and her eyes filled with tears as they met Casey's.

"I let her raise Sean basically without me, and I'll be damned if I'll bail on them now. If that means making some adjustments to my career path, then so be it."

Casey shook her head in disbelief. Had Jacqueline lost her mind? As prideful as Owen was, he wouldn't stand for her speaking to him that way. She started to turn away to give Jacqueline privacy to finish her call, but Jacqueline crossed the room quickly, grabbed her hand, and pulled her close. Casey wrapped her arms around Jacqueline's waist and rested her cheek against Jacqueline's.

"Shit, Owen. I don't know. I need to figure some things out. I can't go back to Atlanta right now. In fact, I won't be in the office the rest of this week. Can we talk on Monday?" Jacqueline trembled in spite of her confident tone. Casey held her tighter and pressed her lips to her jaw, just in front of her ear. She closed her eyes and concentrated, not on Jacqueline's conversation, but on the love flowing through her own heart. The decision she'd made in the bedroom only moments ago crumbled.

Even after Jacqueline hung up the phone and set it on the counter beside them, Casey held on, not saying anything.

"Casey—"

Casey kissed her. Jacqueline's lips moved hesitantly against hers, but she didn't mind. She wasn't trying to escalate this kiss into anything more than a simple expression of gratitude. Jacqueline sighed against Casey's mouth, then eased back and rested their foreheads together. She cupped the back of Casey's neck in a way that had always made Casey feel safe—protected.

"Don't do anything rash, please. You've worked very hard for the career you have. I don't want you to throw that away," Casey said.

"I wasn't making idle threats." Jacqueline's fingers tightened and she pushed harder against Casey's head, as if trying to get closer. "You, Dad, and Sean—you mean everything. I'm so sorry I ever lost sight of that."

Casey stroked Jacqueline's face. She hadn't planned to have this conversation first thing this morning. But Jacqueline's call with Owen might have been the catalyst for their future. "I—you came home."

"Sean told me that you and Dad were fine. But I just—had to see you."

Casey hadn't noticed Sean when she passed through the living room. He'd left a note on the kitchen counter—an entire sheet of haphazardly torn notebook paper that had only "school" scrawled across it. "You were in Atlanta."

It wasn't a question, but Jacqueline nodded anyway.

"Did you see Marti?"

"I was with her when Sean called." Casey started to pull away, but Jacqueline held onto her. "I'd just told her I couldn't be involved with her anymore."

"You had?"

"Did you really think I could just go sleep with her, given how we'd left things?"

Casey shrugged.

"Well, then, just so there's no doubt. I didn't sleep with Marti. I haven't slept with anyone since before you and Nina broke up."

"Wow. Is that a record?"

"It might be." Jacqueline smiled, and then her expression grew serious. "I know I'm supposed to be waiting for you to be ready to talk. But I need to say some things before we decide what's going to happen between us." Jacqueline released her and took a step back, but she maintained eye contact, keeping their connection strong. "I've made so many mistakes and excuses. I know we had problems before—before Elle, but afterward, I used my job to run away from you. I shut down exactly when we should have been opening up together. And now, I'm scared I'll wake up at seventy years old with a bunch more regrets and wishing I hadn't let you go."

"You're afraid of ending up alone." Casey had heard Jacqueline's apologies before, and she'd made her share of them as well. But somehow they always ended up in the same place.

"No." Jacqueline grabbed Casey's wrist. "I'm afraid of being without *you*."

"Jacq—"

"It's you, Casey. It has been since the day you walked into our poker game in that ridiculous scarf."

"It wasn't ridiculous."

"It hid your cleavage."

Casey smiled.

"The point is, I loved you almost immediately and every day since, in one way or another. Yes, I've learned how to live without you. But my life is fuller with you in it. Please, give us another chance?" Her expression was sincere—but more than that, she was incredibly open. Jacqueline had put herself out there farther than at any other point in their relationship.

"I want to try," Casey said, but when Jacqueline stepped toward her, Casey put her hand on her chest, stopping her. "But I don't know how I'll ever get over you again."

"You won't have to."

"You think we're different enough?"

"Yes. I'll never put my job in front of my family again. I don't know yet what that means for me professionally, except that I've decided I don't want to chase Owen's job only to get it and find out I'm lonelier than ever." Jacqueline took Casey's hands in hers. "I know I said you'd have to beg if you wanted me back. But I never did a good enough job letting you know how much I needed you all of those years—how much I need you now. So, I'm prepared to plead for our future."

"I don't think that will be necessary."

"Then let's try a fresh start, get to know each other all over again, for who we are today. Would you like to go on a date with me?"

"A date?" Casey smiled coyly. "That depends. Where would you like to take me?"

Jacqueline's eyes darkened in a way that always made Casey weak. "While I can think of all kinds of places I'd like to take you, we should probably start with dinner."

Casey struggled to shut out the image of Jacqueline dominating her. When she spoke, her voice sounded unnaturally high and tense. "Dinner?"

"Yes. A quiet evening at my condo. I'd like to cook for you."

"Okay. I think I can handle that."

"Yeah."

"Yes."

Jacqueline's smile was so wide and full of love that Casey couldn't help but return it. Jacqueline caught her in an embrace that lifted Casey's feet off the floor. When she set her back down, she kissed her. Giving in to her strongest urge, Casey wrapped her arms around Jacqueline's neck and deepened the kiss.

"When?" Casey asked.

"As it turns out, I'm free for the rest of the week. What are you doing tonight?"

"I have a shoot this afternoon, but I'll be free in plenty of time."

"Are you okay to do that?" Jacqueline glanced at her leg. "Do you need any help? Someone to do the heavy lifting? I think I can still take orders pretty well."

"As much as I hate to turn down free labor, it's a portrait session in my studio, so I think I can handle it. In fact, I should grab my stuff and head home to get ready."

"If you're sure. I think I'll spend the day hanging out here with Dad. So if something changes, call and I can run over there."

"I will. Text me later and let me know what time to head over for this gourmet dinner and what to bring."

"Who said gourmet?"

"Don't worry." Casey rested her hand on Jacqueline's chest and gave her a peck on the lips. "I know you can't cook."

Jacqueline hummed to herself as she returned to the kitchen after she'd showered and changed. She poured a cup of coffee and joined her father in the living room. He sat in his chair, albeit somewhat stiffly, with his own mug. He wore his favorite flannel pajama pants and a black, long-sleeved T-shirt. She searched for signs of injury but didn't see any redness on his visible skin. Sean had said he'd burned his arms and chest.

"How are you feeling?" She settled onto the couch and studied him. He looked tired. He might not have slept comfortably, but it seemed to her like there was more going on.

"Minor burns. Nothing to worry about."

"That's not how I heard it."

"I don't care what you heard. I'm a grown-up and don't need a babysitter—least of all my grandson." The bitterness in his voice surprised her.

"Sean was trying to help." She wouldn't let him diminish the way Sean had stepped up.

He sighed. "I know."

"He did what I wasn't here to do. But that's going to change."

"Quitting your job?" He clearly didn't believe her.

"I don't know how yet. But I'm going to be around more often. For you and for Casey."

"Did she leave already?"

"She has to work. But I'm having dinner with her later."

"That sounds more serious than dinner."

"I hope it will be."

He nodded but didn't say anything more. She didn't push the conversation, respecting his loyalty to both of them. When he sipped his coffee, his mug trembled slightly, and Jacqueline stared at his hand, looking for another sign of weakness.

"She's a good girl." He set his mug on the side table next to him.

Jacqueline laughed. "Yes. She is."

"It'll be good to know that you're not alone."

"Is there something you want to tell me?" She used every ounce of control to keep her tone light while panic tore through her. Either she or Casey had been to every doctor's appointment with him. Could he have a health issue they didn't know about?

He shook his head. "I know I'm not in the best physical health these days. My strength is sapped, and my balance is shot. But I can handle that stuff. I hate how easily I get confused lately. I can't remember what I'm doing from one minute to the next."

Jacqueline nodded, not trusting her voice. She couldn't imagine how he must feel to be aware of the ways his brain was failing him.

"You're having your revelation, I'm having mine. I'm feeling my age, but I'm not going anywhere just yet."

"That's good to know."

"So you don't have to change your life to accommodate me."

She smiled. "I'm doing it for me—adjusting my priorities. This time with you is important to me. As is my future with Casey."

He nodded, and his approval meant more to her than she would have thought possible. All her life, she'd worked hard to make her parents proud. After her mother died, providing for her father had become even more important. At some point, she'd become more his financial support, and Casey had picked up the emotional slack. So, while he was intent on reminding her that he didn't know how much time he had, she was determined to embrace every second of it.

"Hey, Dad. Want to catch a movie or something?" He loved action movies. As a kid, whenever they went to the theater, she and he constantly outvoted her mother's chick-flick choices.

He looked up, clearly surprised. "Don't you have to work?"

"Not today." She stood and picked up their empty mugs. He rose as well, more tentatively, but she resisted the urge to help. "I'll grab my phone and look up the listings. You go get dressed. Just because you're a senile old man doesn't mean I'm letting you run around in public in your pajamas."

He laughed as he walked down the hall to his bedroom. Her heart ached, but for the first time since she'd come home to find him on the floor she felt optimistic. She would focus more on keeping him active, both physically and mentally. She could get him out of the house at least a couple of times a week. She might have reached an age when she had to face the eventuality of losing her one remaining parent, but she didn't have to let go without a fight.

"Come in," Jacqueline called when she heard the knock on her condo door. She'd left it unlocked while she puttered around in the kitchen. She'd just finished checking on the baked chicken and closed the oven door.

"Smells good." Casey handed over a bottle of wine. "I hope white's okay."

"Perfect." She put the bottle in the fridge to chill. "Come in. Sit. Dinner will be a bit longer." She led Casey across the open floor plan into the sitting area by the windows.

"I haven't been here in a while. You've made some changes."

"Furniture and art upgrades. But I didn't choose the art. That's Kendra."

"Of course." Casey wandered around the outside of the room, then stopped in front of one particular piece—a black-and-white photograph of a spiral staircase taken from above and looking down into the stairs. "Did Kendra choose this one, too?"

"Yes."

"I wondered why she insisted on this piece. I knew it wouldn't go in her house."

"I told her I wanted one of yours. I let her decide which one." Jacqueline tried to appear casual as she sat on the couch, but her stomach was in knots over what her admission revealed. She fought her instinct to hold a part of herself back to avoid getting hurt. This was Casey. If she wanted to have a chance, she had to put everything out there.

Casey nodded but didn't say anything more. She joined Jacqueline on the couch, still looking at the room around her.

Suddenly Jacqueline didn't know what to talk about. How was she supposed to act on a first date with a woman she'd known for twenty years? "So, um, did your shoot go well today?"

"It did. And how was your day with Teddy?"

"Really good. We're going to have more days like that." She brushed her hands along her thighs, then folded them in her lap, suddenly unsure what to do with them.

Casey smiled. "You're adorable."

"What? Why?"

"What are you nervous about?"

"I'm not—what?"

"Does tonight feel awkward to you?" Casey slid closer. She put her hand over Jacqueline's and squeezed, encouraging her to unclench her fingers from each other.

"A little."

"Why?"

"I want this to go well, I suppose."

"I love that you care enough to be nervous." Casey leaned in, her breath whispering against Jacqueline's neck as she spoke. "So, what can I do to relax you?" When her lips touched Jacqueline's skin, she jumped.

She should ease away, slow down whatever this was. "I thought we agreed to baby-step this thing."

"You invited me over, cooked me dinner, lit candles, and put on that amazing dress—"

"This old thing?" Jacqueline pulled at the hem of the flared skirt that lay across her lap. She'd picked up the plum-colored dress for a work function but then hadn't worn it. It might be a bit fancy for dinner in her own home, but she'd chosen it to make herself feel more confident.

"All of that makes it very hard for me to hold back." Casey slid her hand under the edge of the skirt and over Jacqueline's knee.

"Are you like this on all your first dates? If so, we may have figured out why you've always been such a popular girl."

"Not all of them." Casey kissed a trail down the side of Jacqueline's neck. "I haven't really had very many first dates, anyway."

"No?" Jacqueline slid her hand around to Casey's back, resting it just above the waistband of her slacks.

"No. Just a handful in the past eight years, and before that—well, I was with the most amazing woman. I didn't have much need for dating."

"Amazing, huh?"

"Mmm." Casey's response was muffled as she opened her mouth low on Jacqueline's throat and bit lightly.

"That's a lot for me to live up to."

Casey shook her head. "I'm certain you can handle it. Besides, I'm not comparing past to present. I plan to enjoy what's in front of me right now."

Casey kissed up her jaw, and Jacqueline lowered her chin until their mouths met in a soft, exquisitely tender kiss. Jacqueline threaded her fingers into Casey's hair and ran her tongue over Casey's lower lip. When Casey opened to her, Jacqueline moaned into her mouth. For eight years, she'd been a jigsaw puzzle in a box—five hundred pieces of something whole. But when Casey touched her, the pieces fit together and she became a beautiful landscape.

"Casey." Jacqueline moaned again when they broke apart. "Wait." She grasped Casey's shoulders. "It's not that I don't want that, because believe me, I do. But I meant what I said about a fresh start. And if us doing this," she waved a finger between them, "is going to jeopardize that in any way, I'm willing to wait."

"You could do that? Just stop right now." Casey smiled.

"I could try." She didn't sound as confident as she wanted to. "Admittedly, keeping my hands off you these past years was easier when you didn't want me."

"I'm not sure I ever didn't want you. But I know what you mean." Casey touched Jacqueline's cheek. "This is not jeopardizing anything. As long as you don't plan to call it a mistake in an hour on your way out the door." Casey winked.

"I'm not leaving." Jacqueline grinned. "This is my place."

"I'm not leaving either. So stop distracting me from where I was headed a moment ago." Casey guided Jacqueline to straddle her lap. She slipped her hand back under Jacqueline's skirt and up her bare thigh until she palmed her panties. "Have I mentioned how much I like this dress?"

"I think you did." Jacqueline was wet already, and Casey's fingers pressing into her threatened her self-control. She closed her eyes, barely managing not to grind against Casey's hand.

"It bears repeating." Casey pushed her underwear aside and dragged a finger through her folds. "I love anything that makes you this accessible."

Jacqueline laughed. "That's so romantic."

"I brought wine. How much more romance do you need?"

When Casey entered her, Jacqueline planted her hands on the back of the couch behind her. "Keep doing that, and I don't need any romance at all."

Casey stroked her maddeningly slow, until Jacqueline began controlling the pace. She rose and drove her hips back down, searching for just the right leverage to ease the tension coiling inside her. Seeing Casey's satisfied grin, Jacqueline forced herself to stop, ground against Casey's hand, and paused.

"What's wrong?" Casey tipped her head back to look at her.

"Absolutely nothing." Jacqueline reached between them and unbuttoned Casey's shirt. With one of Casey's hands trapped between them, she had her at a disadvantage. She slipped her hand inside Casey's shirt and cradled her breast. Her nipple pebbled under Jacqueline's thumb as she rubbed the cup of her bra. Jacqueline squeezed, and Casey's groan made Jacqueline clench around her fingers.

She held her, bracing her other hand on the back of the couch, and moved again. This time, as Casey matched her thrusts, she couldn't have stopped if she'd tried. She released Casey's breast and wrapped her arms around her shoulders, pulling her close. Casey kissed Jacqueline's neck, and Jacqueline's movements quickened.

"Let go, sweetheart. I've got you," Casey whispered into her hair.

Losing control, Jacqueline bounced in Casey's lap. Her head swam with the feel of Casey filling her, and when Casey's teeth raked her neck, she came apart. She stiffened and cried out, grasping Casey desperately as she drove onto her fingers a couple more times, milking the pleasure out of each thrust. Breathing hard, she collapsed against Casey and closed her eyes.

"Jacq?" Casey's low voice vibrated the nickname, and Jacqueline's muscles tightened around Casey's hand.

"I don't think you're allowed to call me that anymore." Jacqueline lifted her head lazily.

"Is something burning?"

Jacqueline took a second to process those words before they sank in. "Shit! Dinner." She rose as carefully as she could, letting Casey withdraw before she jumped off her lap and ran to the kitchen.

She pulled the chicken out of the oven amid a billow of smoke and slid it onto the top of the range. The smoke detector started beeping. She grabbed a towel off the oven handle and waved it toward the alarm on the ceiling.

"Do you think it's salvageable?" Casey cocked her hip against the countertop. Her eyes sparkled with suppressed laughter. Her shirt gaped open, revealing a tempting glimpse of white cotton and skin.

"Absolutely." Jacqueline wanted Casey as much today as she had twenty years ago.

Casey pushed off the counter, crossed the kitchen, and poked at the burnt skin of the chicken with a fork. "I'm not sure. It looks pretty dry."

"No, the food's trashed." Jacqueline peered over Casey's shoulder. She wasn't even going to try to eat that chicken.

"Then what were you talking about?" Casey turned her head and Jacqueline captured her mouth. Casey spun in her arms and embraced her.

"Us," Jacqueline said against her mouth. "Totally salvageable."

"I'm glad you think so," Casey murmured back, her lips buzzing against Jacqueline's.

"I guess we're ordering in." Jacqueline took her hand, not ready to let her go yet, and led her back to the couch. Once they were settled, she flipped open her laptop. "Any requests?"

"Pizza. You know what I like."

Jacqueline clicked through the online menu and ordered their food, then set her computer on the coffee table. "We have thirty minutes or less."

"What should we do while we wait?"

Jacqueline nudged Casey's still-unbuttoned shirt open with one finger. "I can think of a few things."

"Do you think you can beat the pizza guy?"

Jacqueline grabbed Casey's waist, flipped her onto her back on the couch, and moved between her legs. "It's your turn. I should be asking you that."

"I'll do my best."

Jacqueline opened the fly of Casey's pants. Casey lifted her hips as Jacqueline jerked them off and threw them over her shoulder. "I have faith in you."

Chapter Twenty-two

Casey knocked before opening the door to the small room down the hall from the chapel where Kendra and Gavin would exchange their vows. "Is everyone decent?" She curled around the door and pretended to sneak inside.

"I know you're hoping I'm not, but you're too late." Kendra turned from the full-length mirror on the far side of the room.

Her elegant gown hugged her torso, then flared slightly at the waist and fell to the floor in a loose-flowing skirt. The lace cap-sleeves added the only ornate touch on an otherwise simple design that flattered Kendra's figure. Someone with very talented hands had woven her hair into an intricate updo that looked both effortless and complex at the same time.

"You are gorgeous, my friend. I would hug you, but I'm afraid I'll mess something up." Instead, she lifted her camera and fired off several candid shots. "I came to take some pictures of you getting ready. Sean is doing the same with Gavin and the guys."

"By himself?"

"Don't worry. They'll be great. He came up with some creative ideas, and I let him run with them. He's got talent."

"Our boy's going to be a doctor. Stop trying to make him into an artist," Jacqueline said as she came into the room behind Casey.

"Does a veterinarian still count as a doctor?" Kendra asked, teasing.

"Yes. And it makes him smarter than both of us. So leave him alone." Casey turned toward Jacqueline, and her final word nearly turned into a moan. The V-neck of Jacqueline's champagne gown plunged deeper than was decent and exposed the soft swells at the inside of her breasts.

Kendra turned back toward the mirror and fussed with the skirt of her dress.

Jacqueline stepped closer to Casey and kissed her cheek. "You look great."

Casey had opted for a solid-black, wide-legged jumpsuit that allowed her the freedom to move during the ceremony. Jacqueline's eyes dropped to her chest and to the floating pearl necklace she'd given Casey for her birthday a month before. When she lifted the single pearl, her fingers brushed Casey's chest, and Casey shivered.

"I want some shots of you two pre-ceremony." She tried to force her mind back to work. As they both looked at Kendra, Casey rested her hand in the middle of Jacqueline's back, surprised to encounter bare skin. She glanced over Jacqueline's shoulder. The folds of chiffon draped nearly to her waist. "Are you kidding me with this dress?"

"You don't like it?"

Casey had seen the dress on the hanger, but Jacqueline had refused to model it for her, saying only that it would be worth the wait. She was right. "It's amazing. I thought you weren't supposed to be more stunning than the bride?"

"I heard that." Kendra glanced back at them both. "You're not helping my nerves."

"Don't listen to her, Kendra." Jacqueline winked at Casey, then joined Kendra at the mirror. "She's unable to be objective. It's not her fault that I've so thoroughly seduced her."

Casey couldn't even argue. In the two months since they'd agreed to that first dinner date, their relationship had grown stronger than ever. As planned, they'd managed to take things slow, starting with a couple of dates a week. Jacqueline hadn't pushed to accelerate things. In fact, she seemed hesitant—as if she were waiting for Casey to indicate she was ready for more commitment. Casey had told her to leave all those years ago. Though Jacqueline had asked for them to try again, maybe she needed Casey to set the timeline for the final step.

The only area they hadn't held back was their physical relationship. Once Casey had permission to put her hands on Jacqueline, she hadn't been able to restrict herself. And Jacqueline didn't seem to mind at all.

Then, as the frequency of their time together increased, they included Teddy and Sean as well. Casey had been apprehensive when they began to feel too much like a family, waiting for something to go wrong. Their first disagreement had been blown up much bigger than it should have been. But after they'd both calmed down, they acknowledged that their nervousness had caused them to overreact. They both wanted this to work so badly that they saw the first sign of conflict as failure. But when they stopped being so careful with each other, things felt more natural—they had good days and bad ones, and that was okay.

Jacqueline moved behind Kendra, bracketed her waist with her hands, and rested her chin on Kendra's shoulder. "Don't worry. You will be the most beautiful woman in the room. Gavin won't be able to take his eyes off you, and isn't he the only one who matters?"

Kendra grinned at their reflections. "Of course not, it's my wedding day. I want to be the center of everyone's attention."

Casey took several pictures, moving to capture a different angle. She focused on the mirror and got a great shot with their backs in the foreground. She caught a moment when Kendra and Jacqueline looked at each other and the bond between them beamed over both of their faces.

Casey focused on Jacqueline through her viewfinder. If she'd had any lingering doubts, they would have melted away in that moment. She'd shot more weddings than she could count—capturing the beginning of forever for so many couples, as she would now for Kendra and Gavin. Jacqueline glanced over her shoulder at Casey. As she clicked the shutter—freezing the love in Jacqueline's expression—she knew that this woman was her forever.

❖

"Don't let me fall down the aisle," Kendra said to her father.

Jacqueline glanced over her shoulder and smiled. "You'll be fine. But just in case, do you want me to take a dive so no one notices if you do?"

"Okay, smart-ass, it's your turn." Kendra nodded toward the doorway in front of them. The bridesmaid before Jacqueline had already gone through.

Jacqueline took Gavin's brother's elbow and they started forward. Just inside the door, she caught Sean in her peripheral vision. He knelt behind the last pew, looking adorably professional in his shirt and tie with his camera raised in front of his face. She knew he'd worked a bunch of weddings with Casey, but she'd never seen him in this element.

As she walked down the aisle, she smiled at the family and guests in the pews on either side. Up ahead, Casey had found a position that afforded her a clear shot as the wedding party approached the altar. When their eyes met, Jacqueline nearly stumbled. Casey stared back at her and for a moment the room receded.

Jacqueline had enjoyed discovering the ways Casey had grown and changed over the years. At the same time, the things she'd always loved about Casey were still there. Though they still hadn't made long-term plans for the future, she had no doubt that she would do whatever she had to do to hold onto Casey. And seeing the love in Casey's eyes right now, she let herself hope Casey felt the same.

For the past two months, Casey had been holding back, despite her agreement to try. Oh, she'd been giving their relationship an honest chance, but she still hadn't relinquished that last millimeter of her heart. And Jacqueline felt its absence more acutely than when they'd been broken up completely. But she'd vowed not to push. She couldn't make Casey trust her, so she waited.

Before she could analyze what she was seeing in Casey's eyes now, Casey blinked, then slid back behind her photographer persona. Jacqueline reached the front of the sanctuary and took her place next to the other bridesmaids.

The music changed just before Kendra and her father moved into the aisle. Kendra's gaze darted around nervously, but Jacqueline knew the moment she saw Gavin. Serene happiness overtook the anxiety in her expression. Jacqueline snuck a glance at Gavin and found a similar dopey look on his face.

When Kendra and Gavin recited the vows they'd written for each other, Jacqueline wiped away tears. After a tender kiss that made several guests say "aww," Jacqueline followed the happy couple back down the aisle. Swamped with emotion, she avoided looking for both Casey and Sean, as she suspected making eye contact with either of them would likely reduce her to sobs. She would take a minute before the reception to get herself together so she could be present and celebrate with Kendra.

❖

"Your glass is empty," Kendra said as she came to stand next to Jacqueline with two fresh glasses of champagne.

"Thanks." Jacqueline clinked their glasses together. "Where's your husband?"

"I do love the sound of that. He's dancing with my mother." Looking every bit the respectable son-in-law in his tuxedo, Gavin guided Kendra's mother around the floor.

"They make such a cute couple."

"Almost as cute as those two." Kendra nodded toward Sean and Casey on the dance floor.

Casey had wrangled him into one dance by agreeing that Kendra's would be the last wedding he worked for her. She'd already signed up with the art school to provide an internship in studio work for a photography student next semester.

"Yeah." Jacqueline smiled at Sean's begrudging participation. He didn't like dancing anyway, but she assumed if he had to, he'd much rather be dancing with his date, Gemma.

Jacqueline searched for Gemma and found her talking to one of Kendra's nieces, who was about her age. Gemma was a sweet girl, and after meeting her only a couple of times, Jacqueline and Casey already approved.

"You should probably go cut in—save that boy."

"In a minute. I'm enjoying this."

"Tell me you wouldn't rather be holding her."

"I didn't say that."

"You two have restored my faith in forever," Kendra said in an overly dramatic tone.

"Shut up."

"Seriously. It's good to see you together. How are you doing?"

"Very well. We've been communicating. It's not perfect—we're not perfect, but I kind of like that, you know. If we suddenly didn't have any more issues, I don't think it would feel like we were being authentic. That wouldn't fix any of our problems."

"That makes sense."

"But I've made some huge changes. I know what's important to me now." She looked at Casey again.

Though she still had to travel, she'd tightened her schedule and managed to spend more time in town. But she didn't like spending nights alone in her condo. She hadn't realized that she'd gotten so used to being gone that she would tack on an extra day to her trips here and there. Those days added up until she'd spent more time away than she did at home. Home. Her condo wasn't home.

Now, instead of traveling to avoid her solitary residence, she visited her father. She shared dinner, did projects around his house, and took him out for a movie or ice cream once in a while. She'd resumed her semi-regular walks around his neighborhood—presumably for exercise and stress relief. If she passed Casey's house early in her route, that was mere coincidence. And if Casey was waiting on the porch to join her for the rest of her walk, that was probably happenstance as well.

Owen didn't hide his disappointment when she tried to talk to him about her change in career plans. When she told him she needed to travel less, he argued that she could have time with her family when she retired. Since he was only a few years away from that time, she understood why he didn't think that was a big deal. But she wouldn't step into his shoes and spend the next fifteen to twenty years waiting for the someday that might not come. In the end, he'd begrudgingly agreed that as long as she handled her business, she could get as creative with her schedule as she wanted to. But if she screwed up again, he wouldn't back her.

In his view, he'd offered her the brass ring—his tutelage and eventually his job—and he couldn't comprehend her turning that down. But she could handle losing his favor. The reward—her family—was well worth the price.

"Now my kid will have godparents who can stand to be in the same room together." Kendra glanced toward the dance floor, where Casey had relinquished Sean into Gemma's arms. "And who knows, maybe you'll have a little grandkid the same age for mine to play with."

"Not funny."

Kendra laughed.

"No, seriously, that's not funny."

From behind Jacqueline, Casey wrapped her arms around her waist. "What's not funny?"

"Nothing."

"Okay." Casey moved to her side but didn't release her. Jacqueline draped her arm around Casey's shoulder. "Kendra, it was a beautiful ceremony. Are there any more shots you want before I head out?"

"You're leaving?" Jacqueline asked.

"It's time." Though she was responding to Jacqueline, she glanced at Kendra. Jacqueline thought she saw a shared look pass between them, and then Kendra nodded slightly.

Casey pressed closer and met Jacqueline's eyes. "Come home with me."

"Home?" She understood the concept of home, of course, but something in Casey's voice told her the request went deeper than just tonight.

"Yes. Our home. Move back in."

"Are you sure?" Jacqueline kept her voice low despite the excitement singing through her.

"Completely. I'm tired of missing you. You belong at home with me." Casey picked up her purse from the table and pulled out a small ring box. She lifted the lid to a gorgeous diamond solitaire nestled against a familiar titanium band. "And if you'll have me, I'd like us to share something we couldn't the first time around."

"Casey, what—"

"Marry me."

She stared at the band—a ring she'd taken off eight years ago but couldn't bring herself to part with. "The last time I saw this ring, it was in my dresser drawer. How did you get it?"

Casey glanced at Sean, who'd joined them when Casey pulled out the box, and he grinned. Having everyone around at this moment suddenly reminded Jacqueline what was on the line if they handled things badly this time.

"Are you sure?" she asked again.

Casey nodded. "Two months ago you asked me for a fresh start—to get to know each other all over again. And while I agree we've grown and changed and need to respect that, I've also learned that we aren't so different. You're still the same woman I fell in love with that first time. That's why there are two rings. One from our past and a new one for the future." She brushed her fingers over Jacqueline's cheek.

"Oh, sweetheart, I know this face. I've studied it more times than my own. I know the birthmark on the lower lid of your right eye, small, like the point of a pen. I know the dimple that shows up when you smile—the real smile, not the polite one. I know the way you tense your jaw when you're trying not to cry." Casey stroked her jaw, and she realized she'd been clenching her teeth for just that reason. "I'm asking you to marry me and I've never been more sure."

Sean angled close to Jacqueline's ear and whispered loudly enough for everyone to hear, "Say yes, Mama."

Jacqueline smiled and pulled Casey against her. She kissed her, then rested her cheek against the silk of Casey's hair. With tears in her eyes, she said, "Yes."

About the Author

Erin Dutton grew up in Upstate New York, but has made Tennessee her home for over seventeen years. In 2007, she published her first book, *Sequestered Hearts,* and hasn't wanted to stop writing since. In addition to ten previous novels, she's also a contributor to multiple anthologies. She's a proud recipient of the 2011 Alice B. Readers' Appreciation medal for her body of work.

When not working or writing, she enjoys playing golf, photography, and spending time with friends and family.

Books Available from Bold Strokes Books

A Class Act by Tammy Hayes. Buttoned-up college professor Dr. Margaret Parks doesn't know what she's getting herself into when she agrees to one date with her student, Rory Morgan, who is 15 years her junior. (978-1-62639-701-9)

Bitter Root by Laydin Michaels. Small town chef Adi Bergeron is hiding something, and Griffith McNaulty is going to find out what it is even if it gets her killed. (978-1-62639-656-2)

Capturing Forever by Erin Dutton. When family pulls Jacqueline and Casey back together, will the lessons learned in eight years apart be enough to mend the mistakes of the past? (978-1-62639-631-9)

Deception by VK Powell. DEA Agent Colby Vincent and Attorney Adena Weber are embroiled in a drug investigation involving homeless veterans and an attraction that could destroy them both. (978-1-62639-596-1)

Dyre: A Knight of Spirit and Shadows by Rachel E. Bailey. With the abduction of her queen, werewolf-bodyguard Des must follow the kidnappers' trail to Europe, where her queen—and a battle unlike any Des has ever waged—awaits her. (978-1-62639-664-7)

First Position by Melissa Brayden. Love and rivalry take center stage for Anastasia Mikhelson and Natalie Frederico in one of the most prestigious ballet companies in the nation. (978-1-62639-602-9)

Best Laid Plans by Jan Gayle. Nicky and Lauren are meant for each other, but Nicky's haunting past and Lauren's societal fears threaten to derail all possibilities of a relationship. (987-1-62639-658-6)

Exchange by CF Frizzell. When Shay Maguire rode into rural Montana, she never expected to meet the woman of her dreams—or to learn Mel Baker was held hostage by legal agreement to her right-wing father. (987-1-62639-679-1)

Just Enough Light by AJ Quinn. Will a serial killer's return to Colorado destroy Kellen Ryan and Dana Kingston's chance at love, or can the search-and-rescue team save themselves? (987-1-62639-685-2)

Rise of the Rain Queen by Fiona Zedde. Nyandoro is nobody's princess. She fights, curses, fornicates, and gets into as much trouble as her brothers. But the path to a throne is not always the one we expect. (987-1-62639-592-3)

Tales from Sea Glass Inn by Karis Walsh. Over the course of a year at Cannon Beach, tourists and locals alike find solace and passion at the Sea Glass Inn. (987-1-62639-643-2)

The Color of Love by Radclyffe. Black sheep Derian Winfield needs to convince literary agent Emily May to marry her to save the Winfield Agency and solve Emily's green card problem, but Derian didn't count on falling in love. (987-1-62639-716-3)

A Reluctant Enterprise by Gun Brooke. When two women grow up learning nothing but distrust, unworthiness, and abandonment, it's no wonder they are apprehensive and fearful when an overwhelming love just won't be denied. (978-1-62639-500-8)

Above the Law by Carsen Taite. Love is the last thing on Agent Dale Nelson's mind, but reporter Lindsey Ryan's investigation could change the way she sees everything—her career, her past, and her future. (978-1-62639-558-9)

Actual Stop by Kara A. McLeod. When Special Agent Ryan O'Connor's present collides abruptly with her past, shots are fired, and the course of her life is irrevocably altered. (978-1-62639-675-3)

Embracing the Dawn by Jeannie Levig. When ex-con Jinx Tanner and business executive E. J. Bastien awaken after a one-night stand to find their lives inextricably entangled, love has its work cut out for it. (978-1-62639-576-3)

Jane's World: The Case of the Mail Order Bride by Paige Braddock. Jane's PayBuddy account gets hacked and she inadvertently purchases a mail order bride from the Eastern Bloc. (978-1-62639-494-0)

Love's Redemption by Donna K. Ford. For ex-convict Rhea Daniels and ex-priest Morgan Scott, redemption lies in the thin line between right and wrong. (978-1-62639-673-9)

The Shewstone by Jane Fletcher. The prophetic Shewstone is in Eawynn's care, but unfortunately for her, Matt is coming to steal it. (978-1-62639-554-1)

A Touch of Temptation by Julie Blair. Recent law school graduate Kate Dawson's ordained path to the perfect life gets thrown off course when handsome butch top Chris Brent initiates her to sexual pleasure. (978-1-62639-488-9)

Beneath the Waves by Ali Vali. Kai Merlin and Vivien Palmer love the water and the secrets trapped in the depths, but if Kai gives in to her feelings, it might come at a cost to her entire realm. (978-1-62639-609-8)

Girls on Campus edited by Sandy Lowe and Stacia Seaman. College: four years when rules are made to be broken. This collection is required reading for anyone looking to earn an A in sex ed. (978-1-62639-733-0)

Heart of the Pack by Jenny Frame. Human Selena Miller falls for the domineering Caden Wolfgang, but will their love survive Selena learning the Wolfgangs are werewolves? (978-1-62639-566-4)

Miss Match by Fiona Riley. Matchmaker Samantha Monteiro makes the impossible possible for everyone but herself. Is mysterious dancer Lucinda Moss her own perfect match? (978-1-62639-574-9)

Paladins of the Storm Lord by Barbara Ann Wright. Lieutenant Cordelia Ross must choose between duty and honor when a man with godlike powers forces her soldiers to provoke an alien threat. (978-1-62639-604-3)

Taking a Gamble by P.J. Trebelhorn. Storage auction buyer Cassidy Holmes and postal worker Erica Jacobs want different things out of life, but taking a gamble on love might prove lucky for them both. (978-1-62639-542-8)

The Copper Egg by Catherine Friend. Archeologist Claire Adams wants to find the buried treasure in Peru. Her ex, Sochi Castillo, wants to steal it. The last thing either of them wants is to still be in love. (978-1-62639-613-5)

The Iron Phoenix by Rebecca Harwell. Seventeen-year-old Nadya must master her unusual powers to stop a killer, prevent civil war, and rescue the girl she loves, while storms ravage her island city. (978-1-62639-744-6)

A Reunion to Remember by TJ Thomas. Reunited after a decade, Jo Adams and Rhonda Black must navigate a significant age difference, family dynamics, and their own desires and fears to explore an opportunity for love. (978-1-62639-534-3)

Built to Last by Aurora Rey. When Professor Olivia Bennett hires contractor Joss Bauer to restore her dilapidated farmhouse, she learns her heart, as much as her house, is in need of a renovation. (978-1-62639-552-7)

Capsized by Julie Cannon. What happens when a woman turns your life completely upside down? (978-1-62639-479-7)